Stephen E. Moss

THROUGH THE EYES OF A SOLDIER

A WORLD GONE MAD:
THE LIFE OF WILLIAM RUDOLPH

STEPHEN E. MOSS

Stephen E. Moss

THROUGH THE EYES OF A SOLDIER

A WORLD GONE MAD:

Part 1

The Life of William Rudolph

POLSTON HOUSE
PUBLISHING

STEPHEN E. MOSS

Published by Polston House Publishing LLC
www.Polstonhouse.com

Book design copyright © 2022 by Polston House Publishing, LLC. All rights reserved.

Published in the United States of America

CHAPTERS

PART 1:

Stephen E. Moss

OFF TO A GOOD START

My name is William Rudolph. I was born on June 12, 1899, to James and Elizabeth Rudolph. My Father has been in the service of the United States Army for all of my life. I am the oldest of five children. My siblings and I had the benefit of life on an Army post both here and abroad. It was a good life that I enjoyed greatly. When War broke out in Europe, there was never a question as to whether I would serve or not. I planned to sign-up as soon as I was able. How it would turn out, only the Lord Almighty knows. The future and my fate, of course, is a mystery. To this end, I decided to write down as much as possible. But, I'm getting ahead of myself. Let us look at the beginning.

I was born at Fort Riley, Kansas. My Father, James Rudolph, had recently returned from his campaigns in the War of '98. Soon after my birth, he left for service in the Philippines. I saw very little of my Father during my youth. My Mother, brothers and sisters were the only family that I knew. When he did return, James was more of a stranger to us than a Father. It was Mother who raised us and served in both roles as mother and father.

My great-grandfather, Daniel Rudolph, died in 1902. I have no memory of him. I am told that he was a splendid soldier, having served in the cavalry through the War Between the States and the Frontier Wars.

One of my earliest memories took place in April, 1906. We were living in Montana and our teacher, Mrs. Taylor, interrupted our morning class to tell us of a great event that had happened on April 18. There had been a great earthquake and fire in San Francisco, California. Mrs. Taylor read a newspaper article account of the event and had us find San Francisco on the map of the United States. For the remainder of the school year, Mrs. Taylor would read to us additional articles as they were printed.

My only interest was in the fate of my grand-father, Benjamin Rudolph who was posted at the Presidio in California, near San Francisco. Mother read to us a letter from Grand-father telling us that he was well and that all was as well as could be expected. This came as wonderful news to me.

Another event of great magnitude happened shortly after my ninth birthday, in 1908. There was noise and celebration the likes of which I had neither seen nor heard before. This was far greater than the Fourth of July would normally have been. I soon found out that all of the excitement was over the admission of the Oklahoma Territory into the Union. A new state, a new star for a new flag was the cause for great celebration. This brought the number of States to 46.

In 1912, when I was twelve, came news of a different nature. In the spring, I heard Mother talking about a great ship that sunk and all of the people who died. At first, I did not understand why this was so different from the other ships that have sunk before. I later read in the newspaper about this great unsinkable ocean liner named HMS Titanic. I remember thinking how ironic it was that an unsinkable ship didn't even make its maiden voyage across the Atlantic. I was sorrowed that so many lives, over 1500 I believe, were lost in such a grand show of arrogance. It put me in mind of the Tower of Babel.

This great sorrow was later off-set by great joy as not one, but two new states joined the Union. New Mexico and Arizona had joined the Grand Union, bringing the number of States to 48!

Apart from these events, life was regular and well ordered. We played, we attended school, we raised crops in our garden, we read, we sang, and we did all of the normal things a family would do together. Although, being a military family, we moved about considerably more than a regular family. This afforded us the opportunity to see more of this great land of ours. It did make it a bit difficult to maintain friends, though.

During the Mexican Revolution, head of state Victoriano Huerta was struggling against forces in the south led by Emiliano Zapata and forces in the north led by Venustiano Carranza. It was these forces in the north that threatened United States business interests at Tampico. The Tampico Affair as it came to be known began on April 9, 1914. United States Armed Forces stepped in to stop the fighting and occupied near-by Veracruz for six months.

The ABC Powers (ABC stands for Argentina, Brazil, and Chile. The three most powerful countries in South America) were asked to negotiate a settlement to avoid war between Mexico and the United States. This was done at Niagara Falls, Canada on May 20, 1914. The formal treaty was not signed until May 15, 1915.

On June 28, 1914, the Archduke of Austria, Franz Ferdinand, and his wife were assassinated in Sarajevo. The sequence of events that followed lead to war between the Triple Alliance (German Empire, Austria-Hungary Empire, Kingdom of Italy) and the Triple Entente (British Empire, France, Russian Empire). The Triple Alliance soon dissolved when Italy did not support Germany and Austria-Hungary. The Alliance quickly reformed as the Central Powers with the German Empire, the Austria-Hungary Empire, the Ottoman Empire, and the Kingdom of Bulgaria. However, by August 1914, fighting spread through-out Europe, Africa, Near-east Asia and Far-east Asia.

President Woodrow Wilson declared that the United States of America would take the stance of neutrality. This stance, however, did not keep hostilities from us.

The Mexican Revolution had continued and hostilities between government forces and revolutionary forces had continued to strain relationships between the United States and Mexico. The ABC Pact of 1915 had nearly no effect. Mexican Revolutionary Forces under Francisco "Pancho" Villa attacked Columbus, New Mexico on March 9, 1916. President Wilson sent General John J. Pershing and 10,000 troops to capture Villa. The Punitive Expedition used three new weapons; the automobiles, aero-planes, and automatic machine-guns. No common bandit will

11

be able to withstand the might of the American Military.

Public out-cry over the sinking of the RMS Lusitania on May 7, 1915, by a German U-Boat ("U" for Untersee or Underwater), and Germany's diplomatic efforts to persuade Mexico to declare war on the United States, grew ever stronger.

It became very apparent that our Nation would soon be embroiled in the war in Europe. President Wilson ended America's isolationism on April 6, 1917. The Selective Service Law of 1917, enacted on May 18, 1917, granted the President the power to draft men between the ages of 21 to 30 into military service. Soon men across the land were registering for military service.

It might be noted here that there was a small group of men who tried to avoid their duty. These were conscientious objectors. Those with a true and honest objection based on their religious beliefs should, in no way, be considered in the same group of people that claim objection merely because they are cowards.

Although too young, I didn't want to wait to be drafted. I went to volunteer for military service as soon as I reached my 18th birthday. I said good-bye to my childhood, and faced an extremely uncertain adulthood. It is to that uncertainty and for that purpose that I have decided to record the events that are to follow.

Stephen E. Moss

ON TO ARMY TRAINING

June 13, 1917

Having come of age, I took the buck-board to the near-by recruiting station to sign-up for military service. Since the minimum age for conscription was 21, I was able to volunteer for service by means of a slight slip of the pen. I entered my date of birth as June 12, 1896 and suddenly I'm 21.

Originally, I had thought to join Father's unit. But, I thought that they might know me there and instead decided to trust my service to luck.

Once I was at the recruiting station, the day was spent mostly waiting in line. At the head of the line, I gave my name, occupation, home town, and age. We were then given a short examination, some papers and told that we would receive further information at a later date. This completed my first official work in the United States Army. I returned home to wait for further information of where and when to report for duty. The Recruiting Sergeant told us that we should receive a letter in the mail in a few weeks.

June 14 to August 20, 1917

Life at home continued on as before. There has been no real change to my life, yet.

I had hoped to observe the soldiers here at Fort Robinson, Nebraska. But, there are so few of them, as the bulk have been sent with Father to join General Pershing a little more than a year ago. The few soldiers left here at the post go through their actions of the day with very little drill or ceremony. There was very little for me to learn from observing them.

August 21, 1917

I received notification in the mail, to-day, to report for duty. I am to report to the training camp on the first of September.

August 22 to 30, 1917

I tried to maintain the normal routine of life. This was not to be. The excitement, the anticipation, the packing, and yes, the fear of what was to come was greater than my ability to keep things as they were. Life, for me, is about to change in ways I can't imagine.

August 31, 1917

Mother took me to the railroad station, I checked in with the Military Police, and got onto the train with all of the other new recruits. Together, we proceeded to our new home. The train ride is pleasant enough. The scenery of the surrounding country-side leaves much to be desired. There was nothing out there except wide open prairie. This afforded a wonderful opportunity to relax, read, and catch-up on my journal entries.

September 1, 1917

We arrived at Fort Riley in Kansas. I remember this post as I was born here. Our family lived here for several years and, to me, this was a very nice Post. In many ways, it was enjoyable to see Fort Riley, again. It was interesting to note that where I started my life was the same place that I am starting my military life.

September 2, 1917

Nothing to-day, no activity as it is Sunday. I spent the day attending church services and walking around the post. There have been very little changes from when I was here last, that I can observe. The rush of memories has brought a smile to my face.

Fort Riley was like a ghost-town. Nearly all of the regular army soldiers are gone. I was told that they had gone to the Mexican Boarder to capture Pancho Villa. Just like the soldiers from Fort Robinson and several other posts, I dare say.

With respect to that, I read in the paper, that General Pershing was unable to accomplish his mission to capture Pancho Villa. Even with all of those modern inventions, the automobile, the aeroplane, the machine-gun, the Army could not bring that villain to justice. General Pershing was taken away from that mission and ordered to organize and lead the American Expeditionary Forces to be sent to Europe.

I wonder if all of those troops, and Father, will be returning home, soon. I would not doubt that his stay at home will be short-lived. As he, too, will undoubtedly be off to bash the Hun.

September 3, 1917

We started our in-processing into the Army.

We waited in the lines to see the various doctors. Each of them poking and prodding in every opening on our body. They had us stand on one foot, then the other, sit down and stand back up. They checked our eyes, ears, nose, and throat. After all was said and done, we were told to wait in a large room.

Later, a Sergeant entered the room and called out a few names, handed them a piece of paper and told them to wait in another room. The Sergeant had the rest of us stand up, an Officer came in, he told us to raise our right hand and we were sworn in to the United States Army. After-wards, we signed our name to some papers and we then waited to be told what we were to do next. Soon, we were sent to the barracks for the night.

September 4, 1917

To-day, we continued with our in-processing. This time, we spent the day filling out papers...papers...and still more papers. You would think that the Army is made-up of nothing but papers and doctors with big, sharp needles.

September 5, 1917

In the morning, all of the new recruits, of whom I am one, were gathered together. We were taken to Camp Funston. We walked over to our new home, and were moved into some tents. This came as a bit of a let-down. We were under the impression that we would conduct our training on the post. Only parts of the camp were completed with wooden structures. Tents were used to finish the necessary structures.

Camp Funston was named in honor of General Frederick Funston, a native of Kansas, celebrated for his intrepid service in Cuba and the Philippines, and no less for his prompt mastery of conditions in a time of great civil catastrophe – the 1906 earthquake and fire of San Francisco. Camp Funston is located on the Fort Riley Military Reservation, near its eastern border and two or three miles from the post. The camp is in a large river flat in a bend of the Kaw River containing several hundred acres.

September 6, 1917

Early in the morning, we formed into a mass formation and were moved to the administration building. There we waited, filled out more papers, waited, answered more questions, waited, walked to the mess hall, waited, ate our meal, waited, walked to the Infirmary, waited, received some shots, waited, wondered what we were doing, waited, walked to the quartermaster building, waited, were issued our clothing, waited, walked back to the barracks, waited, changed into our new uniforms — which consisted of a hat, blue denim overalls, shoes, socks, and undergarments — and then we waited, walked back to the mess hall, waited, ate again, waited, walked back to the barracks, waited, were finally told we were to have personal time for the rest of the evening. For the majority of the time we spent our time putting our things away. The new blue denim overalls are interesting, at best.

September 7, 1917

After morning formation and meal, we were formed up again. Sergeant Major Parsons called out names. As the names were called, the soldiers moved to the side and made a new formation. This was the creation of our new units. I was assigned to "E" Company of the 355th Infantry Regiment of the

178th Infantry Brigade of the 89th Infantry Division, the Middle West Division. We are part of a newly formed branch of the Army called the National Army. The U.S. Army is made up of several parts. The United States Army, these are the career soldiers. Then there's the National Guard Army. These are State Soldiers that have been ordered to Federal duty. Then there's the National Army, these are units made-up of draftees. There's also the Reserve Army. These are drafted soldiers who are used to fill the ranks of the garrison and training units. In the event that more troops are needed in Europe, the Reserve Army will be employed to fill that need.

The only difference that I can tell between the National Army and the United States Army is that the soldiers of United States Army get all of the equipment and real buildings.

We were introduced to our Sergeants, the First Sergeant, and the Company Commander. Our lives will never be the same, again.

September 8, 1917

General Leonard Wood, our Commanding General, ordered the units to be formed to preserve state integrity as much as possible. The 353rd Infantry Regiment was composed of Soldiers from Kansas. The men from Missouri filled the ranks of the 354th and 356th Infantry Regiments, the 342nd Field Artillery, and the 314th Engineers. The 355th Infantry Regiment was made up of the men from Nebraska. The balance of units was filled with soldiers from other States. Needless to say, the largest number of Soldiers in the 89th Infantry Division came from Missouri.

The pace of our activities has increased tremendously! Scarcely a second goes by without something for us to do.

We were issued rifles. There are no actual rifles for us, so we were issued rifles carved from wood. We must be quite the sight, marching about in our blue overalls carrying wood sticks for rifles.

September 9, 1917

It is Sunday again, and another day of rest. Here, I will take a moment to mention some of my fellow soldiers.

As I noted earlier, the majority of everyone in "E" Company, as well as the 355th Infantry Regiment came from Nebraska.

Private John Gilmer of Central City, Nebraska is a tall, red-headed, lanky fellow. He has a splendid personality and good leadership qualities.

Private Joseph Farrell is a quiet sort of fellow. He is a hard worker and does what he is told without complaining.

Private John Patton of Lincoln, Nebraska is a rather humorous lad. We can always count on John for a witty comment or a good story to help brighten our day.

The rest of the members of our squad I have yet to become acquainted. I shall make observations and entries as I learn more and more about them.

Sergeant Thomas is in charge of us. That can not be an easy task. All we know of him is his voice.

We hear it all of the time. Sometimes, I hear it in my sleep.

Our officer is 1st Lieutenant Griffith. We have very little contact with him. He talks to the Sergeant, mostly.

On the whole, the squad is made-up of a very nice group of soldiers. There are a few that prefer to keep their own council. And a few that it would be wise to keep your distance. But, even for all of that, they are a good group.

September 10, 1917

Training has gotten into a routine. Reveille is at 5 o'clock, Physical Training by 6 o'clock. Breakfast is at 8 o'clock and the days training get started by 9 o'clock. Lunch is from noon to 1 o'clock and then it is back to training until dinner at 5 o'clock. I am not certain why I need to write down the times, or even why I should carry a watch at all. There are bugle calls to tell us where to go all of the time, and Sergeants to tell us what to do once we got there.

September 11 to 30, 1917

We continue to train and drill as more and more new recruits join our formation, every day. I have never seen formations as large as what we are becoming. Every new recruit must go through the same indoctrination once they are assigned to our unit. They have to fill out a mountain of paperwork, go through the medical inoculations, more paper work, be issued their overalls and wood rifle, more paper work, find their bunks, and receive a warm and heart-felt greeting from their new best friend, the Sergeant.

October 1 to 31, 1917

Our ranks, now fully manned and outfitted (in a manner of speaking), can now prepare to begin our training in earnest.

We were taught everything we needed to know to be soldiers; how to stand, how to walk and run, how to salute and even how to rest. We were taught everything in the School of the Soldier. Orders, signals and commands were also part of our schooling. This included voice commands and orders as well as arm, bugle, whistle and flag signals.

Physical training greets us every morning after breakfast. We usually spend 15 minutes setting up for the exercise and 45 minutes of exercise. Once completed, we continue on with the training of the day. By the end of the day, we are ready for sleep.

Once we learned how to be soldiers, we learned how to work together as a team. We are trained in the School of the Squad, the Company, the Battalion, and finally the Regiment. Every time we accomplish one task, we are introduced to another task. And then there are inspections, always inspections. I swear there are times when they inspect us in our sleep!

As supplies come available, we are issued uniforms and equipment. This was a very slow process. When we received our new uniforms, we spent half of a day sorting out and trading with each other the parts of our uniforms to get a better fit. I think the Supply Sergeant just handed to us whatever he placed his hands on, rather than checking for the correct size.

Having traded pants, shirts, jackets, coats and anything that we needed to trade to obtain an issue of clothing that fit reasonably well, we put on our new uniforms. I'm not at all certain that I got the right size after-all. It will take a while to get use to the feel of these trousers. They feel like the legs were put on backwards. It will also take some time to get use to the itchy, olive-drab wool that was used to make these uniforms. The wide brimmed hat and canvas leggings seem a bit outdated as they were part of the uniform at the turn of the century. Maybe some day we will be issued modern uniforms and equipment.

In addition to the new uniforms, we received new buildings. We moved out of the tents and into the new buildings as they were completed. Unfortunately, the only thing that was completed was the walls.

Our training consists of digging ditches, close-order marching, police call, guard duty, and the occasional classroom instruction. By-in-large, there is nothing new, nor different to write here. There is one exception. When they planned and organized this division, several foreign Officers were brought over from Europe. They designed and over-saw the construction of a training area that is an exact copy of the trenches that we will be occupying. They also trained our Officers and Sergeants in what they can expect. In this way, they will be able to better prepare us. This was possibly the best training that we could receive.

In addition to our regular training, we are routinely assigned temporary additional duties. Some of these additional duties include Kitchen Police (KP), where we assist in the kitchen; guard duty, where we walk an assigned post, or area, until properly relieved; latrine officer, which speaks for itself; fire watch, where we take two hour shifts at night to ensure that nothing happens at night. There are several other little duties that the Sergeants use to help discipline and motivate us.

Sergeant Thomas spends the days, trying to convert this group of civilians into a cohesive, working, fighting, military unit. We spend the nights trying to hang on to memories of what it was like to be a civilian. We sing songs, play games, write letters to loved ones back home, and generally engage in any kind of activity that will help us to forget the trials and tribulations of the day. It is interesting to watch this test of wills. The Sergeant's will prevail. They must for us to win on the battlefield. But, how long can the individual hold-out.

The worst part came when a severe cold snap arrived. The temperature dropped to twelve degrees! Fortunately, we were no longer housed in tents. The wooden buildings were finished and that offered some protection from the wind. But, we had neither steam heat nor electricity. Many of the buildings did not have running water. This made for some EXTREMELY uncomfortable days. Our heavy, itchy, hot, wool uniforms and blankets provided a bit of relief, but not enough.

November 1, 1917

To-day started a new phase of our military life. We began weapons training. This could be the most dangerous thing we have done, to date.

We turned in our wooden rifles and were issued a nice, new, greasy M1903 .30 Caliber, bolt action, Springfield rifle, a M1910 dismounted cartridge belt, and a M1905 bayonet with a M1910 scabbard. The first order of business was to clean our new weapons.

November 2 to 9, 1917

We spent the majority of the week drilling, marching, and generally doing the same things we did before. Only, we did everything with our heavy, new rifles. This was to get us use to carrying them with us all of the time.

The only change to our routine was the addition of bayonet training. The addition of actual bayonet and rifles when we did our trench training made a significant difference, too.

November 10, 1917

To-day, we marched to the range to receive our initial instruction in marksmanship. We lined-up in a firing order and lay down on the ground. One-by-one, the Sergeant moved down the firing order, giving personal instruction on proper firing technique. Then issuing the soldier one round (bullet) and having the soldier fire at the target some 100 feet down range. The range detail at the targets would then mark the target where the bullet hit. More times than not, the round missed the target. Maybe the Germans will be scared by the noise our rifles make. Still, that is why we practice, so as to improve our skills.

November 11 to 20, 1917

We certainly have had plenty of opportunity to practice. The past week or more has been spent at the rifle range. The only exceptions were the days that the weather would not permit. On those days, we worked and trained in the barracks.

On the whole, the marksmanship skills of the Company have improved greatly. It is entirely possible that we will survive on the battlefield.

November 21, 1917

GREAT NEWS!! We have been granted leave to return home for the Holidays! We spent the day preparing for our journey home.

November 22, 1917

We traveled by truck from the camp to the railroad station. My train arrived on schedule. I am so excited to be going home.

November 23, 1917

I have arrived at home! Mother and everyone came to the railroad station to meet me and take me home.

November 24, 1917

Father, too, has come home for the holidays. Father arrived at the railroad station to-day. We all went to the station to greet him. Mother and Father have commented on how much I have changed. I suppose that they are right. Everything at home appears to be the same to me.

<u>November 25, 1917 to January 3, 1918</u>

My time spent at home was most enjoyable. I enjoyed it so much that I did not feel like writing any of it down. I preferred to experience every moment of it, instead.

<u>January 4, 1918</u>

The time to return to Camp Funston has arrived, unfortunately. All good things must come to an end, I suppose. It was a most splendid time, though.

<u>January 5, 1918</u>

The entire family rode with me to the railroad station to see me off. It was a very touching scene. It was enough to bring tears to my eyes. Not only mine, but Mother's and Father's as well. I have never been so moved in all of my life.

I hope to see them all, again.

January 6, 1918

I have returned to Camp Funston.

All of the other members of our unit have also returned. A great time was spent, exchanging stories and the fun that was had by all.

January 7, 1918

Life at Camp Funston has returned to normal, already.

January 8 to March 2, 1918

Our Camp life has settled into a very set routine. Our level of proficiency at soldiering has increased daily.

Private Gilmer was promoted to Corporal and made assistant Squad Leader. This was an excellent choice. Corporal Gilmer has been respected and well liked by all of the men.

March 3, 1918

The war took a drastic turn for the worse. The Czar signed a treaty with the Kaiser. The Treaty of Brest-Litovsk ceded vast areas including Finland, the Baltic States of Latvia, Lithuania and Estonia, Poland and part of the Ukraine to the Central Powers. Hostilities between the Russian Empire and the Empires of Germany and Austria-Hungary have come to an end. Now the Russian Revolution is the only fighting on that front.

We need to get there and even the score.

<u>March 4 to May 20, 1918</u>

Our training intensified with the urgency of getting into the fight.

Finally, we received the word to pack our equipment and prepare to move. We are on our way, Over There!!

Stephen E. Moss

OFF TO WAR

May 21, 1918

Having completed our training, the 355th Regiment is now ready to fight. We loaded onto some trucks at 10 o'clock and rode to the train station. We then got off of the trucks and waited at the train station for about 2 hours. Our train finally arrived and we proceeded to board. Everyone was given their bunk assignment. Mine is C-23-B, sleeping car C, bunk 23, wall side. The aisle side of the bunk is occupied by Private Andy Robinson from Omaha, Nebraska. He's a short, rugged kind-of guy that lived on a farm all of his life. He may not be very worldly, but he knows more about crops and harvesting than I'll ever know. This is the first time he has ever been away from his farm. It is fun to watch his wide-eyed excitement and amazement at every little thing.

May 22 to 24, 1918

The train takes a few days to travel to New York City. It is enjoyable not having to march everywhere. Most of our time is spent reading, playing games, talking or looking at the country-side. Occasionally, First Sergeant Peterson would have some information to give to us. Altogether, we had a very pleasant journey.

May 25, 1918

We arrived at Long Island Train Station late on the evening of the 24th. By the time we deboarded, formed up into our sections and marched to Camp Mills, it was very early in the morning of the 25th. By the time we received our tent assignment, staked out our cots, and unloaded our packs, it was time for a late breakfast. Almost time for lunch, actually. After we ate, we went back to our cots and finished organizing our equipment. By the end of the day, we were exhausted!

May 26 to June 2, 1918

Life at Camp Mills has been very relaxed. We would rise to the melodic tones of the bugle, do our calisthenics, clean-up, eat breakfast, go over to the drill field and do the training of the day (close order drill, bayonet drill, classes, etc.), eat lunch, continue with our training, eat dinner, go back to our tents for personal time until it was time for lights-out. All of this was done to the rhythmic tunes of the bugle and the soothing sounds of Sergeant Thomas. This went on for a week.

June 3, 1918

The time has come to move again. We packed our rolls and were transported to Hoboken, New Jersey. There, we boarded the transport RMS Adriatic. I located my berth and settled into a fun-filled sea voyage to England.

June 4, 1918

We sailed past Bartholdi's Statue, "Liberty Enlightening the World". We stood on the deck to get a glimpse of her as we sailed by. It seemed a bit strange to me that we were passing from behind her, as if she were seeing us off on our journey. The damage to her skirt was visible, as was the twisted remains of the dock were the explosion occurred. I had heard rumors that the ammunition that was detonated on that day, a year ago, might not have been accidental. That it might have been the result of sabotage by German agents. Even if that were true, they still could not dim the light of liberty. All who saw her were inspired by what she stands for as we sail forth to our grand and glorious mission. Private Robinson just stood there with a smile on his face. He stood there until we could no longer see the Lady Liberty. He stood there for a long time after, as if he could still see her. Later, he told me that he had never seen anything so beautiful in his life. I must say, I had to agree with him.

June 5, 1918

The sights and sounds of the United States of America fade away beyond the horizon. Only the seagulls remind us of that which we have left behind. Before us, the future lies as vast as the ocean we travel. But, just as we are certain to reach the opposite shore, we shall certainly defeat the Kaiser and return home once again!

June 6, 1918

The seagulls finally stopped following our ship. Just as long as no albatrosses show-up, we should be fine. We definitely do not want to suffer the same fate as Mister Coleridge's Ancient Mariner. I fear we might face a greater danger from the U-Boats than from an ill-omen.

June 7 to 11, 1918

Our daily routine is a simple one. We rise, eat, spend some time on the deck, read, talk, play games, sing songs (all in no particular order), and go to sleep. The turns on deck are enjoyable for the chance to stretch your legs and get some fresh air.

The ocean offers a view other than the bulk-head and the sun is enjoyable. On several different days, I watched a school of dolphins swim along side of our vessel. I had never seen anything so wondrous and beautiful before in my life. What marvelous and graceful creatures are these dolphins!

Another strange and curious sight occurs when we look out across the sea to the other ships. They are painted with bright colors in a most unusual pattern. One of the ship's crew told me that this was called "dazzle paint". I guess it is meant to dazzle the enemy.

June 12, 1918 My Birthday

To-day was my 19th Birthday. I celebrated it by sitting in a deck chair for the majority of the day. By this time next year, we will have beaten the Hun and we should be on our way back home. I must remember to do this again next year.

June 13 to 15, 1918

We are approaching land, again. The seagulls have returned. There were a few days of concern when we thought that there might be German U-Boats in the waters around us. We had heard that those

Wolf Packs were to be feared. We're still keeping a sharp eye out for periscopes or anything unusual.

June 16, 1918

We arrive at Liverpool, England early this morning. After disembarking the Adriatic, we proceeded to Camp Woodley. But, we are staying only for the night. We are departing in the morning.

June 17, 1918

This is going to be a VERY long march!

We formed up early in the morning and marched out of Camp Woodley, headed for Southampton and a steamer for France. It was a short march, only 230 miles! We will be doing about 30 miles a day. We should arrive in a week. That is, if our feet can hold up.

June 18 to 23, 1918

I can not tell which hurts more, my feet or my shoulders. I suppose this is one way to get us prepared for the rigors of our upcoming adventure.

June 24, 1918

We made it to Southampton! I have never been so tired in my life! We embarked onto a steamer and crossed the channel. The rest, though only for a little while, is greatly appreciated! We arrive at Le Havre, France. The trip across the channel took only a couple of hours. Our next destination is Paris, France. It is a short 120 mile march.

June 25 to 28, 1918

Here we go again! My legs and shoulders are numb. This does make it easier as I do not have to think about the pain. I am, how-ever, getting quite good at taking naps while we march. As long as the column does not change direction, I am able to stay in formation.

June 29, 1918

We arrived at the Fourth Training Area (at last!), just out-side of Paris. We moved to our tents and collapsed. I am extremely thankful I had broken-in my shoes when I did. I do not think my feet would have survived had I not. Several lads had not taken care of their shoes and neither their feet. You can tell who did and who did not take care of their feet. Those who did not are at the Surgeon's tent and in great pain!

Along the way to the Fourth Training Area (also called the "Reynel Training Area"), we saw several new sights. The picturesque French countryside gave us a splendid view as we marched. We also had our first glimpse of Germans. There were several prisoners being guarded by a Poilu or two. A Poilu is a French soldier.

June 30, 1918

To-day has been assigned as a day of rest. I think it might be because of the large number on sick-call.

July 1, 1918

We spent the day doing light duty and recovering from our journey, thankfully.

July 2 to 3, 1918

We returned to our regular training schedule with the addition of imaginary battles. We would fight long, furious battles, Company fighting Company. Then an Officer with a white ribbon on his hat and arm would step out from behind a bush and declare a winner.

July 4, 1918 Independence Day

We celebrated Independence Day, to-day. Passes were given to a few soldiers. Taxis were available to take them to Paris. Corporal Gilmer, Privates Farrell, Patton, and I were given passes and went to the Eifel Tower and Notre Dame Cathedral. There was a stirring parade. We had the most wonderful time of our lives. It was a shame that we had to return to camp.

Andy was telling me that soldiers at the camp spent the day playing baseball and listened to speeches. Everyone enjoyed the day.

July 5 to 31, 1918

The intensity of our training has increased. Daily imaginary battles and large troop movements are used to get us ready for battle conditions. We were also issued new equipment. That was just what we needed, more equipment to carry. The good thing about all of this is that it will be over shortly. The filthy Hun will never be able to stand-up against our mighty forces.

We have a new division insignia. As we are called the Middle West Division, our insignia is a circle with a letter in the center that if you look at it like one way, you would read M for middle. Turn it like a cart wheel, and you would read W for West. With it turned to read W, the center forms a shell. Different brigades use different colors for the shell. The artillery uses red, the 177th Infantry Brigade uses sky-blue. We in the 178th Infantry Brigade are identified with cobalt-blue.

August 1 to 2, 1918

We were issued new equipment, a helmet, a gas mask, and leg wraps. We're finally ready to go to the front. The helmet has an odd feel and one size is meant to fit everyone. The gas mask will take a bit of getting use to, also. This is a necessary evil, however. The leg wraps were not the easiest things to figure out, either. The first time that I tried was a complete fiasco. After several more attempts, I finally stumbled upon a method that produced a good-looking, well fitted wrap that doesn't fall down. That was NOT an easy accomplishment. Many of the other lads wet their putties so that the lower side would shrink to form-fit around their legs. Sometimes this worked. Other times were not so successful. It took a couple of days and a great deal of practice to get to the level of proficiency where–by we look like real doughboys.

Everyone wanted to place the new emblem on their equipment and on their helmet. This would boost morale and unit pride. The problem was spies. The filthy Hun spies could track our movement, strength, morale and lots of other things that spies do. Therefore, to confuse these spies, units in the rear will use the insignia and the troops in the trench won't be wearing any markings other than their collar disks. In addition, we were ordered not to keep journals for fear that sensitive or vital information might fall into enemy hands. I must remember not to let anyone see me writing or I could be court-marshaled.

August 3, 1918

We packed up our kits and prepared to move again. We loaded onto a fleet of trucks and headed off to hammer the Boche. Boche is what the French call the Germans.

August 4, 1918

We arrive at the front to-day. I do not think that any amount of training could have prepared us for what greeted us. I could spend days and books trying to describe the trenches and still not paint an accurate picture. Instead, I will describe bits and pieces as they would enhance the surrounding situation.

Through the night, we passed the town of Beaumont. It seems that every time we move or do any thing of interest, we do it at night. I suppose there is a good reason for this. My thoughts are that the brass-hats like to hear how the war went while they slept, or that they're a bunch of night owls. It was difficult to see any of our surroundings as we moved in the darkness. With the glow of the early morning light to assist, I could make out more of the landscape. I could see the field hospital as we passed-by. The roads in the rear were in good condition as the heavy artillery pieces and supply trains traveled them continuously. The engineers kept them in good repair.

Soon, we came upon some artillery emplacements, French 75s mostly. Some of them were so well camouflaged that one could walk right up to it and not realize that they were there. The closer you move toward the front, the more shell-holes pock-marked the roads and the surrounding landscape. We passed several signs cautioning drivers to proceed slowly to reduce the amount of dust raised on the road and prevent detection by the enemy.

You also see more camouflage as you near to the front. As we approached the trenches, the number of shell-holes and camouflage along the road increased. Also increasing were the number mangled and grotesque corpses of animals. By now, the roads are not much more than muddy ruts in the ground, made nearly impassable from all of the shell holes and dead animals.

We entered the trenches. They run for miles and miles in a zigzag manner, as far as the eye can see. They are cut 8 to 10 feet deep into the earth. For the most part, they are lined with wood and high stacks of sand bags. About every 20 to 50 feet, the line turns, left or right, runs for a while, then the trench turns back. We were led through connecting or communication trenches to the secondary line. This line was much like the one that we had just passed through. The slimy mud in the bottom of the trench was getting deeper and the over-all condition was more run-down.

As we passed through the communication trench, moving toward the front line, we were cautioned to be as quiet as possible while in the trench as the German listening posts were a mere 30 or 40 yards away. Nearly every one of us couldn't resist the temptation to pop our head over the top to have a look at No Man's Land. Rows and rows of barbed-wire cover No Man's Land. In addition to the barbed-wire, debris and bodies also cover the devastated land. The front line is also crowned with barbed-wire and dotted with rifle parapets and an occasional machine gun nest creating a strong point. All along the trench are shelves carved into the wall. Placed on the shelves are hand-grenades and bombs of all shapes and sizes to be used during attacks. The width of these over-grown ruts is scarcely wide enough for two men to pass each other. Several beams span across the trench to hold the top of the trenches back and to hinder the Hun from entering. Though I'm not certain they are very effective in that respect. In the bottom of the trenches are the bodies of dead Huns scattered about. The smell is horrific. The debris of years of conflict is scattered about everywhere to complete the scene.

August 5, 1918

We spent most of the day trying to get settled into our new surroundings. We relieved the boys of the 82nd Infantry Division who held these trenches before us. I heard that these trenches were occupied since the beginning of the war. I guess that might be true, several areas appear as though it would take years to construct with the tin roofs and re-enforced walls for the bunkers. There are also several small notches cut into the walls of the trench. These "dug-outs" or "digs" are our home-away-from-home. Everyone looked about to find the best that they could. The Officers and Sergeants usually scarf-up the larger, better built bunkers.

I claimed my hole and proceeded to set-up house-keeping. I think a family of badgers lived here before me. One of them even wrote his name in the wall. 'A YORK' is carved in the side like a signpost. This York fellow must be from the back-woods or up in the hills somewhere, considering the condition of this dug-out.

Everyone was issued a can of emergency rations and a tin of bully beef with the strict order not to open them except when ordered to do so.

August 6, 1918

We continue to improve our surroundings and try to learn all of the lessons of the fight. Important things such as keeping your head down, how to look over the top without getting your head blown off, when to flop and when not to flop from artillery, how to tell high-explosive from shrapnel from a "gasser" (that's a helpful one), what all of the different rocket and flare signals mean, the sound of a gas attack alarm, and much, much more. There are far too many things for anyone to learn at once. All we can hope for is to learn enough to stay alive until we can learn more.

August 7, 1918

It is an unsettling set of circumstances that we live under. The constant roar of artillery shell flying over head punctuated by the occasional rifle shot. Maybe a burst from a machine gun will sound off, just to make things interesting. There was a whiz-BANG of a mortar round landing near-by. The earth-shattering BOOM and smell of gun powder from an artillery shell that landed a little too close. Most definitely, there are far too many sounds to make getting any sleep possible. I wonder how long before the Boche decide to test our mettle.

August 8, 1918

That didn't take long. The Hun hit us last night, at about half past 10 o'clock, with a gas attack. It lasted almost until midnight. There was a second attack that started at 1 o'clock A. M. and lasted for two more hours.

I had just gotten back to my dug-out after spending 6 hours on watch when I heard the gas rattler and everyone yelling "GAS"!! I put on my mask, dropped the gas-curtain and waited for the attack to end. It was nearly dawn before Sergeant Thomas came by, telling everyone that it was safe to take their masks off. I took off my mask and put it away. I stepped out into the trench and looked around.

It's extremely un-nerving sitting in a black hole, straining to hear anything and realizing that a bullet or bayonet could come ripping through the curtain at any time. I'll not make that mistake again. I would rather take my chances in the trench than live through that hell again. At least I can move about and see what is happening around me.

August 9, 1918

No attack. I guess last night's gas attack was just a friendly greeting, a sort of, "Welcome to the war". We'll have to return the favor soon.

It is a very strange environment that we now find ourselves. Except for the occasional explosion and standing deep in the earth, one might forget that there's a war on.

I heard that a few boys got gassed in the attack, yesterday. That's a shame. They'll miss the whole war.

August 10, 1918

Last night was an odd experience. The whole night was spent on pins-and-needles. I imagined every little sound to be a German patrol of some sort or another. I do not think that I got more than a few minutes of rest all night long. If it were not one thing, it would be another. There are the enemy probes and raids, the artillery barrages, the standing watch all night long, and my incredibly uncomfortable digs to name but a few of the things that conspire to keep me from getting a good nights' sleep. Sooner or later, I'll just pass out from exhaustion.

August 11, 1918

Every day seems to be very much like the next. The sun comes up, the morning dew mist burns off, standing in a hole all day long, the occasional burst of machine-gun fire, the searing heat of the day, the odd whiz-bang and artillery duel, aero-planes flying over-head and firing at each other or at us, dusk and sun-set, the severe temperature drop, the enemy probes and night attacks, the flairs and the flashes from the cannons lighting up the night sky, and the ever present knowledge that at any time a sniper's bullet could take you out. Not to mention the absolutely horrendous stench that permeates everything. And there's the smoke and fog that could hide an elephant.

Why, this is just like being at home! That is if I lived in a steaming pile of horse manure. I'm being sarcastic, of course. I'll be glad when I return home.

August 12, 1918

To-day was just another fun-filled time in France. Through the night, there was a German raid in the trench, near-by. A couple of boys from Company "F" were taken prisoner. Pity the poor lads.

August 13, 1918

Slowly, but surely, I have gained the ability to sleep through almost anything. It was either that I develop this skill, or have a break-down. One of the old-timers was telling us a' few useful bits of information. How to sleep during an artillery attack, how not to sleep during a gas attack, when to flop and when not to flop were some of the more useful things for us. You can't worry about if you'll live or die. As they say in the trench, "If a bullet's got your name on it, there's nothing you can do".

<u>August 14, 1918</u>

I wonder when we'll get the chance to give the Hun a darn good thrashing.

<u>August 15, 1918</u>

I guess I should be careful about what I wish for. I'll be joining the raiding party, to-night.

I'll try to get some rest. Just before we head out, we'll go through an equipment check a brief from Sergeant Thomas. Then we'll move to our staging area and we'll be on our way.

<u>August 16, 1918</u>

THAT was exciting!!

We gathered together for our sortie just after sun-set and received our instructions and last-minute information from Sergeant Thomas. Just before mid-night, we slipped over the top and made our way toward the German line. We moved slowly and quietly across No Man's Land. The closer we came to the Huns, the slower and quieter we became until we were so close that we could see the enemy trench clearly and hear Fritz snoring in his bunk.

We found an unprotected stretch of trench and slipped in, looking for a prisoner or two. We didn't have to look too far. A couple of Hinnies came stumbling through the trench. We over-powered them quickly and with as little noise as possible so as to not arouse anyone else.

Sergeant Thomas used a bit of rope and a gag that he had brought with him in case the Huns gain consciousness before we got them back to our line. They were a bit heavy to carry. But, using two raiders to carry one prisoner we were able make our way back across No Man's Land. I suppose they were the lucky ones. The war was over for them.

Soon, we returned with our trophies and headed off to our bunks for a bit of well earned rest.

I was so keyed-up that I couldn't go to sleep for hours. I just kept remembering everything that we had just gone through.

August 17, 1918

That raid was a bit of fun. It's a shame to have to return to the serenity of the trench. We definitely need to go and do that again as soon as possible! Apart from that, life in the trench is back to normal.

August 18 to September 6, 1918

I have nothing much to say, here. Every day is much like the one before, with the exception of the occasional patrol or detail. Sometimes, I feel like jumping over the top and having a go at Fritz. That, at least, would be exciting. I'm beginning to understand a poem that someone carved into the wall of the trench:

THE GERMAN GUNS

Boom Boom Boom Boom
Boom Boom Boom
Boom Boom Boom Boom
Boom Boom Boom

I am beginning to understand and appreciate trench humor. It is actually starting to be funny. Trench superstitions make a little sense, too. Some carry a bullet with their name carved in it. If you own the bullet with your name on it, you won't get hit by it. Some believe that shaking hands with a corpse hand sticking out from the wall of the trench will bring them luck, especially just before a battle. Others believe that carrying a rabbit's foot with them will bring them luck. Though I can't help but think that wasn't very lucky for the rabbit. Nearly everyone believes in one thing or another that will help them stay alive.

Everyone believes in God.

September 7, 1918

It started to rain, to-day. That is something different. I still dare not pop my head over the top for fear of getting it shot off. I can not believe how foolish and reckless we were when we first entered the trench, peeping over the top as we did. I'm surprised that no one was killed that morning.

To keep our heads on our shoulders, we were issued a very useful piece of equipment. Corporal Gilmer came by and gave everyone a trench mirror. You attach it to the tip of your bayonet and hold it up, over the top of the trench. This provides a safe way to have a look at Fritz without risking your nut. Corporal Gilmer also issued to everyone a leather jerkin. It's helpful against the elements and rugged environment of the trench. As before with our uniforms, we were issued a jerkin without regard to our size. We were left to our own means to find one that fits (normally through trade). Those who were unable to secure a jerkin that fit, found other useful means to employ them (dugout liner or curtain, tailoring or modification of all shapes and sizes). Any way you looked at it, every scrap of material in the trench is used.

September 8, 1918

More rain.

The floor of my dug-out is turning into a quagmire. It is to the point that I have to stand up to get some rest. Nearly everything that I own is drenched. All of my clothes, my equipment, my food; everything that I have is soaked. Maybe I will get lucky and there will be a vacancy in a bunker.

September 9, 1918

Rain again. To-night is my turn at duty as OP/LP. That's short for Observation Post/Listening Post. I shall explain more when I return.

I hope that the rain ends soon.

September 10, 1918

I have returned. And, it is still raining.

Duty in the OP/LP entailed a well rehearsed procedure. First, the soldiers reports to the company headquarters to receive a briefing. Then, the pair of soldiers move-out to the OP/LP to relieve the other soldiers that have been on duty. The OP/LP is a hole in the ground some 50 yards in front of the trenches. It is connected to the front line trench by means of a narrow slip-trench or sap.

Johnny (Private Patton) and I reached our post and started our duty. We tested the telephone. Fortunately for us, it worked. We lay there all night, observing, and listening. I guess that's why they call it an observation post and a listening post. We did not observe anything. We heard plenty, but nothing of interest.

We were told to return to the trench at dawn. We had no difficulty obeying that order. We informed 1st Lieutenant Griffith of everything that we had seen, or rather not seen. Then we headed back to our digs for a bit of a rest.

Stephen E. Moss

<u>September 11, 1918</u>

Guess what? More rain.

The bottom of the trench is like a deep, slimy mud river. There's not a dry place to stand, or sleep.

Sergeant Thomas gave us the news to-day; we attack at dawn.   During our brief, Sergeant Thomas referred to the twelfth as D-Day. We are to climb over the top at 6 o'clock A.M., H-Hour as he called it. This reference to D-Day and H-Hour was a new phrase we had not heard before. It must be part of this new code talk that everyone is using.

I'll try to get some rest before the attack.

<u>September 12, 1918</u>

WHAT A DAY!!! I'll try to recall all.

The entire night was charged with excitement, getting ready for the dawn.   Everyone was so excited, we hardly got any rest. We checked our equipment and weapons.   Making certain that everything was in proper working order and ready to go, off for the big push (that's what we call the start of battle).

The boys of the assault battalion had worked through the night clearing obstacles, removing mines, cutting paths through the barbed wire, and working diligently to prepare No Man's Land to make it easier to cross and improve our attack.

The artillery barrage lasted for about an hour. The noise and pounding from the impact was tremendous! It was hard to imagine that anything could survive such a devastating onslaught.

We lined up against the wall of the trench and waited for the signal. 6 o'clock and the shrill of the whistles sounded. We climbed up and over the top!

That's as far as our good fortune lasted. We had not gone more than a couple of yards when we were up to our knees in some of the worst mud and goop that I have ever seen. We made our way past the barbed wire, moved through the mud and shell holes full of water, across the field until finally, we reached the German line.

A near-by machine gun opened up and its fire had us pinned down. I dug as deep into the mud as I could. For the first time, I had a chance to look around and take stock of the situation. Our boys were scattered all over the field. There was no way to tell who was alive and who was not.

Something caught my eye. Several large iron-clad motor cars and many smaller ones were making their way across the field. Unfortunately, it appeared that the majority of them were stuck in the mud. I have no doubt that, under dryer circumstances, those armored motor cars would be of great assistance in an attack. A burst of machine gun fire hitting near me quickly brought me back to the situation at hand.

No sooner had I started to form an idea about what to do to silence that machine gun when I saw someone jump up and run straight toward the Boche gun, throwing hand grenades, firing his revolver and encouraging us to follow him. It was Corporal Gilmer. He cleaned out that machine gun nest. But, not before they cut him down. That had to be the bravest act I have ever seen.

Out of rage over Corporal Gilmer going down, several of us got up and ran toward Jerry. We climbed to the top and jumped into the Hun's trench and fought them hand-to-hand. That was the worst fight I have ever been in. It was so crowded at times that you couldn't swing your arm to get in a good punch. Our trench knifes came in mighty handy. Several times, we couldn't tell who was a friend and who was a foe. Soon, we were the only ones standing in the trench.

Sergeant Thomas gathered us together and told us that we were going to continue the attack. We checked our equipment and ammunition, and started to move through the Mort Mare forest. That was one dense forest. It seemed like there was a Machine gun nests hidden behind every tree. I took some doing, but we cleared Mort Mare.

The vast open field beyond the forest was a welcome sight. Our objective was the town of Beney some 6 miles away. We reached our objective around 3 o'clock P. M.

There was a road, but it was of no use. There were artillery pot holes, the corpses of dead Germans and horses, wrecked wagons and carts making the road impassable.

When we reached Bouillonville, a few of the civilians crawled out of their hiding holes. The wide eyed look on their faces was something to behold. At first, I couldn't tell if it was the look of shock or fear. Their look soon changed when they saw that we were Americans! The look became one of joy as they realized that the hated invader had at last been driven out. The way they greeted us with feelings almost too deep for expression was felt in the very bottom of our hearts.

The fires were still burning in the stoves of the military kitchens. We found huge kettles full of food. No doubt a lot of German stomachs went empty that night. We enjoyed a fine meal. Afterwards we set up a defensive line just north of town. The first day of the assault came to a close. Today was a day of a lot of firsts.

September 13, 1918

We continued our assault.

The Boche put up a fight from hastily dug fox holes and shallow trenches. We knocked the Krauts on their heels and sent them running. Many of them surrendered. Fritz looked like he was tired of fighting.

We passed by the village of Xammes. There was another jerry kitchen and fires under kettles full of food and another fine meal. We filled our stomachs and then our pockets with as much food as they could hold.

By the end of the day, we had advanced about a mile.

September 14, 1918

Sergeant Thomas told us to stop after only a mile. We started digging fox holes and improving our positions.

The 2nd Infantry Division on our right was clearing some woods and had fallen back. Remembering the Mort Mare forest, I don't doubt that they might be having a rough time of it.

September 15, 1918

We continued to improve our position. The Germans fired on us every now and again. The 2nd Infantry Division on our right came on line.

September 16, 1918

More improvements were done to our position. We strung some wire and put out some tangle-foot. It's starting to look like the trench where we began. Before we arrived in France, we were told that men were fighting and dying for yards over the last three years. Our first fight and we advanced eight miles! That's American know-how. I still can't believe Corporal Gilmer's gone.

September 17, 1918

Everything looks very much like the trenches from where we started. Even our digs are coming along nicely. Unfortunately, one obvious difference is that all of our personal gear and equipment is not with us. All that we have is what we carried with us. I'm beginning to think that it might have been a good idea to wear my backpack.

Also, our supplies are running low. Most notably is the food. The kettles of food that we captured was the last that we had to eat and that was four days ago. All of our emergency rations have run out, too. Where are those supply trucks?

We've scrounged as much as we can. We've taken all of the spare ammunition from the wounded and the dead that we can find. We've also taken as much food off of the Hun prisoners and anything we can find from the corpses. We did anything that we needed to do to survive.

September 18, 1918

Still, the supply trucks have not arrived. I'm feeling a bit gaunt. It's hard to keep in mind that we are here to fight a war. Also, the lack of artillery is ominous. The silence is very unsettling.

September 19, 1918

Where is that Supply Sergeant? It's been a week! It only took us three days to walk this far, and we were fighting the Hun! Are they lost?

Many of the boys are foraging for anything that they can find or catch. The only thing that there are plenty of are rats. It's not much. But, it's better than nothing. You just have to close your eyes, hold your breath and think of something else, anything else.

I'm thinking that the Germans are just as tired and hungry as we are. Otherwise they would have attacked by now. We are told the German defense before us is the Hindenburg Line. From what I can see, it is not very much. Much of it is less than what we have managed to build over the last week. The trenches were unfinished and in some places they had not even begun to dig them. Somehow, that doesn't seem to match with the image we were given of this great defensive fortification, the Hindenburg line. Had we been given enough supplies and support, we could have punched through it with no difficulty at all.

September 20, 1918

We received good news to-day, we are being relieved! To-night, we'll leave the line and go into reserve. All I can say is that I hope the field kitchen is operating!

September 21, 1918

It was. That was the best meal I have ever had in my life!

We were told to rest for the remainder of the day. That was one order that no one argued or complained about.

September 22, 1918

I feel much better! We spent the day cleaning our equipment and ourselves. There was a truck loaded with all of our packs from the trench where we started. We sorted through and tried to find our own. The fellows that picked up the packs didn't take care to get everything. Nor did they handle what they did pick up with care.

I'll have to keep this in mind for the future. If I want to keep any souvenirs, I'll have to hide them, pack them, or carry them with me. Otherwise some administration clerk in the rear will have a trophy that they didn't earn.

Several doughboys received good news. Orders for promotions were handed out. Private Joseph Farrell is now Private First Class Farrell. Private Andy Robinson is now Corporal Robinson. He certainly has come a long way from his farm near Omaha, Nebraska.

September 23, 1918

More refitting, resupplying, and replacing doughboys we lost in the battle. No one could ever replace Corporal Gilmer or the other lads that we lost. I'm certain that Corporal Robinson will perform in an exemplary manner. Additionally, we received several fresh new troops to fill our ranks.

We began training to get the new troops used to the trenches and for us to get used to the new troops. One thing that I have noticed is how quickly the new troops have picked up cooties. Everyone is scratching themselves. The straw that we sleep on, the clothes that we wear, everything that we have is infested with cooties. I am certain that I have a family of them living on me.

September 24 to 29, 1918

This time was spent training and preparing to return to the line. I took the opportunity to look around. There really is a lot of death and destruction all around. In spite of all of that, there is a lot of natural beauty, too.

September 30, 1918

Our little rest is over. We go back in the line to-night.

October 1, 1918

"Once more, into the breach" as Mr. Shakespeare said. Not much has changed. Fritz appears to have improved their position greatly. We were told of a raid on the enemy in Bois de Dommartin that took place on the night of 25-26 September, 1918, by a group of 100 lads from the 354th Infantry. This, along with raids all along the American line, was to confuse the Germans as to the location of the actual attack in the Argonne.

October 2 to 7, 1918

Life in the trench is back to normal. Everything is just as it was before.

The Artillery duels, the occasional dog fight and air attack, and the nightly raids and probes keep everyone on their toes.

October 8, 1918

We were relieved by the 37th Division to-day. They had recently been engaged in the Battle in the Argonne. They looked tired.

We marched back some twenty to thirty kilometers to the vicinity of Commercy. We were far enough back that we could take off our gas mask and tin derby and hang them on a nail. A rest would be nice. But the fight is in the Argonne and that's where we need to be.

October 9, 1918

Our rest is over. We loaded on 40/8 cars. They're called 40/8 because of a marking on the side of the rail car, indicating that the car can carry 40 Hommes (men) or 8 Chevauxs (horses). I'm sure the 8 Chevauxs are much more comfortable than the 40 Hommes. They are rough, crowded, filthy, and the stench is beyond description.

The train moved across the country-side to our staging area near Verdun itself. We then loaded onto French trucks that took us to our training area where we refitted and trained for our upcoming fight.

October 10 to 12, 1918

We spend five hours a day training and preparing for what we can expect in the fight to come. The tactics and drills incorporate many of the lessons that we learned at St. Mihiel. One item in particular was that every man was issued two extra bandoliers of ammunition and at least two hand-grenades. This will greatly enhance our ability to continue the fight.

In addition to our training, we also received several new troops that came from the 86th Division. The

86th Division was broken up and used for replacement purposes upon their arrival in France. These replacements were fine stalwart men from Michigan and Wisconsin. These men appear eager and well qualified to stand alongside the veterans of the 89th.

October 13, 1918

We spent the day moving forward, past bombed out buildings, wrecked stone walls and tree stumps, past endless lines of wire and trenches and through the shell torn area that had once been No Man's Land, until at last we came to bivouac in the mud near Epinonville. The roads were so blocked with traffic that the kitchens were unable to keep up with us. Oh well.

October 14 to 18, 1918

Here we waited for orders to move up into the line. We didn't have long to wait. We received word that we were to relieve the 32nd Infantry Division.

October 19 to 20, 1918

Through the night, we replaced the 32nd Infantry Division in the line. At this, we have achieved a level of very high proficiency. We were able to relieve the 32ⁿᵈ so quickly and quietly that we accomplished the task in half the allowed time and without the use of Guides to show us the way. A very impressive action, indeed!

Our fresh troops, though new to the trench, performed in an exemplary manner. I'm certain that they will handle themselves equally well when the order to attack comes.

Once again, we were back in the line. The battle has been raging for nearly a month. Great gains have been made, but at a great cost. The boys who started the attack are worn out and in desperate need of some well deserved rest.

We had little time to rest ourselves. We were immediately tasked with clearing the Bois de Bantheville. "F" Company was selected to lead the assault with us following closely behind. H-hour was 2 o'clock P.M. Around noon, "F" Company formed up in front of our position. There was a delay of sorts and "F" Company didn't jump off until their revised H-hour of 8 o'clock P.M.

They immediately encountered strong resistance. We could hear the heavy machine guns. But, there was no stopping the brave lads of "F" Company.

They fought their way through the Hun all through the night and well into the next day.

October 21, 1918

"F" Company continued their attack. By 3:30 P.M., they reached the southern slope of the hill about a kilometer from where we started when several machine guns opened up on them. "F" Company was spent and down to the strength of a Platoon. We took up the attack.

We charged through the woods and up the hill, dislodging those jerry guns. We reached our objective, the northern edge of the woods, by 4:30 P.M. Here we halted and started to construct our defensive positions. That was a day to remember!

October 22, 1918

We continued to improve our positions. Here, we faced a new threat, air raids. German air planes appeared almost continuously over our lines, machine gunning and dropping bombs on us completely unopposed. Where is our air service? All air and no service, I guess. It was easy to spot the gloriously colored planes of the "Richthofen Circus".

Stephen E. Moss

October 23, 1918

Johnny Patton was hit, to-day. We managed to patch him up and got him into an ambulance. I hope that he'll be alright.

October 24 to 30, 1918

This week went by with little change. The Circus in the air, the shells on the ground, the gas attacks, the raids and counter-attacks go on and on.
We did lose two of the new lads during this time, what a pity.

October 31, 1918

Word reached us that the time has come for the big push. The 177th Brigade will take the attack while we will be close behind in reserve. D-day is November 1, 1918; H-hour is 5:30 A.M. At 10 o'clock P.M. the Artillery barrage began and continued through the night.

November 1, 1918

The early morning fog covered the battlefield, the signal flares burst over head, the whistles shrilled and our boys went over the top!

The 177th Brigade jumped off right on schedule. They attacked by Battalion in depth with 1000 meters between the front element and the rear element. The 353rd Regiment was in front of us.

The soul-shattering din of the artillery, supported by every trench mortar on the line and insistent tap-tap-tapping of the machine guns made for a truly awe inspiring sight. Just before H-hour, smoke rounds were mixed in with the high explosive rounds shrouding the Hun's position and obscuring out forces as they advanced. The attack elements advanced tightly behind the barrage and battered down any resistance that manifested itself along the way. The Germans put up a vigorous defensive with their artillery. But, they must have gotten their lines crossed because they heavily shelled the wrong area. Our lads advanced almost untouched.

All of the objectives of the first day were accomplished on schedule! We had advanced some 8 kilometers and captured the Heights of Barricourt in the face of fierce German resistance.

November 2, 1918

The barrage to-day was not nearly as thunderous as yesterday. Instead, our troops successfully advanced against bitter resistance of the enemy in strong and well-prepared positions across the open with the use of practically nothing, but the doughboy's own weapons.

German artillery was fierce. They rained high explosive and gas down on top of us every step of the way.

In spite of all of these disadvantages, the 353rd Regiment reached their objective just after night fall. Our troops advanced three more kilometers and captured the cities of Barricourt, Tailly, and Nouart. But the cost was high. The 177th Brigade was spent. The order came through for us to pick up the fight in the morning. Our lads are ready.

November 3, 1918

9:00 A.M. We passed through the lines of the 177th Brigade through the night jumped off on our attack. We met light resistance, initially. We were able to reach our objective by 9:30 A.M. So we pressed on. Enemy resistance increased as the day wore on. Even with increased resistance, we were able to take Beauclair and Halles (Halles was originally in the 90th Division's sector to our right) by night fall, four kilometers from where we started.

November 4, 1918

We started the day's attack at 8:30 A.M. against strong resistance.

To our great delight, we heard that Beufort, about two kilometers to our right, had already been taken. Some of our boys had advanced through the night and taken the town by dawn. This enabled us to concentrate on reaching the Foret de Dieulet some three kilometers away.

Fritz just doesn't want to give up! We reached the forest and fought our way through. The spectacular artillery support we received at the start of this attack is but a distant memory.

The Hun machine gun nests were well hidden. We didn't see one until it opened up on us. Pvt. 1cl. Farrell was practically cut in two. We cleaned out that nest and many more besides.

We reached the far edge of the forest with enough time in the day to mount an attack on La Neuville.

This we did and took the town by night fall. One unfortunate discovery that we made was that the main bridge to Stenay has been destroyed. That might cause a bit of a problem in the morning.

We've now been back in the line for 15 days and advanced some 25 kilometers against extremely dogged defenses. Our casualties have been high. But, our morale is higher. Jerry's on the run and there's an overwhelming feeling in the air that the end is near!!!

November 9, 1918

I'm not sure that I comprehend the events of the last few days. I'll try to recount as much as I am able.

I remember the morning of the fifth. We had to ford the river on our way to Stenay as the bridge was out. As we approached Stenay, the German resistance stiffened greatly. It seemed as every building and ditch was fortified and turned into a machine gun nest or strong hold. We were just outside of town when a machine gun opened up on us. We flopped into a near-by ditch. It is here where everything becomes a blur.

For reasons unknown to me, I jumped up, out of the ditch, and ran towards the machine gun nest. I threw a hand grenade through the opening and silenced that gun. No sooner had that happened than someone started shooting at me. I fired back and ran towards them. This series of events repeated itself two or three more times. Someone would fire at me, I would fire back, and the shooting would stop. Then there came a blinding light, unbelievable din, crushing pain, and finally darkness.

It is in that darkness that I really do not understand. Everything was like a dream, or night-mare. I saw the trenches that we lived in for so long. I saw many, many doughboys all around. I thought that I recognized Corporal Gilmer. Darkness set upon me again. The next dream that I remember was a bombed out building with ragged curtains over what use to be windows. The darkness and dreams continued with neither rhyme nor reason. Most of these I can't remember.

Slowly, I returned to consciousness. Little by little I became aware of my surroundings. At first, I thought that I might be in Heaven. Then I was hoping that I wasn't in Hell. As my level of consciousness increased and I could see more around me, I became aware that I was in a building of some kind. The lights were bright and everything was white (sort of). I started to become aware of the sounds around me at about this time. It took a while until I realized that I must be in a hospital. But who's hospital, ours or theirs?

I tried to look at the other patients near-by. I was unable to move enough to see anyone. So, I must wait until someone comes to check on me. Maybe then, I could learn more. I did.

The nurse came to check on me. I have never seen such a beautiful sight in my life. All I could think was, "I hope she's not German". She wasn't.

She's French. I had been taken back to one of our field hospitals. Then, darkness fell upon me again.

I returned to consciousness again. Only slightly confused this time, I soon remembered that I was in a field hospital. I managed to stay awake long enough to ask some questions. I was indeed in a field hospital. To-day is November the ninth. I had been here for three days. My wounds are expected to heal. I should be able to return to my unit soon. There was very little else that I could get from the nurses. They spoke English for the most part. Either they didn't understand my questions, didn't know the answer, or wouldn't tell me the answer. I'm not certain which one applies here. Much to my surprise and delight, my journal was in with my kit! Also, to my great fortune, my hand was free and able to write.

November 10, 1918

I'm still trying to piece together a frame of an idea of what happened since November fifth. I have written what I can remember, but there are still gaps, a whole day, in fact. And then there's that angel that I saw. Did I dream her? When I ask about her, no one knows whom I mean.

I tried to get a better assessment as to the extent and severity of my wounds. I have all of my limbs, thank the Lord!!! There are several bandages, mostly on my left side. The pain is not nearly as bad as I would have imagined. Maybe I'm not that badly wounded. Then again, it might be the medication.

November 11, 1918

THE WAR IS OVER!!!

Word reached us that at 11:00 A.M. a cease fire was declared. German delegates crossed over No Man's Land to surrender! This will be a day to remember, the War to end all Wars is over. I wish I could have been out there with our boys, instead of laid-up here in this hospital. I hope I can re-join them soon.

On a different front, I'm still trying to understand the events of the past week. I think the missing day might have been spent in an aid station or something to that effect. I suppose it doesn't matter. It's just that I would like to know what happened.

The celebration and jubilance continued throughout the day. Doctors, nurses, orderlies, and patients alike were cheering and carrying on in such a manner. I was no exception. I had to be careful not to open my wounds and start bleeding. Everyone who could move about, on foot, with crutches, or in a wheelchair was doing so. Through the crowd of people in the ward, it happened. I caught a glimpse of my angel.

At first I wasn't certain that I had seen her. After all, I was unsure if she existed at all. Then, I couldn't be sure it was her, or if she was as pretty as I remembered. She came by my bed. She was more beautiful than I had remembered. She spoke to me. I had never heard such glorious tones before. It was pure music to my ears. She asked how I was doing. She told me how she had kept nearly constant vigil over me since I had arrived. It was her that I remembered seeing! This was a day that I would never forget.

Her name is Mademoiselle Annette d'Arcy. She is a nurse here at the Field Hospital. She had been gone for the past few days to visit her parents. That explains why I hadn't seen her recently. It doesn't explain why no one knew of her when I made inquires.

November 12, 1918

I suppose that I should correct one item. The Germans have not surrendered. They signed a ceasefire agreement in order to work on a treaty. Hostilities could resume at any time. We must still be on our guard. Still, they have given their word and the formality should follow soon.

November 13, 1918

Mlle. d'Arcy spends a large portion of her days checking on how I'm doing. I couldn't be doing any better if she spent all of her time with me. I often consider feigning an illness, just so she would stay longer.

November 14, 1918

Mlle. d'Arcy brought me a newspaper, The Stars and Stripes. She said that she noticed that I wrote considerably in my journal and thought that I might enjoy having something to read. The Stars and Stripes was the only thing written in English that she could find. She said that she would try to find some more, if I would like. I wouldn't care if she brought me something written in German, as long as it was from her.

The paper was dated September 25, 1918. There was an article about the Battle of St Mihiel. That seems like a life time ago. The article talked about the large use of the heavy metal automobiles that I remembered seeing. The article called them tanks. They are a fierce looking contraption. I can definitely see their usefulness on the battlefield. There was also a mention of the day and time of the jump off of the attack. I remember the mention of the use of D-Day and H-Hour for that morning. It said in the article that this was first time that these terms had been used. I guess this war is full of firsts.

The article went on to describe the problems that the artillery and supply trucks had in keeping up with the speed of our advancement. The engineers tried to build new roads. They met with limited success. Having crawled through those shell holes and crossed those knee-deep muddy fields, I don't doubt that they had a rather difficult time trying to traverse that countryside. That would also explain why it took so long for us to be re-supplied, and fed.

<u>November 15 to 27, 1918</u>

Mlle. d'Arcy continued to bring me anything that she could find that was written in English.

One article wrote about an entire battalion that was trapped behind enemy lines. Some 590 men of the 77th Division had advanced a mile behind the German line and held on to a 600 meter long pocket for five days. That had to be a real thorn in Jerry's side to have a Lost Battalion sitting there for such a long time. This too happened during the Argonne Offensive, beginning around the second of October, 1918. There certainly was a lot of action in that offensive. I still have not read anything about our efforts.

Another article of interest was about a hero of the Argonne Offensive. A Corporal Alvin C. York and seven men had taken 132 Germans prisoner! It happened about the same time as we moved into the line on the seventh of October, 1918. I remember an "A YORK" carved into the post of my first digs. I wonder if this is the same person.

November 28, 1918

The Doctor removed several stitches and many of my bandages to-day. From what I could see, my wounds are not very bad. Even the scars are not very noticeable. I will truly be blessed if this is the extent of my wounds.

I made inquiries into how I received my injuries. The doctor was able to tell me the nature of my wounds, fragmentation mostly. As to how I received them, he could only speculate. He said that most of my injuries appeared to have been caused by shrapnel. By either a shell or hand grenade going off near me. There were some other lacerations and abrasions that might have been caused by flying or falling debris. The doctor also said that I should be able to rejoin my regiment soon. I was excited to hear this last piece of information. I noticed, though, that Mlle. d'Arcy appeared rather unhappy. Perhaps I read too much into her facial expression. Perhaps I imagined that there might be more than a simple nurse-patient relationship.

November 29 to December 9, 1918

I watched Mlle. d'Arcy closely over the next several days. I just had to know if what I thought that I saw in her eyes was real, or was it just my imagination.

The closer that I observed, the further away the answer seemed to be. I would watch as she attended to her duties with cold, distant, detachment. I'm certain that any relationship that we might have is strictly professional. Then I would see how her whole face would radiate when she would look my way. The way her eyes would sparkle and shine, how her beautiful lips would curl into such a soft, warm smile, the spring in her step, the music in her voice, this couldn't be my imagination. This is enough to drive a man insane! I must know. I shall taunt myself no further. I will ask her when next I see her.

December 10, 1918

I can't believe it! I simply can not believe it! I was resolved to ask Mlle. d'Arcy if she had any feelings for me. I had steeled myself for a cold, hard truth of nothing beyond that of a nurse for her patient.

Instead, I received the warmest hearted response of "yes"! She did care for me more than just as a patient.

She was afraid that I might not care about her. The sorrow and occasional coldness that I had noticed in her expression came from when she thought of my returning to my unit. She feared that she might never see me again.

What joy! My mind is a whirl! I feel as if my heart is going to burst out of my chest! I shall write more when I calm down.

December 11 to 24, 1918

I'm still all a flutter.

Annette spends every spare minute that she has at my bed side. We spend hours upon hours talking about everything and nothing.

Annette told me that she made a promise to herself when she became a nurse that she would not get involved with a patient. And, as the war dragged on, she was right to make such a pledge. The number of soldiers that came through the hospital was unimaginable. Some of them were sent home after they were healed, mostly without limbs or sight or some other mutilation. Many of the brave lads died in the hospital. The rest were sent back to the line. Annette would never know the fate of any of these young men. She was able to keep herself at a professional distance, until she saw me. She told me that there was something about me, that from the moment I arrived in the ward that she could not pull herself from my side. She continually told herself not to get involved, that nothing good could come from such an affair. With the end of the war and when I told her how I felt, she could hold back her emotions no further.

December 25, 1918 Christmas Day

The day's celebration got off to a wonderful start. I awoke to find Annette sitting beside me. That alone was the best present that I could have received. With the war causing shortages in everything, there was little left for gifts. However, she had more surprise for me. From her pocket, she pulled out a sprig of mistletoe and held it above us. Simple gifts of the heart are often the best. We utilized her gift several times throughout the day.

December 26, 1918

The doctor removed more bandages and changed the remaining ones to-day. I'm feeling stronger every day. Although that might be due to the excellent care I've received from my nurse. Annette's personal care has been instrumental to my recovery.

The doctor also mentioned that he would have to operate to remove some of the large pieces of shrapnel. I notice the look of sorrow on Annette's face again. I hadn't seen that look for some time.

December 27 to 31, 1918

We returned to a normal existence. Annette would make her rounds of the ward then spend the remainder of her time with me. We would then spend our time talking about anything and everything. I showed her some of my journal entries. She noticed the gap just before I came to the hospital. She told me that she would try to learn what happened. That would be wonderful. But, I fear she might not meet with much success.

January 1, 1919 New Year's Day

May this bright, New Year bring joy and happiness to all.

The earnest, heartfelt joy that everyone celebrated with seems to be a continuation of the jubilation first felt from the end of the war. After so many years of sorrow and suffering, the out-pouring of such emotions is quite understandable.

Everyone celebrated the New Year with song and noise makers. Annette and I celebrated in our own way, privately, as privately as an open ward would allow.

January 2 to 10, 1919

These days have been some of the best days of my life, certainly the best within recent memory. Annette and I spend every moment together. Time seems to stand still when we are together. We would spend hours talking and getting to know each other. We learned about each other's likes and dislikes and how we felt about anything and everything. With every conversation, I fell more and more in love with Annette, and she with me.

Annette has been assisting me in learning to speak French, as I have been assisting in improving her English. One curious expression that I learned in the trench is "sortie". We used it to refer to a patrol. Annette told me that it means "exit". I suppose that whoever came up with that usage of the word was referring to us "exiting" the trench when we went on patrols.

Day by day, I felt myself growing stronger in body and heart. I never thought that this sort of thing to be possible. Perhaps I am manifesting my elation at the cessation of hostilities in the form of Annette. No matter what it is, I intend to enjoy every moment that comes my way.

January 11, 1919

Annette was very sad this morning. She told me that I was to go in for surgery this after-noon. I think now I understand the sorrow behind Annette's beautiful eyes. Recently, she told me how time after time she witnessed wounded Soldiers go in for surgery only to die or return dismembered or disfigured. She fears greatly that this will happen to me. I attempted to reassure her that this would not be the case. Unfortunately, my words do not even convince me. Oh how I hope she is wrong!

January 12, 1919

I do not believe that I have been that frightened in my life!

As I regained consciousness, I remember a wash of lights and colors. One by one, shapes became recognizable. Next, there came confusion and fear. With the realization that I was in a hospital came the remembrance of why I was there and my fear grew. I was alive, but in what condition and do I have all of my limbs. Annette, where's Annette?

I saw Annette right beside me. The moment I looked into her eyes, all of my fears disappeared. The happiness that I saw let me know that everything went successfully and that everything would be alright. Relieved, I slipped back into darkness.

January 13, 1919

I awoke to find Annette sitting right where I remembered seeing her.

As I regained the use of my arms and hands, I explored the extent of my new injuries. The bandages indicate chest and arm wounds. Annette also mentioned that there was some surgery done on my back. She also told me that the doctor believed that I would have a complete recovery with minimum scarring. That would explain the happiness in her eyes.

January 14 to 31, 1919

I can not begin to describe the joy and ecstasy each day brings. I can not wait until to-morrow for each day brings new levels of rapture! I want nothing more than to spend every minute with Annette! What's even more unbelievable is that she appears to want to be with me!

Annette did make some inquiries for me as to the nature of how I came to be in the hospital. She was unable to obtain any particulars as to the details. She was able to learn the whereabouts of my unit, the 89th Infantry. They had moved on and are now in Germany. It was a bit difficult to obtain any particulars due to language barriers and a natural suspicion of foreigners on the part of our boys. She did hear of one rumor regarding the 89th Infantry.

Annette had heard that the 89th Infantry had attacked a village after the cease-fire of 11:00 A.M. on the eleventh of November, 1918. I can't believe our stalwart boys would do anything so dastardly deliberately. In the unlikely case that there is any truth in these stories, I'm certain that it would be as a result of the orders not being received in time. Most likely it's just some Hun propaganda meant to discredit our lads or cause dissent between our troops.

An even weightier matter exists. With the end of the war, our victorious forces will be returning home to America. For the time being, while awaiting our departure, my unit is located in Germany. This troubles me greatly as I don't wish to leave Annette. There must be a solution to this dilemma.

February 1, 1919

A solution might be at hand. An Officer went around the ward, calling for volunteers to join a unit remaining in Europe. It is a unit in the Regular Army and there is the possibility of promotion. The National Army units like the 89th Infantry will demobilize when they return to the United States. Transferring to the Regular Army would keep me gainfully employed. This could afford me the opportunity to remain near Annette for a time sufficient to affix a more permanent situation.

Perhaps I should take up residency here and seek my fortune in France. I've already learned a great deal of the language and Annette could assist me to learn more. Still, France is in a shambles and its job market is almost non-existent. I must remember to be open to any and all possibilities.

February 2, 1919

I thought it through and have decided to join the unit remaining in Europe. I submitted my transfer request. I can't say that Annette was too happy. But, she was pleased at the prospects of my staying in Europe versus returning to America. She also agreed that there would be poor prospects at finding employment. All things considered, this was the best option available.

February 3 to 19, 1919

My stay in the hospital is drawing to a close. The majority of my wounds are healed and the doctor has indicated that I should be ready for discharge soon.

Still, all that concerns me is to be with Annette.

February 20, 1919

An interesting coincidence occurred to-day. My discharge from the hospital arrived at the same time as the approval for my transfer. I won't be returning to the 355th Regiment, I am now assigned to "E" Company of the 12ᵗʰ Infantry Regiment of the 8ᵗʰ Infantry Division. My orders will soon follow and I will take up my new station. With any luck at all, I won't be very far from Annette.

Annette told me that she is planning to stay with her parents in Reims after she is released from service. Perhaps she could get a position with a hospital considering her abundance of experience.

Annette confided in me that she feared that I would forget about her, that this was just one of those "war-time" romances. I tried to assure her that that was certainly not the case. I promised to write to her as soon as I reached my new duty station. I would use her parents address until she has a place of her own. As a safe guard, I gave her my parents address. One way or another, we would be able to stay in contact with each other. Or at least our parents will get to know each other. This seemed to ease her mind and humor her.

The crushing weight in my chest was almost too much to bear. I just wanted to hold her. I did not want to go. But, duty calls and I must obey. I gathered up my kit bag and waited outside of the hospital for my transportation to arrive. I took a moment to see where my new duty station is located. It is in a place called Siberia.

Stephen E. Moss

ON TO SIBERIA

February 21, 1919

Annette and I said our fare-wells. I loaded my bags onto the truck and climbed on board. As the truck pulled away from the hospital, I continued to wave and watch her until I could see her no more. I then continued to stare at the spot on the horizon where I had last seen her. The jolt from a pot hole and the chiding from the lads in the truck soon brought me back to the situation at hand.

While traveling to the rail station, we had the opportunity to observe the carnage and destruction this war wreaked upon the countryside. Never would I have thought it possible that man was capable of such atrocities.

We arrived at the train station. Sergeant McKinney introduced himself to us by calling us together and reading of a list of names to ensure we had all arrived. We were all present. Captain Anderson introduced himself and told us that we were to re-enforce our troops in Siberia. He also told us that more information would be forth coming.

The train arrived. We climbed aboard and settled in for our journey.

February 22, 1919

We headed eastward, ever toward the rising sun. I wonder just how far this Siberia could be.

Our Detachment wasted no time and started doing what doughboys do best; entertaining themselves. Cards and chess boards were brought out. Books and the odd instrument added to the gay atmosphere. The majority of our group is new troops who arrived in Europe too late to take part in the fight. There are maybe a dozen veterans of the trench. These soldiers are easy to spot in a crowd; they are the quiet ones.

February 23, 1919

Our train stopped near the German border. We got off of the train and on to some trucks. Again, we were headed eastward.

There was a striking contrast as soon as we crossed into Germany. First, and most notably, was the fact that the signs were no longer written in French. Everything was now written in German. Secondly, all of the road-sign posts had been broken off. Perhaps that was done by the retreating Germans in an attempt to confuse the advancing allied forces. Another difference that was soon noticed was that the German roads were not nearly as well built as the French roads. Riding over the poor condition of the roads had us shaken up more than an artillery attack.

We finally arrived at the train station at Trier. As we got off of the trucks, I recognized the sign over the platform. It was the rolling "W" of the 89th Infantry Division. I figured that we would have a few minutes before our train arrived and went to the reception office just on the off chance that I might see someone that I knew. Much to my surprise, I saw Corporal, now Sergeant Robinson sitting behind the desk.

He was extremely surprised to see me. He, like everyone else in our old unit, thought that I had died from that fight at Stenay. I congratulated him on his promotion and I assured him that I hadn't died, that I had been in the field hospital and am now on my way to Siberia.

Sergeant Robinson told me what he remembered from that morning. He told me that he saw me dashing about from machine gun nest to machine gun nest and German strong hold, throwing grenades and firing an assortment of weapons until there was no more resistance. No sooner had everyone else jumped up to advance than an explosion went off throwing me 20 feet into the air. When they reached me, they expected to find me dead. Instead, I was still alive. They quickly fashioned a litter team and took me to the nearest aid-station. He left me at the aid-station and returned to the company. That was the last that he had seen of me until now. I listened to this account with complete wonderment as if I were hearing the story of someone else. Only occasionally did his story spark a memory or sound vaguely familiar.

Sergeant Robinson told me that I had been cited for gallantry. He also happened to have a copy of the citation, which he gave me. He said that they still had much of my things.

I gave him my parents address and dashed off a quick letter to Mother explaining the circumstances so that she would not worry. I asked Sergeant Robinson to send anything that he might have of mine to her.

I thanked him and said good-bye as our train had arrived and I had to be on my way. It was marvelous to see him again.

February 24 to 28, 1919

These German trains are not too bad. They are a bit slow as we made several stops along the way. Every where you look, you can see the hardship that the years of war have taken upon the German people. Whenever we stop at a town or city, you can see the people wrapped in rags, digging through rubbish bins for anything that they can find. Among them can be seen wounded veterans. They are not exempt from this hardship, even though they have suffered enough already. Now-and-then they would look at the train and recognize us as doughboys. Always, there comes an instant look of hatred in their eyes. As if we are to blame for their misfortune.

Beyond this, the German countryside is very beautiful. I would certainly enjoy a visit here sometime in the future.

March 1, 1919

We reached the Russian border. Again the language on the signs changed. I can't even describe the Russian alphabet.

While we were waiting for our ride, Sergeant McKinney had us take our weapons apart and hide the pieces in our kit bags. He also distributed all of our supplies and ammunition among everyone and instructed us to hide everything in our bags, too.

While we were doing this, Captain Anderson gave us another briefing. We knew about going to re-enforce our forces in Russia. Captain Anderson explained that those forces had been sent to Siberia in August, 1918 to help protect the Trans-Siberian Rail Way. Ever since the Russian Revolution, several groups were vying for control. The principle forces are the Bolshevik Red Army, the Czarist and Provisional Government White Army, the Ukrainian Nationalist Green Army, and the Ukrainian Anarchist Black Army and Black Guard. Additionally, there are several war-lords and bands of Cossacks all trying to claim as much land and power as they can. As if this is not enough, there are an unknown number of marauding bandits using the situation as an excuse to loot and pillage. Many Allied Nations have sent troops to protect areas of interest. Britain, France, Czech-Slovak, Japan, Finland, and Italy are a few of the countries that have sent troops.

The carts arrived. We loaded up and continued on our trek.

March 2 to 10, 1919

Transportation is a mixture of carts, trucks and trains. The roads are little better than dirt trails or cart paths. We were stopped several times by all types of marauding bands of people. The ones that spoke English tried to gain intelligence on our mission and equipment. The ones that didn't speak English just made a lot of noise and waved their weapons in the air. All of them appeared to be surprised to find that we were American soldiers. I think that might have frightened them.

We finally arrived at the train station in Moscow and the Trans-Siberian Rail Way. I thought that we had reached our destination, but Captain Anderson informed us that we were waiting for the train. Our duty station was at the other end of the line, at a place called Vladivostok.

March 11, 1919

While waiting for the train, we huddled together for warmth. We are FREEZING! I don't think I have ever been this cold. I can barely write in my journal, my fingers are so cold. I think that family of cooties on me has frozen to death. I'm not scratching as much as I did before. That is good as

I wouldn't be able to scratch through all of these clothes.

The train arrived and we boarded. We were given spaces in the luxury cars. I guess they were luxury because they had benches and windows. Actually, compared to the 40/8 cars we rode in back in France, these are very luxurious.

At least it's warmer than standing outside.

<u>March 12 to 25, 1919</u>

We departed the train station and made our way down the line. Generally speaking, we made very good time. The only times that we stopped was for scheduled halts such as stations and mail stops. We also stopped for unscheduled reasons. This could be due to snow covering the tracks, herds of animals blocking our way, mechanical break-downs or damage to the tracks. Still, all things considered, we made excellent time.

Our trip across the Russian countryside was a mixed bag of emotions. The cold created a thick frost on the windows. This was both beautiful and dangerous as one young lady found out. She fell asleep, leaning against the window. When she awoke, her hair was frozen to the glass. She had to have her hair cut off to free her from this predicament. I must remember not to do that as I do not have that much hair to spare. The beauty of the land and the charm of the occasional horse drawn sled were peaceful and serene. This was in stark contrast to the fear we felt when we were raided by various groups or factions (another unscheduled stop).

When these groups appeared, they would halt the train, board and check everyone's identification papers. The Russian passengers had to be quick and clever. Nearly everyone carried identification papers for all of the different forces and governments. They had to figure out which group was checking papers and present the right ones. If they guessed wrong, they were taken off of the train and shot. We were advised not to interfere or we would meet with the same fate.

The other standard practice that was used to ensure our safety was to bribe the inspectors. This was usually accomplished with a small trinket such as a watch, a badge or medal, and such. We were concerned that we might run out of items before we reached our destination. We have been traveling for over a month and must have covered thousands of miles. I feel so far from Annette. I have written a letter to her every day since we parted. I just have not had the opportunity to post them. How much further must we travel?

<u>March 26, 1919</u>

We arrived at Vladivostok. I have never been so tired of traveling in my life. We gathered together our equipment, formed up, and marched to the Headquarters building. Major General Graves greeted us and briefed us on the situation and our mission.

"Our aim is to be of real assistance to all Russians in protecting necessary traffic movement within the sector on the railroad assigned to us... All will be equally benefited, and all will be treated alike by our forces..."

Maj Gen William S. Graves.

The need to transport military supplies and maintain communications for White Russians had recently produced the Inter-Allied Rail Way Agreement. This agreement divided the Trans-Siberian Rail Way (all 6000 miles of it) into sectors to be protected by different Allied forces. We are here to protect the far eastern end of the Trans-Siberian Rail Way, from Vladivostok to the Amur River (the 27th Infantry Regiment was assigned this area) and from Vladivostok to the coal mines in the Suchan Valley (the 31st Infantry Regiment had this duty).

The other Allied forces in our area that have sections to protect are France, England, a Czech-Slovak Legion, and some 70,000 Japanese Soldiers. Additionally there are a large number of German and Austrian-Hungarian troops. These are soldiers who escaped, or were released, and decided to join us. It is still a little unsettling to me to be standing alongside men that a few months earlier I had been trying to kill.

Our American forces are made up of the 31st Infantry Regiment (the Polar Bears), the 27th Infantry Regiment (the Wolfhounds), and Detachments from the 62nd, 13th, and 12th Infantry Regiments. These last two were formerly assigned to the 8th Infantry Division and came along with General Graves. The other Regiments were taken from units in Hawaii and the Philippines.

The nickname of Polar Bears for the 31st Infantry Regiment was apparent, considering the extreme cold weather. The Wolfhounds for the 27th Infantry Regiment was not quite as apparent. I learned that this nickname was given by the Russians. Shortly after their arrival in Siberia, the men of the 27th Infantry, while assisting the Japanese on a reconnaissance mission along the Trans-Siberian Rail Way, were told of a large concentration of Bolsheviks headquartered in the Ussuri Valley. These forces threatened Vladivostok. The doughboys crossed the rugged countryside in frigid temperatures for over 1000 miles in pursuit of the retreating Bolsheviks and capturing the town of Blagoveschensk. The drive so impressed the Russians that they nicknamed the 27th Infantry, the "Wolfhounds".

The main conflict is between the White Army and the Bolsheviks. The Bolsheviks are loosely made up of Partisans and Cossack guerillas. The worst of these Cossacks is a warlord called Kalmikov. Kalmikov appears to be nothing more than a pathological murderer that hides behind the guise of Bolshevism to commit murder, decapitate innocent Siberians, rape, and torture to spread fear and set up a reign of terror to get his way. No soldier or civilian is safe.

An even more distressing bit of information is that the Japanese financed many of these Cossack guerillas and condoned similar acts of violence against the Russian people. It is no wonder why the Russians constantly plead with us for protection. Most unfortunately, these pleas are beyond the limits of our orders.

And it is just as well because we have no idea who is on which side. Near the village of Sviyangino, for example, Bolshevik Partisans frequently wreak havoc with the tracks and telegraph poles. It was discovered that several locals who sold our boys milk and vegetables in the morning, tried to kill them at night. What kind of a situation is this?

<u>March 27, 1919</u>

The first order of business to-day was to go to the Supply Sergeant and receive our issue of clothing and equipment to replace the woefully inadequate items that we brought with us. The continuous 60 degree below zero temperature requires a completely different way of thinking and taking care of ourselves and our equipment. For example, our water-cooled machine guns are worthless when the water freezes. The bolts on our rifles will freeze solid if there's the slightest amount of moisture. And exposed skin will freeze in a matter of seconds.

<u>March 28, 1919</u>

A bit of nastiness had developed only recently. Partisans had attacked a Japanese unit, killing 247. I guess they got confused and forgot which side were "friends" and which side were "foes". The Japanese want us to join them in a counter-attack. General Graves refuses to participate. I wonder what kind of ally these Japanese are. They appear to serve no one but themselves.

March 29 to April 7, 1919

The routine here is simple, wake up, freeze, eat, freeze, eat, freeze, eat, freeze, and go to sleep, shivering. On a regular rotation, we go out to patrol the track. Much more often, we go out to repair the track or telegraph lines. Every now and again, Cossacks or Partisans will attack and give us some excitement. Unfortunately, there is such a problem with supplies (fuel, food, ammunition, and similar necessities) that we are unable to mount any kind of offensive, even if we were allowed to.

Nearly everyone has frost-bite. Only the most severe cases go to the hospital. The hospital is one in name only. It is little more than butchery. The typical means of treating heavy frost-bite is amputation. Many a doughboy will go home minus a hand, foot, arm, or leg. Not from the heat of battle, but more from the lack of heat in the hut.

There have been some recent developments at the Suchan Valley coal mines. The Red Army has been inciting the miners to strike. We have increased our presence in the area to try to regain stability. The mine owners want us to fire on the striking miners or at least arrest them. General Graves refuses to issue such an order. Again, our mission is to protect everyone. This does not sit well with the mine owners. They are accusing General Graves of being a Red sympathizer.

The bleak situation and intolerable weather has taken a heavy toll on the men's morale. There is little to do and no reason to do it. Many doughboys have taken to visiting the Vodka Houses. Vodka is a Russian alcoholic drink. Many of the lads use it to help deaden the pain of surroundings. There are many prostitutes in these Vodka Houses, too. They help ease the pain of being so far from home with personal companionship, for a price, of course. I miss Annette.

<u>April 8, 1919</u>

Grim news, the French forces located at Odessa have left. They packed up and left the country without a fight. I have very mixed feeling over this action. I would certainly leave, given the opportunity.

However, our mission is here and we must stay and see it through to the end.

April 9 to May 22, 1919

The situation grows tense day-by-day. The attacks grow in intensity and frequency. We have our hands full fending off these attacks.

May 23, 1919

More news from the Suchan mines. The Bolshevik leader, Yakov Triapitsyn (who was assisting the striking miners), has threatened to murder every American unless we withdraw from the area. Of course we can not do this. We are the only neutral force in the area. If we leave, the Bolsheviks will take control of the major source of fuel in the region. This must not happen. Millions of innocent Russians will starve and freeze to death. Not that the Bolsheviks ever cared about anyone but themselves. I'm not even sure that they care about themselves.

May 24, 1919

General Graves' response to Triapitsyn's demand came quickly. Gen Graves ordered that all Partisans be removed from the area by force.

May 25 to June 24, 1919

We've made several attempts to fulfill General Graves' order. But the continuous plague of fuel and ammunition shortage has severely hampered our efforts. The daily operation of patrolling and repairing the line appears to be the most we can handle for the time being. At least it is warming up a bit.

June 25, 1919

A little something different happened to-day. We were out on a dawn patrol when Cpl. Brodnichi of the 31st Infantry staggered out of the near-by woods. He was severely wounded. He said his Detachment had made camp near Romannovka when Partisans attacked them around 4:00 a.m. this morning. Everyone dove for cover or for protection in near-by log houses. Cpl. Brodnichi implored for us to come to their aid. Lieutenant Lorimer agreed and we were on our way with Cpl. Brodnichi showing us the way.

We arrived at the camp around 8:00 a.m. and surveyed a dire situation. Our lads must have been out numbered twenty to one. The Partisans were in firm control of the battle and poised to annihilate our forces. They did not witness us taking up a position on their flank. The Partisans were very surprised when we opened fire and sent them running. A handful tried to take cover behind a small knoll and return fire. Private Johnson and I rose up from our position without order and charged the Partisans killing all of them.

In the aftermath of the battle, we tended to the wounded and gathered the dead for burial (as soon as the ground thaws). We lost 32 soldiers. Most of them, about 26, died in the opening moments of the fight. Several were found still in their cots where they died. The Partisans losses were 100 dead and there's no way of knowing how many wounded as they fled. Those who could not flee were executed by their own people. One of the dead Partisans was recognized as the villager who regularly sold them milk. He had done so only the day before.

We set things right and returned to Vladivostok with the wounded.

June 26 to July 3, 1919

Our excitement over, we returned to our normal routine.

<u>July 4, 1919 Independence Day</u>

We tried to hold a little celebration. But we have no fireworks and dared not fire off any weapons as the villagers might think that there was an attack.

<u>July 5 to 24, 1919</u>

Summer is here. At least we have something other than snow to look at. Unfortunately it also means that there will be an increase in Bolshevik and Cossack attacks.

<u>July 25, 1919</u>

That butchering Cossack, Kalmikov has struck again. He and his men kidnapped a Captain and a Corporal in the town of Iman, just north of Vladivostok. The Captain escaped to notify us of their peril. The Corporal was not as fortunate. He remains their captive.

Major Shamotulshi with 150 men and machine guns were dispatched to Iman to demand the release of the Corporal.

The Japanese, still annoyed with General Graves, have threatened to side with the Cossacks.

July 26 to 28, 1919

We stood fast by our resolve. We are determined to gain the release of the Corporal. There have been a few tense moments with the Cossacks and the Japanese. For the most part, the Japanese have been keeping to a safe distance away from the town.

July 29, 1919

The Cossacks have backed down and released the Corporal. The poor lad had been badly beaten and tortured and was barely alive. The Japanese also withdrew. The words and actions of the Japanese definitely left us with the impression that they orchestrated this whole incident. Cossacks do not normally kidnap people. Normally, they just kill.

July 30 to August 10, 1919

The rise of Cossack attacks has renewed our order to remove the Partisans from the Suchan Valley.

August 11, 1919

A 40 man detail (including yours truly) was sent to the coal mines to remove all Partisans by force. The Bolshevik leader, Triapitsyn, and his men retreated immediately and the miners ended their strike and returned to work. Hopefully there will be no further problems at the mines.

August 12 to September 11, 1919

The attacks by the Bolshevik, Partisan, and Cossack have increased noticeably. We're constantly running hither and yon, reacting to any and every attack. This can't continue. It seems that the strategy of the Bolsheviks and Cossacks is to keep us running around in circles, wearing us down so that we can not gain a decisive victory.

September 12, 1919

It appears that the General came to the same conclusion. The Headquarters at Spasskoe ordered us to use our entire force against any Cossack attack.

September 13 to November 10, 1919

The new tactic of concentrating our forces has met with success. In the early days, the Cossacks were surprised to be confronted by such a large force. We defeated the Cossacks easily. The results were the same against the Bolsheviks. We routed them every time. Their casualties were so heavy that the frequency of attacks has dropped off sharply. At the present rate, there will soon be no attacks at all.

November 11, 1919

To-day was an exceptional day, indeed. It was the first anniversary of the end of the war to end all wars. However, the real exceptional part came from an award ceremony. To my complete surprise, I was called out to receive a promotion and a medal. I was promoted to Corporal and awarded the Distinguished Service Cross for my actions on the 25th of June when we came to the aid of the Detachment of the 31st Infantry. I have never been so thrilled and excited. There were many others who also received awards and promotions. But, I don't remember. I am so giddy, that even now, at the end of the day, I'm still light-headed, smiling, and have butterflies in my stomach. It is absolutely unbelievable. My only regret is that Annette isn't here to share in my joy.

November 12 to 14, 1919

It took a while, but my thrill finally wore off and I returned to the normal day-to-day schedule of activities.

November 15, 1919

News has reached us that the Red Army captured Omsk yesterday. This definitely will disrupt the White Army's hold in this area.

November 16 to December 18, 1919

The attacks in our area have dropped off almost completely. The lack of action leads to long and uneventful days. I can't help shake the feeling that something is afoot. We have not driven off all of the Cossacks and Partisans. The fiends certainly would never give up willingly. They must be planning something. Since we increased our force, they must increase their force to defeat ours. They also need to hoard their supplies and ammunition to sustain their attack.

December 19, 1919

Apparently I am not the only one to make the same assessment of the situation. With the White Army effectively eliminated in Siberia, we have lost a large portion of our support. With the reduction of our forces, there is an imminent danger of a massive enemy assault. We have been ordered to abandon parts of our sector to take up a stronger defensive position.

December 20 to 24, 1919

We proceeded to reposition our forces to strengthen our defenses. This was fortuitous in many ways. Attrition had taken its toll. Our supplies, food, ammunition, and worse of all, number of men, had all fallen to dangerously low levels. By reducing the amount of area that we needed to defend, we increased the number of men available with which to defend.

December 25, 1919 Christmas Day

To-day is a day of joy and celebration. Though there doesn't seem to be much to celebrate. I can not help but remember the joy and celebration of Christmas Day a year ago with Annette. The happiness of that day lies in stark contrast with the dismal, desperate and depression of to-day is far beyond mere mortal description. I have written to Annette every day since last I saw her, often two or three times a day. But alas, there has never been a means to post them. No train has ever successfully delivered any westbound shipment. Likewise, nothing has ever been received.

December 26 to 31, 1919

Firmly in the grips of another Siberian winter, we steadied ourselves by any means possible. Needless to say, the Vodka Houses are doing a robust business.

January 1, 1920 New Year's Day

It's a new year and a new decade. I can only hope that things will improve. They certainly couldn't get much worse.

January 2 to February 15, 1920

This winter has been severe. The news that we have been receiving of late has been severe for the White Army, too.

It would appear that the Bolsheviks have decided to use their renewed strength against the White Army rather than us. News has arrived of great battles in the west. The White Army was victorious in some of the battles as has the Red Army in others. Neither side seems to be able to gain a decisive victory over the other.

February 16, 1920

The White Army has suffered a decisive defeat along the Volga front in the west. Reports are that the White Army is in full retreat. This can not bode well for us. The Siberian Government is shaky, at best.

February 17 to March 1, 1920

The news continues to be bad. The White Army attempts to regroup and mount a counter-offensive only to be defeated. The level of anxiety among the local population has risen to a state of near panic.

March 2, 1920

The Siberian Government has collapsed! People have gathered together what possessions they can carry and are heading toward the docks, hoping to gain safe passage away from here.

March 3 to 12, 1920

The situation continues to deteriorate daily. The remnants of the Czech-Slovak Legion have entered Vladivostok in preparation for leaving. There have not been military attacks recently. This is most fortunate. With the amount of chaos and congestion in the town, any attack would have catastrophic results.

March 13, 1920

A call went out for volunteers. We are to withdraw from Vladivostok by sea. A five man team will try to make their way to the American forces at Arkhangelsk on the Baltic Sea. The purpose is to deliver dispatches to the American Expeditionary Forces in Northern Russia, detailing our situation and decision to leave. In the event that the American forces were no longer there, the detail would make their way back to America via Europe. Needless to say, presented with the chance to return to Europe, France, and Annette, I volunteered for the mission.

I was promoted to Sergeant and placed in charge of the detail.

March 14, 1920

My team of volunteers has been assembled. Corporal Hamilton will be my assistant leader. Private Varanasi will serve as interpreter. Privates Anderson and Horace will complete our team.

We can no longer be assured safe passage on our journey. To this end, we will wear our locally purchased civilian coats over our uniforms in an effort to appear to be local peasants. We will wear our uniforms to avoid being shot as spies should the situation arise. I have our dispatches and have sewn them into the lining of my coat. We shall carry neither weapon nor equipment to assist in our deception. We will also carry additional amounts of gold and currency should we need to buy our way out of a tight spot.

Our level of speaking and understanding Russian varies. All of us speak enough to be able to communicate. We also have our documents and passes in multiple copies should someone decide to keep our papers. We have tried to prepare for every possibility. We depart in the morning.

<u>March 15, 1920</u>

We gathered our belongings together and set out for the rail way station. The remainder of my equipment was packed up and turned in to the Supply Sergeant to be taken back to the United Stated via boat.

As we made our way toward the station, we passed several people (Czech-Slovak legionnaires,

American soldiers, White Army soldiers, Russian civilians) making their way to the docks in hopes of gaining safe passage to anywhere but here. The look of despair and fear on the faces of the Russians was very much like that on the faces on the Germans after an Artillery barrage.

We boarded the train and prepared for a very uncertain journey and future. The train departed on schedule. Hopefully that is a sign of good things to come.

<u>March 16 to 24, 1920</u>

The journey has been nearly uneventful thus far. There was the occasional obstruction (snow, fallen trees, wandering herds of animals, landslides, etc.) on the track, causing a slight delay as we cleared them away. And the stray Partisan attack that failed when the train didn't stop. I couldn't help but think that had we our weapons, the five of us could have easily defeated such disorganized, half-hearted attacks. But, we are to keep our presence on this train a secret. We press on.

March 25, 1920

Horror and disgust! I can't think of any other way to describe the events that we witnessed to-day. Absolute detestation!!

We were halted by a Red Army group. They went through the cars, looking at everyone. All of the passengers, including us, dutifully had their papers prepared for presentation. But, the Red Army Captain did not look at any of them. He just walked through the cars, selecting specific passengers who were rapidly and roughly hustled off of the train. At first I thought that the Captain might have been pulling off known White Army sympathizers. But then I noticed that too many were being taken off to fit that concept. Then I thought that they might have been doing a conscript, pressed service for the Red Army. But a closer inspection of the people did not support that thought either. I couldn't think of what purpose they had in mind. Then they took Private Horace. It was all that I could do to keep from attacking those Bolsheviks! I could not compromise our mission. Such a rash action would surely doom us all.

We soon learned what they had in mind. Everyone taken off of the train, were moved to a spot about thirty feet away from the train. Then they were executed. In plain view of everyone on the train, the filthy bastards shot about forty unarmed civilians in cold blood. Including Private Horace!! I am absolutely sick to my stomach.

The train began on its way, but it was barely noticeable over the din of the wailing and crying from the passengers. My head is still swimming in a fog from these events.

March 26, 1920

I still can not understand yesterday's events. Between the waves of nausea and disgust, I replay the events, over and over in my mind. Was there anything I could have done to prevent Private Horace from being killed? Did he do something to give himself away? What could I have done differently? I can't think clearly. The only thing that I keep coming back to is that it was a completely random selection, that there was nothing any of us could have done. Had the passengers resisted, everyone on the train would have been executed.

Much to Private Horace's credit and bravery, he did nothing to compromise our mission. Our only stroke of good fortune came when the train departed before the bodies could be searched. Had Private Horace's true identity been discovered, the murderous swine would have searched for the rest of us until we were found. Private Horace's bravery in the face of death can be directly credited to the mission being able to carry on. This event will be reported, should we survive. It is my sincere hope that Private Horace's sacrifice will not go unrewarded.

March 27 to April 4, 1920

The remainder of our trip went relatively uneventful. I still have a hard time understanding what we witnessed. I've seen soldiers blown to smithereens. I have killed and seen men killed. I have had friends die in my arms. However, that was in battle. Everyone knew the risks and we accepted them. This was cold blooded murder. I have never seen anything so cruel in my life. I hope never to see it again.

April 5, 1920

We arrived at the railway station in Moscow. It will be four days before the train heading north arrives, if it arrives at all.

We looked for lodging and found an empty corner of a bombed out building. There's no coal, wood, or supplies of any kind left. Everything has been scrounged by the poor citizens to survive. There was some recent news posted on a near-by wall. Private Varanasi and I read it over to see what intelligence we could learn. We discovered two items. First, the bulk of the fighting was in the south, around the Crimea. This is good news as it should allow us to move about easier. Second, all of the foreign intruders have been driven out of Russia. This is a much more critical piece of information. Should it be true, it means that the American Expeditionary Forces that we are going to rendezvous with have gone. Private Varanasi and I returned to our digs to discuss our options with the rest of our group.

We had to be on our guard. Should someone suspect that we were foreigners, we would be turned in to the Political Office and executed immediately. We talked in low tones as one kept watch. To keep the talking to a minimum, I wrote the situation and our options on some paper and passed them around. Everyone read them, wrote their comments and observations, and passed them on. Soon everyone had read all of our options, made comments and read everyone else's comments.

The situation can be split into two cases, continue north or head west for Europe. Staying in Moscow or heading back to Vladivostok are too dangerous and therefore not options. If we continue northward, there is a good chance that our troops have already left, leaving us stranded and looking for a way home. If we head for Europe, it would be less risky and easier to find safe passage back to the United States. No one can cast a shadow of doubt over the bravery and dedication of every man here. The mission is to get the dispatches safely to our higher command. The way to accomplish this with the highest probability of success would be to head for Europe.

My decision was an easy one, everyone was in agreement. We head for Europe. Our next problem was one of transportation.

April 6, 1920

Corporal Hamilton and Private Anderson stayed in the building to guard our things while Private Varanasi and I went out to find out about transportation to Europe and to scrounge some food. A local merchant was planning a trip to Minsk to sell his wares and welcomed the company and the protection. We sealed the deal by accepting his invitation to dinner. We went back and gathered

Corporal Hamilton, Private Anderson and our gear and went to the merchant's dom (that's Russian for home).

I have my fear of trusting our lot in the hands of a stranger. But, we can't get out without the help from someone. And I have a good feeling about this man.

We arrived at Mr. Bryansk's dom and had a hot meal. That tasted good. The conversation was light and vague. We didn't want to give ourselves away. Fortunately, there was no heat in his house and we had to keep our coats on. Mr. Bryansk asked a few questions about where we came from and seemed very interested when we told him we had just come from Vladivostok. He said that he always wanted to vacation there. But there was something else, something under the surface that he wasn't saying.

My suspicions were further aroused when Mr. Bryansk got a glimpse of Private Anderson's uniform. He acted like he didn't see it. But the momentary expression on his face told me otherwise. Later, when we were alone, I voiced my suspicions to the others of my team. We decided to carry on, but to be on our guard.

April 7, 1920

We arose early and started on our way. Mr. Bryansk seemed very cheerful. The talk was again light, the weather, business, different places that he had seen, nothing about politics or the revolution. All was going well until shortly after mid-day. A small band of Partisans stopped us and asked many questions. Mr. Bryansk did all of the talking. I was sitting next to him on the bench of the wagon. He was trying very hard to convince the Partisans that everything was fine and that we had nothing that would interest them. Despite his best efforts, the Partisans appeared intent on taking everything. They struck me as nothing more than low-life, thieving scum.

I thought that we were in serious trouble when I felt something nudging my thigh under the blanket. I didn't react, but slowly moved my hand to see what it was. I felt the handle of a pistol. I cocked it and prepared to fight. I didn't have long to wait. I felt a movement next to me, pulled the pistol in my hand, out from under the blanket, drew aim, and fired. In less than the blink of an eye, a volley of bullets had been fired and all of the Partisans lay dead in the snow. Not all of them were taken out by my hand, though. That movement that I felt was Mr. Bryansk pulling his revolver out and firing at the Partisans near him.

We thought that it would be better to get moving rather than search the dead Partisans. As we moved away, Mr. Bryansk explained that the shots would bring others. And that the stolen property that the thieves were carrying will satisfy them and keep them from following us.

I held out the pistol to return it to Mr. Bryansk. Vlad, as he asked to be called, told me to hang on to it. We might need it again. He also gave me some more bullets.

Vlad explained that he had been an interpreter for the British forces. He could have left with them, but decided to return to his family in Moscow, only to discover that his family had been killed by the Bolsheviks. Since then he has been wreaking his revenge whenever and where ever he can.

Originally, he had planned to kill us on the trip. But, when he spotted Private Anderson's uniform, he realized that we were Americans and quickly changed his plan. When I told him that we were making our way to France, he changed his plan again. Vlad decided that it was too dangerous to remain in Russia. He offered to take us anywhere we wanted to go.

April 8 to 15, 1920

Once again, I think we have jumped out of the frying pan and landed in the middle of the fire. As we approached Minsk, we found ourselves in the middle of another war. We were taken prisoner by Polish forces and questioned. We were able to convince them that we were Americans and were making our way to France. We were fed and put up in a tent for the night.

April 16, 1920

We were greeted with a mixed bag of events to-day. The Polish Army confiscated Vlad's wagon and all of its contents. In exchange, we were given documents for free passage through Poland. We were also given an escort to the train station.

On the way to the station, our escort told us about the fighting that we had stumbled upon. At the end of the Great War, Poland was established as an independent and sovereign country. For the last year, Polish forces have been fighting for their survival against the Red Army and the Ukrainian

Nationalist Army. To date, the Polish Army has been victorious. I certainly wish them success.

Our escort saw us safely to the station and stayed until we pulled away.

April 17 to 22, 1920

We traveled across Poland, Germany, and into France with no problems at all. The countryside looked better than the last time that I passed through. The Germans still look tired and angry.

When we crossed into France, I told the other members of our group my intention to hold-up in Reims for a day or two or three. This decision met with enthusiastic support. I suspect that others had sweet-hearts that they would like to look-up. Or maybe they wanted to find a sweet-heart for a night or two. I can't say that I blame them.

April 23, 1920

Upon our arrival in Reims, we located a hotel and proceeded to unpack our gear. Vlad lost everything that he had when the Polish Army took his wagon. We need to outfit him. We also need to reorganize our load, prepare for our journey back to the United States of America. Fortunately, I still have most of the money we were given when we left Vladivostok. It should be sufficient to meet our needs and purchase our passage home. I inquired at the train station what would be the cost for four tickets to the coast, also the cost of passage to the United States. The teller had the cost of the train tickets, of course. But, he could only speculate as to the boat fare.

As we proceeded through town, I looked in the shop windows. Not so much at the merchandise, but to get a notion as to the cost of things we might be likely to purchase. Running this information through my mind, adding in the possible hotel cost, food, taxis, and allowing for extras, I came up with a general idea of how much money we would need to continue with our mission.

We went to the bank to exchange our currency. Unfortunately, the exchange rate between Rubles and Francs was not as favorable as I had hoped that it would be. I had to exchange some of the gold to be certain that we had enough money to finance our venture.

Next on our list, find a hotel, maybe one with a bath. Here we received our first piece of good luck. We were able to get five rooms with private baths for less than what I had estimated. I love my team dearly, but I need some relaxation. As I am certain they would like some, too. We will meet later to decide on what we will do next.

April 24, 1920

After a wonderful dinner, a fantastic hot bath, and a marvelous night's sleep, I feel like a new man.

Vlad and Private Varanasi will pick up the supplies that we need, Corporal Hamilton has an address that he wants to find, Private Anderson will stay at the hotel room to catch up on some rest, and I, of course, have a mission of my own. That is our plan for the day. We will all meet back here for dinner. As the hotel is near the Cathedrale de Notre-Dame De Reims, we should be able to find our way back without too much difficulty.

Corporal Hamilton and I looked at a map of Reims. The address he is looking for is in a different direction from the address I need. So we proceeded on our separate ways.

The address Annette gave me is 32 Rue D'avenay. I know that because I wrote it on every one of the 452 letters that I wrote to her, but never had a chance to post. The map indicated that this rue was only a few blocks away. I decided to walk.

I found Rue D'avenay. And it wasn't long at all before I was standing in front of 32. I stood there, transfixed. After all of this time, after all that I have been through, would this crown me or kill me. I don't even know if the address that Annette gave me is the right address. But I know one way to find out. Walking up the steps, ringing the bell, were the last things I did before time stood still. An eternity passed. I rang again, silence. The thought to leave had just entered my mind when I heard some footsteps coming from within the house. I know my heart stood still. The door opened. And there she was, even more beautiful than I had remembered.

In an instant, time and space was transformed and it was as if not a second had gone by since last I saw her. The instant joy that lit up her face told me that she was happy to see me, too.

Her parents were not at home, so we went out for a promenade. Annette had been working at the Hospital since the war. There's a great demand for medical help with all of the wounded poilus (soldiers). We walked and talked for hours, until it was time for her to return home. We walked back to her house. I told her at which hotel that I was staying. Annette would be on duty to-morrow. She asked if I would like to visit her the next day, to meet her parents. I didn't even hesitate to accept. We said our good nights and went our separate ways. This time, it was a much more joyous parting than the last time we had to separate.

On the way back to my hotel room, I was so elated, that I decided that I would ask Annette's Father for her hand in marriage.

April 25, 1920

I awoke, still smiling from yesterday. At first, I thought to visit Annette at the Hospital. But then I thought better of that. I would only be a distraction. Instead, a better use of my time would be to look into what I needed to do to marry Annette should her parents' grant their consent.

After our morning team meeting, everyone agreed that we need to stay in Reims for a while longer. I made a few inquiries and located the American Consulate. Corporal Hamilton (Frederick) and I hailed a taxi. It appears that Frederick's meeting yesterday went as well as mine. We arrived at the Consulate and soon learned what we needed to know. It would seem that we are not the first doughboys who desired to marry a young, beautiful French maid. Both Frederick and I were unaware of any restrictions on immigration. We quickly learned how wrong we were.

There were little to no restrictions on anyone wishing to become an American until the Chinese Exclusion Act of 1882. As the title indicates, this act barred Chinese from entering the United States. Immigration was further restricted by the Gentlemen's Agreement of 1907 with Japan. This agreement regulated the number of Japanese that could immigrant to America. But these laws were nothing compared to the Immigration Act of 1917. While we were off to fight the war in Europe, our legislators back home passed an act that added to the number of undesirables banned from entering the country. The list of undesirables includes, but is not limited to, idiots, feeble-minded persons, criminals, epileptics, insane persons, alcoholics, professional beggars, all persons mentally or physically defective, polygamists, and anarchists. Furthermore, it also barred all immigrants over the age of sixteen who are illiterate. There is also a section that designates an Asiatic Barred Zone. This is a region that includes much of eastern Asia and the Pacific Islands. People from this zone can not immigrate to America. This considerably increases the region of people who can not immigrate to the United States from only the Chinese, first restricted in the Chinese Exclusion

Act of 1882. I think these laws are made just to confuse everyone.

There is a series of documents, forms and tests that Annette and I will need to complete to verify that she does not fit into any of those classifications or areas, before we can be wed. Frederick and his good lady will also need to complete this mountain of paperwork. We remain undaunted in our resolve to be joined with our dear-hearts.

Armed with our arms full of forms and instructions, Corporal Hamilton and I proceeded to our next objective, the City Magistrate, to find out what will be needed to obtain a marriage license. This proved to be extremely simple. We submit an application, pay the fee, and find a Priest to perform the ceremony. All things considered, Annette and I could be married in a week. There remains only one small detail, Annette's parents must agree and Annette has to say yes.

April 26, 1920

I can't believe how nervous I am. I must have taken three baths and changed my clothes five times. Finally, the moment for me to depart to meet Annette's parents arrived. I don't remember if my feet ever touched the ground. I floated down the rue, around the corner, and up the steps to her door. I rang her door bell and held my breath. I didn't have as long to wait as the last time. Annette answered the door almost immediately. I think that she might have been waiting by the door.

Annette invited me into her house and showed me to the front parlor where her parents were waiting. I had feared that this meeting might resemble the Christians and the lions in the coliseum. Au contraire, they were the nicest couple I had ever met. They spoke English very well. They were also very tolerant of my French. We were able to communicate extremely well. They seemed to be impressed with my manners. When I was growing up, Mother spent, what I thought was an inordinately large amount of, time teaching her children proper manners. I am so grateful that she did. It is a wonder to me, that the older that I get, the more her intelligence grows. Or perhaps, I grow to understand her wisdom.

We talked for hours. We then proceeded to the dining room where we dined on an exquisite meal, and retired to the rear parlor were we continued our talk. As the evening wore on, I reached a point where I felt comfortable enough to broach the subject of marriage. M. d'Arcy was clearly uncomfortable, but not surprised. I presented my case. I explained that although I was young and that I would prefer to allow sufficient time to allow them to get to know me and I them, time was not a luxury of mine. I must return to America. In support of my case, I pointed out that Annette and I had known each other for a year and a half.

M. d'Arcy understood and agreed that time was not a commodity available to us. He did confide in me that Annette had talked about me nearly every day that we were apart. Mme. d'Arcy rose and left the room. I was afraid that this might be a bad omen. Shortly Mme. d'Arcy returned with an arm full of letters that Annette had written while I was away. In response, I reached into my satchel and produced an equally large stack of letters that I had written to Annette. The emotion was too much for Mme. d'Arcy. She hurriedly left the room in tears. With his eyes glazed in tears, M. d'Arcy called for Annette to enter the room. He told her that I had asked for her hand in marriage and that he gave his blessing. I could barely see the joy on Annette's face for the tears in my eyes. I was so moved that I got down on my knee right then and there and proposed to her. I don't exactly know what I said or how I said it. The only French I could remember was "je t'aime" ("I love you"). I do remember what she said. She said "oui" (that's French for "yes").

We set a time to meet to-morrow to talk about the arrangements. As I returned to my hotel room, I reflected on the past month. I had experienced everything from the horror of when Private Horace was killed to the exaltation of being engaged to Annette. What a strange and wonderful life I have. I wonder what else life has in store for me.

April 27 to May 2, 1920

These days flew by at an incredible pace. The daily meetings with my team to keep abreast of our situation and our responsibility to the mission, the hourly meetings with Annette and her parents to arrange for the wedding, the minutely meetings to get through all of the forms and documents to prepare for Annette's immigration to America, the secondly meetings I had with myself to remind me that this was real, kept me a little occupied.

May 3, 1920

We completed all of the necessary forms for Annette's immigration and turned them over to the American Consulate.

Now, all we have to do is to wait for her travel visa.

May 4 to June 15, 1920

Ah, what a wonderful time this is. With every passing day, we fall more and more in love with each other. I wish for nothing more than for this time to never end.

June 16, 1920

Time is starting to run out. As much as I would like to stay here, we must wrap up our business and be moving on about our way. Annette and I submitted her immigration application several weeks ago. Hopefully, we will have a response soon.

June 17, 1920

Annette received a letter from the American Consulate, to-day. She is to appear before the consulate next week for an interview. Annette is so excited!

June 18 to 23, 1920

To-morrow is the big day! Annette is a nervous wreck. She is so afraid that she will do or say something that will prevent her from getting the visa. I am constantly reassuring her that she will perform admirably. I have no doubt that she will acquit herself with distinction.

Frederick's lady, Claudette, has her interview in a few days.

I'm certain that she, too, will have no problem in obtaining her visa.

June 24, 1920

We arrived at the Consulate's office well ahead of our scheduled appointment. We waited patiently to be called back for our interview. I do not know who is more nervous, Annette or me. Finally, our moment arrived.

We went into the office and met with the Consulate. He seemed to be a nice enough gentleman, though slightly disinterested. He introduced himself and asked for us to have a seat. He looked over our application and asked Annette a few questions. After what seemed to be an eternity, he handed Annette her visa, congratulated her and wished us the best of luck.

I thought that I had seen joy and happiness in Annette before. But, nothing compared to the glow on her face as we left the office. I don't think that her feet ever touched the ground. She glided above the floor. She talked about everything on her mind. I don't think that I have ever seen someone so excited and in such exaltation, unless it were I.

June 25, 1920

The joy continues. I don't think ten minutes have gone by without Annette looking at her visa. She has memorized every word and smudge on it. She has and will show it to anyone and everyone. It makes me so very happy to see her so very happy.

Now, we need to get our license and make the Church arrangement.

June 26 to July 3, 1920

Arrangements are proceeding well. We have applied for our Marriage License and checked on the availability of the Church. Frederick has also met with approximately the same amount of success. Annette and I have grown close to Frederick and Claudette. Our shared journey and experiences have afforded us the opportunity to get to know each other and allowed a genuine friendship to emerge.

A curious suggestion was offered. In order to conserve time and expenses, it was proposed that we hold a duel wedding. Surprisingly, this idea was welcomed by all parties involved. I must say that I am amazed at both the acceptance of the idea, and how much I enjoy the thought. If everyone else enjoys this ceremonial concept as much as I do, we shall have an extremely memorable event.

July 4, 1920 Independence Day

To me, this would be an excellent day to be wed. We would celebrate our nations' independence and our union at the same time. Needless to say, Annette does not share my enthusiasm for this idea. I think that we will go with her plans.

July 5 to 15, 1920

Arrangements proceed at a most excellent rate. All of the required documentation, permits, licenses and permissions have been acquired. Preparations are all but completed. The great day has arrived. To-morrow, we are to be wed!

Frederick and Claudette will be wed at the same time. Privates Varanasi and Anderson as well as Mr. Bryansk will stand for us. It should be a most splendid ceremony.

July 16, 1920

Joy! Rapture! Bliss beyond compare! The entire day was an ever increasing crescendo of pleasure that culminated beyond anything imaginable. It began when I beheld Annette approaching the altar, looking every inch the Angel that she is, and rose from there. I dare not write any of it down. Any poor attempt on my part to put ink to paper would fall far short of how I feel and would offend all memories. Better to keep the memories and bask in the glow of the day and Annette's love!

July 17, 1920

We had little time to spare to-day. We rose early, gathered together our belongings and proceeded to the rail station. Annette and Claudette's parents met us at the station to bid us farewell. After a three hour train ride, we arrived at the port city of Calais. We made our way to the dock to gain passage on our ships. I say ships, for Vlad has decided to travel to England rather than accompany us to America. He made the decision based on the many friends that he made when he served as an interpreter with the British Expeditionary Force in Northern Russia. We said our good-byes and went our separate ways.

Although we had known him for but a short time, we had become fast friends. I do hope that some day our paths will cross again. The remainder of our group boarded the ship and began our journey home.

OFF TO AMERICA

July 18, 1920

We located our rooms, unpacked our luggage, freshened ourselves and met up on the deck. We waved to the people on the dock. We didn't know any of them, still we waved most enthusiastically. It was not so much as we were waving to an individual, I think, as we were waving good-by to France and Europe. I had arrived just over two years ago. It feels like a life time ago.

July 19 to August 2, 1920

This has been a most enjoyable trip, indeed. These two weeks have gone by entirely too fast.

We spent vast amounts of time just strolling around the deck, looking out over the ocean, visiting with Frederick and Claudette, as well as Darrel (Private Anderson) and Ivan (Private Varanasi), and several other passengers on board the ship that we met.

The stark contrast between this cruise and the last time that I crossed the Atlantic has not gone un-noticed by me. Many of the sights and sounds of our ocean voyage bring back memories of the lads that I made the journey with, before. What a splendid bunch of fellows they were. I can still see their faces, full with high spirits and excitement as we ventured fourth on our great adventure. Even the faces that were green with sea-sickness had a smile on them. Well, in a strange sort of way. I best not think of them, lest I get weepy-eyed. Instead, I shall take great joy in my current situation and look forward to a bright and prosperous future.

August 3, 1920

We were greeted this morning when we went for a stroll on deck, by a most wondrous sight; Lady Liberty was there to welcome us home. Her torch held on high lighting our way home. What a grand and glorious image to behold! We sailed ever closer. Annette and I were absolutely spell-bound. And I think, perhaps, for much the same reasons; for her, I think, a new life; for me, life anew. A wave of joy swept over me.

Shortly after noon, a steward came near, advising everyone that we would soon reach the docks and that we should prepare to disembark. We took his advice and retired to our cabin to ready our luggage and ourselves to dock.
Once completed, we returned on deck. By now, the outlines of the buildings of New York City

completely dominated the horizon in all directions. The ship docked and we proceeded with everyone down the gangplank and onto the dock. Immigrants were lead over to another dock where we boarded a ferryboat to Ellis Island. Upon arrival, we were herded into a large, castle-like red brick building. Once inside the great hall, we waited to see an immigration agent. Fortunately for us, we did not have long to wait. Annette and I were sent to a separate line that handled cases such as ours. We were asked a few questions, showed the agent our documents, he filled out some more documents, stamped everything (several times over), returned our documents to us and welcomed us to America. That was, I believe, the second happiest that I have seen Annette. We exited the building, returned by ferryboat to the main dock, and preceded on our way.

We soon met with Darrel and Ivan. They did not have to pass through immigration and were waiting for us just outside the dock as we had arranged. We talked and joked as we waited for Frederick and Claudette. We did not have long to wait. Having gathered together all of our luggage and belongings, we set forth for our new home with the 12th Infantry Regiment. However, there seemed to be one small problem, we had no concept of where we were to go. As it was getting rather late in the day, we decided that it would be prudent to acquire rooms for the night and start anew in the morning. A hearty meal would also be a welcomed event.

We secured both, and thus concluded our first day home. Once again, we stood on American soil.

August 4, 1920

To-day proved to be a most interesting adventure. It was decided among ourselves, to venture to the nearest Military Installation and attempt to locate our Regiment through them. Little did we realize what a daunting task that would encompass. At first, we feared that there would not be an Army Post close at hand. This proved to be the least of our worries. In fact, there was an over abundance from which to choose. There was Forts Schuyler, Wood, Slocum, Totten, Jay, Hamilton, and Wadsworth near-by and still more across the river in New Jersey. Of these, we determined that Fort Jay would be the closest and easiest to reach. And so, to Fort Jay, we proceeded. Annette and Claudette remained in the hotel room along with our luggage.

In what seemed to be no time at all, we arrived at Fort Jay. In another instant, we located the

Administration Office. We met Corporal Johnson and asked him where the 8th Infantry Division was stationed. We were rather surprise to discover that the 8th Infantry Division had been inactivated years earlier. The 12th Infantry Regiment faired a little better. Corporal Johnson thought that they were stationed at Fort Howard in Maryland. While we were waiting for confirmation and direction to reach Fort Howard, I asked Corporal Johnson what was the cause of this disorganization. He told me that after the war, while we were in Siberia, the returning doughboys were mustered out of the service in vast numbers. The resulting Army was but a shadow of its' former size. The high command also had the notion to reorganize the standing Army with the Division as the basic unit, rather than the Regiment as it had been before. They also incorporated higher echelons above the Division, the Corps and the Army. It seems peculiar that the general staff would create a larger organization for the Army at the same time that they cut the number soldiers to the minimum. The over-all atmosphere throughout the Army was one of confusion.

Corporal Johnson was a most informative and helpful soldier. Armed with the knowledge we had sought, we returned to our hotel rooms and prepared to depart for Fort Howard in the morning.

<u>August 5, 1920</u>

We rose early, packed, and departed for Grand Central Terminal. We proceeded through what was, most certainly, the largest building that I have ever seen in my life! How we were able to find our way to the ticket booth, purchase our tickets, and make our way to the correct level, platform and track, is quite beyond my poor powers of comprehension. Our train was on time (as was expected). We boarded and were on our way. As I write these words, Annette is sitting across from me, looking out of the window with a wide-eyed expression, in a gaze of child-like wonderment. Her giddy excitement is contagious. I, too, am getting excited seeing all of the scenery anew as if I were seeing everything through her eyes.

In what seemed to be no time at all, we arrived in Baltimore, Maryland. We secured a taxi to take us to Fort Howard. Unfortunately, by the time that we finally arrived at Fort Howard, the duty day had ended. We were able to secure rooms on post. In the morning, we should be able to report in our Regiment, provided that they are stationed here.

Through the Eyes of a Soldier: A World Gone Mad

August 6, 1920

This was certainly a day of surprises. After a while of searching, we located the Orderly Room for the 12th Infantry Regiment. Once there, we had a most difficult time convincing the Orderly of who we were. He seemed to be very confused. We waited in the front room as he disappeared into other rooms, only to return and ask us our names again. As the morning wore on, more and more people came into the room, each asking the same question and looking just as confused as the one before. We had to repeat to several people who we were. I noticed that the rank of those coming into the room was increasingly higher; Corporal, Sergeant, First Sergeant, Lieutenant, Captain, Major, Lieutenant Colonel. Finally, we were asked to walk to another building. In there, we were soon ushered into an inner office where we were presented to Colonel Warren, the Regimental Commander.

Colonel Warren asked to see our documents. He examined them and us very closely. Finally, he declared that he had never met such healthy dead men in his life. He explained that shortly after the group had returned from Siberia, we were reported as "Missing – Presumed Dead". Apparently, we were sent on a suicide mission to distract the Russians. We were not expected to survive. I reported that, in fact, Private Horace had been killed. The Colonel said that there would be time to hear the entire story. But, for now, we needed to be re-indoctrinated into the Regiment. This we did for the remainder of the day.

<u>August 7 to 8, 1920</u>

I awoke to a pleasant surprise. It's the weekend, we are home, and we have nothing to do. For the first time in years, I can relax. I'm not exactly sure that I know how to do that. I feel certain that we will find something to do.

We did. For the majority of the day, we were busy getting organized and touring around the Fort.

<u>August 9, 1920</u>

An interesting day we had, to-day. We spent the entire time going through indoctrination. I don't remember it being this difficult the first time that I went through it. The one big difference that comes to my mind is that I'm a little wiser this time.

August 10, 1920

We were issued new uniforms and equipment, to-day. This was greatly appreciated as our old uniforms were becoming rather thread-bare. Also, the pattern and style of the uniform had changed in our absence. Our older pattern uniforms were a bit of a stand-out.

August 11 to 13, 1920

Slowly, day-by-day, we are returning to the regular life style of a Soldier. It is not quite the life that we had left behind when we departed for Europe. But, in many respects, this life is far superior.

One question from my former life remains: my parents. I must contact them as soon as possible. I can only hope that they still reside at Fort Robinson, Nebraska. I have written them a letter. Not only to find out where they are located, but to let them know where I am. The other information regarding Annette, I will tell them once communication has been established.

August 14 to 17, 1920

A routine is beginning to take shape, not only in our duty-days, but in our home-life as well. Annette is continuously excited over each and every aspect of her new life and her new home. I, too, find myself getting excited from seeing her so happy. It is as if I were seeing the world anew through her eyes.

August 18, 1920 Ratification Day

The Nineteenth Amendment to the Constitution of the United States of America was ratified to-day. In order for this to be accomplished, a proposal must be passed by the House of Representatives and also by the Senate. Once this is accomplished, three quarters of the States (36) must ratify the proposal. This is the procedure for a proposal to become part of the Constitution. Tennessee became the thirty-sixth State to ratify the proposal to-day. The Tennessee General Assembly passed the proposal by one vote, making this the Nineteenth Amendment to the Constitution. The amendment states "The right of citizens of the United States to vote shall not be denied or abridged by the United States or by any State on account of sex". Additionally, "Congress shall have power to enforce this article by appropriate legislation".

August 19 to September 24, 1920

The routine of the day has returned. I have been placed as third Squad Leader of second Platoon. My Assistant Squad Leader is Corporal Williams. Together we are responsible for twelve Privates. They are a mixed bag of lads. Corporal Williams and I will get them sorted out. Our daily activities are not anything like those in neither France nor Siberia. I am extremely grateful over that fact.

Annette continues to be the light of my life.

September 25, 1920

WHAT A DAY OF SURPRISES!

We arose to what we thought would be a normal Saturday, when there was a knock at the door. It was Mother and Father!

Apparently, my letter finally reached them. They no longer live at Fort Robinson. Father is now stationed with the 3rd Cavalry Regiment at Fort Myer, Virginia. That's a scant 60 miles from Fort Howard. We could travel that in three hours.

We spent the day catching up on everything that has happened to us. Of course, the largest topic of discussion was Annette. Mother seemed a might apprehensive at first. But, as the day wore on and she learned more about Annette, Mother became very accepting. Annette, of course, was charming and entertaining. I could sense that she was cautious, though. However, she too, became more comfortable talking with my parents as the day progressed. By the end of the day, we were all family.

As I said earlier, what a day of surprises!

<u>September 26, 1920</u>

I am still all a flutter over yesterday. To-day was a continuation. We spent the morning together until they had to depart for their home.

Among the information that my parents provided was a sad piece. My younger brother, Charles, died of influenza. It appears that there was a very devastating out-break that killed tens of thousands. Annette knew of this out-break. She said that beginning in the final year of the war and continuing for years after, thousands died in France from the influenza epidemic. I had heard nothing of it while I was stationed in Siberia.

Apparently, this epidemic is only now beginning to subside.

Mother informed me that Charles died shortly before they received notification of my presumed death. This double-dose of bad news was most disturbing to Mother. Understandably, she was elated when they received my letter. At first, she thought that it might have been in error. Perhaps it was a letter that had been misplaced and was only now being delivered. But, it was soon obvious that the letter was a current letter and that I was alive. This is what prompted them make the journey to visit me, immediately.

In addition to their visit, my parents brought with them the collection of my belongings that had been sent to them. There were the parcels that I had sent along with ones sent by my unit, both the 355th and 12th Infantry Regiments. I'm not certain who was happier, me for receiving the items or Mother for being able to give the items to me.

Before my parents departed, I was certain to obtain directions to their house. All too soon, they were on their way home. Annette and I soon resumed our normal routine. We continued to discuss the events of the weekend. Annette was so delighted to have met my parents, as was I. She told me that my

Father and I were very much alike, although I did tend to favor my Mother in facial features.

I took some time in the evening to sort through the boxes that Mother had brought. There were a lot of memories in these packages, both good and bad. There were also several items that I had never seen before, such as photos, orders and awards. Again, a day of surprises!

September 27 to October 15, 1920

The days are stable and simple. The drilling on the Parade Field, the administrative work, and the now-and-then trip to the range, all of these items blend together to fill the hours of the day. And Annette fills the hours of the night.

I did check on my service record to see if everything was properly annotated. Not surprisingly, they were not. Fortunately for me, I had the vast majority of the missing documents. It did take some time, but the clerk was able to transcribe everything and make the proper entries to my record. The few documents that I did not have with me will be added at a later date, as soon as they can be located.

Annette and I have made arrangements to visit Mother and Father to-morrow. It will be nice to travel beyond the boundaries of our Post and view the country-side. I feel certain that Annette will enjoy the journey. We are also in high spirits in anticipation of seeing my parents, again.

October 16, 1920

We awoke early. That is to say, I awoke early. I don't think Annette slept at all, she was so excited. After a hearty breakfast, we gathered our luggage and called for a Taxi Cab. We proceeded to the Railroad Station. We arrived on time and the train was equally punctual. It was a smooth and comfortable journey. The city soon faded into country-side. The joy and wonderment on Annette's face makes me feel happy, like a child again. Every day is a new day through her eyes.

The hours rolled by quickly and we soon arrived at our destination. Another Taxi Cab ride and we were knocking on my parents' front door.

We spent the remains of the day continuing our getting to know each other, reviewing matters of the family that occurred in my absence, dinning, and a tour of Fort Myer. It was quite an event filled day.

October 17, 1920

The first half of the day was an on-going extension of the day before. Our enjoyment was ever rising. Until, all too soon, it was time for us to depart. We gathered our belongings and began our long journey home.

While riding in the Taxi Cab, the thought struck me; "How affordable would an automobile be to own?" It certainly would be much more convenient to be able to travel according to our schedule rather than to adhere to that of others'. Whether or not it would be cost effective would depend on the cost of the vehicle. The journey back to Fort Howard was every bit as enjoyable as it had been the day earlier. Having completing our weekend, we prepared for the week before us.

October 18 to November 1, 1920

Life goes on in a very normal manner. Since I have been paying attention, I have noticed an ever growing number of those automobiles on the road. The vast majority of these automobiles appear to be those made by Mr. Ford. Not only is it interesting from a practical form of transportation, but it is intriguing from an investment point of view. I wonder how one would go about investing in something like that. I wonder if it is even possible for an average person to invest. I would suppose that research would be the first step.

<u>November 2, 1920 Election Day</u>

It is peculiar to me. With everything that is going on around the world and has happened within recent years, I finally have the opportunity to express my opinion in the form of a vote. Additionally, with the recent ratification of the Nineteenth Amendment to the Constitution earlier this year, Annette can also partake in her first election. She is highly excited over the prospect of participating in a national election to select our President.

The candidates are;

Democratic Party: Ohio Governor James M. Cox, running-mate Assistant Secretary of the Navy Franklin D. Roosevelt.

Republican Party: United States Senator from Ohio Warren G. Harding, running-mate Massachusetts Governor J. Calvin Coolidge. I read where General Leonard Wood, my former Commanding General, had bide for the Republican nomination. After 20 ballots at the Convention, Mr. Harding was finally chosen as the party candidate. General Wood was an excellent officer and I feel that he would make a fine President.

Social Democratic Party: Former Indiana Senator Eugene V. Debs

The platforms are;

Democratic Party: Continuation of the progressive work of the Woodrow Wilson Administration.

Republican Party: Return to normalcy, the laissez-faire approach reminiscent of the William McKinley Administration.

Social Democratic Party: Not entirely clear as the candidate was arrested and convicted in 1918 under the Espionage Act of 1917.

The campaign has been filled with slander and accusations. The most notable was the rumor that Mr. Harding's great-great-grandfather was a West Indian. By the "one-drop rule" (anyone with one drop of African blood in them is considered African), that would classify Mr. Harding as African. Neither Annette nor I can believe that this is an issue or that such a rule exists.

Apparently though, this is important to others, enough so to warrant it being mentioned.

Annette appears to have her mind decided. As for me, I know not which way to cast my ballot. I shall decide before this day is through.

<u>November 3, 1920</u>

These are wondrous times in which we live. Through the miracle of the radio we are able to learn the results of the election in a day rather than weeks. Mr. Harding was elected with the largest margin of victory in history. He received 60% of the National vote. The people have spoken. They wish to return to the days before the Great War.

<u>November 4 to 10, 1920</u>

The people may wish to go backwards, I prefer to move forward. Those were some very difficult days. I do not wish to return to them. Nor do I have any desire to live through them again. I must do everything within my power to ensure that these soldiers under my command are properly trained and prepared for what-ever may come.

November 11, 1920 Armistice Day

This day is known as Armistice Day in America and France. This day is also known as Remembrance Day in other countries such as Great Britain and her Commonwealth. No matter how it is known, it is a day that is to be remembered and all who paid for this day with their lives.

November 12 to 24, 1920

The weather has turned cooler as of late. It is true that winter is approaching. And yet, the temperature seems unseasonably low. Perhaps it is just in my imagination.

November 25, 1920 Thanksgiving Day

What a wonderful day!

My parents, brother and two sisters came to our house to celebrate Thanksgiving. Andrew traveled in from Philadelphia. Jean and Leah live in New York City. That is to say, Jean lives in the city and Leah lives in Hoboken. Annette arose early to prepare our meal. It was magnificent!

This was a wonderful opportunity for Annette to meet my brother and sisters. It was also the first time in three years that I had seen or spent some time with my family.

Altogether, it was a very enjoyable day and we had much for which to be thankful.

<u>November 26 to December 19, 1920</u>

It is a constant amazement to me how every day is very much like every other day. The only bright point in my day is when I return to home to be with Annette. I mark the passage of time through her eyes.

One such event was when we received word that her parents were planning to visit us for the holidays. Annette could scarcely contain her joy, each day climbing to new heights until their arrival. Their ship, S.S. Nieuw Amsterdam, is scheduled to dock to-morrow at 3:00 pm. We shall be there to greet them and bring them back to our home.

December 20, 1920

I must commend Annette on her composure. She was able to keep her enthusiasm under control. That is, until we saw her parents from the dock. They were standing on the deck of the ship, scanning the crowded dock for us. Through some miraculous turn of fate, we made visual contact. Annette began calling to them. I doubt seriously that they could hear anything over the horrendous din of the thousands of others calling to each other, the ship's engines, and whistle signaling their arrival to name but a few of the sounds that surrounded us. Time seemed to stand still as we waited to catch a glimpse of them coming down the gang plank. They did appear and we proceeded to the far side of the custom house and wait for them to clear through customs.

Soon, we were making our way back to Fort Howard. How wonderful to see Annette's parents again.

December 21 to 24, 1920 Christmas Eve

During the day, M. and Mme. d'Arcy were not alone. It actually worked to our advantage that I had to work. This allowed Annette time alone with her parents. I do appreciate how valuable that time can be.

December 25, 1920 Christmas Day

What a wonderful day of celebration! The morning was spent with Annette's parents. By the afternoon, my parents had joined us. It was exciting to have the opportunity for our parents to meet. They appear to have gotten along very well. They will have a few days to get to know each other better as my parents have planned to spend the next two days with us.

December 26, 1920

Our joy and celebration was carried on through the day. Everyone enjoyed themselves. To-morrow, M. and Mme. d'Arcy's ship, S.S. Eastern City, departs at 12:00 mid-day. We will need to arrive at the dock in plenty of time to ensure that they will be able to board.

December 27, 1920

Annette and I accompanied M. and Mme. d'Arcy to the docks and watched as they boarded their ship. We stood and waved until we could no longer see them on the ship. Then we stood and watched until we could no longer see the ship. Finally, Annette and I turned and proceeded back to our home. What a wonderful holiday season this has been.

December 28 to 31, 1920 New Year's Eve

With the holidays behind us and everyone returned to their homes, Annette and I can look forward to peace and quiet.

ON TO PEACE

January 1, 1921 New Year's Day

Here we are at the start of another year. Let us hope for all that is good in the world to come forward and take its' rightful place in the hearts and minds of mankind.

January 2 to 5, 1921

I do so enjoy this time of the year! The bounty of joy through the holidays now has one more to join their revels.

January 6, 1921 Annette's Birthday

I now get to add the enjoyment of celebrating this joyous day along with all of the events of the season!

January 7 to March 3, 1921

The normal routine of our daily life continues unabated. It is of increasing concern to me, as I suppose it is to everyone, that the number of unemployed Americans continues to rise, and the price of commodities continues to fall. Yet, there are some good things that have come from these hard times. I have a steady income and, through careful money management, we can afford some of the new luxuries such as a radio and an automobile.

The radio, an RCA, is a wondrous invention. We are able to tune-in stations as far away as Philadelphia, Pennsylvania. Instead of reading news events in the newspaper days after they occur, we can hear about them that same day.

The automobile, a Ford Model-T, took a little longer to save the $290.00. However, we were successful and are able to travel with greater independence. The additional expense (gasoline, oil, tires, et cetera) is out-weighed greatly by the freedom the automobile offers. We are able to visit with my parents or travel on a short expedition or journey with little or no outside co-ordination.

<u>March 4, 1921 Constitution Day</u>

This is also Inauguration Day as Warren G. Harding was sworn in to-day as the 29th President of the United States of America. We were able to listen to his speech on the radio. Father was present for the inauguration as his unit participated in the celebrations.

If the accusation made during the campaign about his great-great-grandfather is true, that would make him the first American President with African ancestry.

March 5 to May 29, 1921

The continual un-rest in the world is continuously on my mind and in the news. The Russian White Army captured Mongolia from China on March 13. The Russian Red Army crushed a rebellion in Kronstadt on March 17. Having seen the cruel, heavy hand of the Red Army in person, I can well imagine what atrocities occurred in that kind of action. There have been assassinations and revolts all around the world. It seems that every day you hear or read of unrest somewhere in the world.

On the positive side, the Second Peace of Riga was signed on March 18, between Poland, Soviet Russia and Soviet Ukraine, ending the Polish-Soviet War. This is the same war that had begun when we crossing the frontier on our way to France. I am very pleased that Poland has successfully defended them-selves and established their independence.

In April, the Reparations Commission of the Allied Nations announced that Germany had to pay 132 billion gold marks for the war. This is to be paid in annual installments of 2.5 billion gold marks. That will take Germany 53 years to complete.

In addition to all of this unrest, on May 19, the Emergency Quota Act was passed by Congress. This act limits the number of immigrants allowed to enter the United States to 3% of the number of persons from that country, living in the United States in 1910, according to the census. I certainly am glad that Annette was able to get her citizenship. It would be much more difficult to do so, to-day.

May 30, 1921 Decoration Day

This day is also known as Memorial Day. This is a time set aside to decorate the graves of those who have fallen in the service of our nation. Originally, this marked the anniversary of the end of the Civil War. Since the Great War, this is a day to remember all who have served.

May 31, 1921

In the sports news, Tommy Milton won the International Sweepstakes in Indianapolis, Indiana yesterday.

In the national news, there were some very disturbing news reports on the radio about some unrest in Tulsa, Oklahoma.

June 1, 1921

The news reports from Tulsa, Oklahoma continue to be disturbing. There are reports of dozens of people being injured or hospitalized. It is still unclear exactly what is happening or how it began.

June 2, 1921

The picture in Tulsa is beginning to become cleared, and it is not a pleasant picture.

As best as I can determine, there was an incident between a nineteen-year old black shoe shiner named Dick Rowland and seventeen-year old white elevator operator named Sarah Page on Decoration Day. Mr. Rowland was arrested and taken into custody the next day. A crowd soon gathered outside of the courthouse, demanding that

Sheriff Willard M. McCullough turn Mr. Rowland over for lynching. The Sheriff refused. The crowd would not be dissuaded. The size of the crowd continued to grow. A group of men from the near-by black community of Greenwood arrived to support the Sheriff and his Deputies defend Mr. Rowland. But their assistance was refused by the Sheriff in fear that it might worsen the situation. However, things did worsen through the afternoon until gun fire erupted in the evening and continued through the night. By the morning of the first, it was a full-blown battle. The neighborhood of Greenwood, also known as "the Negro Wall Street" because of its prosperity, was isolated and ablaze. There are reports of airplanes being used in the attack. By noon, the Oklahoma National Guard had arrived to restore order. There is no word, as of yet, as to the number of casualties. However, Annette and I agree that it would most likely be in the thousands. There is also no word as to whether the Ku Klux Klan was involved or not. Again, Annette and I feel strongly that they were.

I have seen what an attack of this nature can do to civilians. The memories of the battlefields in both France and Siberia are all too fresh in my mind. The deaths, the destruction, the shock, the horror, the hollow-eyed stare of disbelief of the survivors, are images that continue to haunt Annette and me to this day. I fear that they will remain with us for the rest of our lives. We suffer these memories because we had a job to do. Why anyone would intentionally inflict this tragedy on another is completely beyond our comprehension.

June 3 to 11, 1921

Annette and I endeavor to put those images out of our heads. This is not easy as we are reminded of them daily with the news reports of rebellion and unrest from around the world. Scarcely a day goes by without us hearing about there being trouble somewhere around the globe.

Annette does seem to be light-hearted of late, though. It is a curious thing.

June 12, 1921 William's Birthday

I had nearly forgotten my birthday. Annette is determined to celebrate it and I can not disappoint her. It does come as a welcome relief from all of the pain and suffering that we read in the paper and hear on the radio. For Annette's sake, we will celebrate this day and I will enjoy it, if only to see the excitement in her eyes.

<u>June 13 to July 3, 1921</u>

That was a brief respite, but an enjoyable one.

One interesting piece of news was that President Harding signed a joint congressional resolution yesterday, declaring an end to the state of war between the United States of America and Germany and Austria-Hungary. Actually, it would be both Austria and Hungary as the empire Austria-Hungary exists no more. Strange that it took the politicians four years to put on paper what it took us one year to accomplish on the battlefield.

<u>July 4, 1921 Independence Day</u>

To-day is our nations' 145th birthday. We have planned a splendid day of celebration and fireworks.

<u>July 5 to 15, 1921</u>

That was a very refreshing day of enjoyment. We had a picnic on the parade grounds and listened to the Regimental Band play a number of stirring, patriotic tunes. In the evening, we watched a wonderful display of fireworks. It was so enjoyable that we were in a good mood for the remainder of the week.

July 16, 1921, First Anniversary

I tried to make to-day as enjoyable and memorable for Annette as I could. Since this is a Saturday, I let her sleep-in through most of the morning. I made breakfast for her and brought it to her in bed. I had her gift wrapped and ready to present to her. I had planned to make this day as relaxing and enjoyable for her as I could. There was one slight difficulty; she had planned to do the same for me. We compromised. I would treat her to breakfast, she would do lunch, and I would do supper. The evening we would share. I like this arrangement.

July 17 to August 11, 1921

The majority of the days go by in a normal manner. The only item of interest was that President Harding and the United States of America declared peace with Germany, formally ending the Great War.

August 12, 1921

Annette and I welcomed a new addition to our family, Frederick Rudolph. He arrived at 9:27 A.M. He's a healthy, handsome lad.

<u>August 13 to September 2, 1921</u>

The outside life goes on in an uneventful manner. One exception would be that in August, the United States of America formally ended the Great War by declaring peace with Germany. Our inside life is completely changed. Young Frederick has brought new levels of adventure and responsibility. Every day (and night) ventures into worlds, the likes of which I never knew existed.

<u>September 3, 1921</u>

I read of some disturbing news. Over in West Virginia, at a place called Blair Mountain, Federal Troops were sent to put an end to fighting that had been going on since August 25. Some 15,000 members of the United Mine Workers of America had gathered near Mingo, West Virginia to free confined fellow miners by anti-union Sheriff of Logan County, Don Chafin. The Sheriff took up a position outside of Mingo on the high ground of Blair Mountain with his private army of around 2000. The union members, who identified themselves by wearing red bandanas around their necks, rednecks one reporter called them, were spurred on by reports that Sheriff Chafin had deliberately fired on union sympathizers in the near-by town of Sharples. Sheriff Chafin was determined to keep the Coal Miners Union out of Logan County. He was backed by the Logan County Coal Operators Association, private aircrafts, President Harding, and General Billy Mitchell with additional aircraft and Federal Troops. The "rednecks", armed only with hand guns and small caliber rifles, made several assaults up the hill, only to be driven back by the higher caliber rifles and machine gun fire from the Sheriff's forces. In the end, some 100 union members were killed against some 30 of the Sheriff's men. Nearly 1000 "rednecks" were arrested. It was the arrival of the Federal Troops that ended the fighting.

September 4 to November 4, 1921

The events in West Virginia disturb me greatly. I had thought that I had left the fighting in France and Siberia. I certainly did not expect to hear of it again so soon and in America.

November 5, 1921

Annette and I departed on a voyage (a journey) to Washington D. C. We will first travel to Fort Myer to join with Mother and Father. From there, we shall all proceed to Washington D. C. We should arrive in only two days. Annette was concerned about taking young Frederick out in public so soon.

She nearly had decided not to go. My parents, however, convinced her that they would like, very much, to visit with their new grand-son.

Ordinarily, my parents would have come to visit us at our home. There is an event that altered our decision. Earlier in the year, I had learned that on Constitution Day (March 4), Congress had approved a resolution to provide for the burial of an unidentified American Soldier. This practice has been adopted by several of our allied nations. The burial site is to be the newly dedicated Arlington National Cemetery. The unidentified remains of an American Soldier have been brought back from France and are currently lying in state in the Capital Rotunda. The remains will be buried on Armistice Day. Father and I feel very strongly that we should attend. Annette agreed and will also attend.

We arrive at my parent's house. They were excited to meet their grand-son. I don't recall ever seeing Mother smile so much. Father smiled quite a lot, too.

November 6, 1921

We continued on our sojourn. I must comment on the condition of the roadways. They range from excellently constructed and well marked to unmarked, muddy ruts reminiscent of the roads behind the trenches in France. There are virtually no accurate maps to guide you on the correct path, either. We used dead-reckoning, dumb-luck, and getting directions every time that we stopped to find our way. We finally arrived and located a hotel.

November 7, 1921

Our first order of business was to pay our respects at the Capitol rotunda. Annette and Mother stayed at the hotel with young Frederick. Father and I were quite surprised and pleased at the turn-out. The body of the soldier has been lying in state for about ten days and yet, there were still thousands of people who were willing to wait in line for their turn to view and perhaps say a prayer over the Unknown Soldier. This spontaneous out-pouring of emotion by so many for this one who represents all who gave their lives in the Great War, is nearly more than one can stand. More than once, I had to fight back tears that were welling up within me. I noticed Father brushing back a tear or two. By the time we finished viewing the remains and remembering those that we knew who fell in the fields of France and Siberia, and returned to our automobile, we were exhausted. We had planned to take in some of the sights of the city. We decided instead to return to the hotel and retire for the day. We will venture forth to-morrow.

November 8, 1921

To-day, Father, Annette and I visited the Lincoln Memorial. Mother stayed at the hotel room with Frederick. The work on the memorial is nearly complete. We were told that they hope to have the dedication in May of next year. Maybe we can return for that. The constriction is nearly completed. One of the men working on the memorial was very informative and answered our questions. He told us that the memorial was first proposed in legislature in 1901. It took six attempts, but in 1910 a bill was passed. Former U. S. President, now Chief Justice of the United States William H. Taft was chosen as the president of the Lincoln Memorial Commission. Construction did not begin until 1916, due to an inability to come to a consensus on the design and location. Even after construction began, several changes were made. The most recent change being the addition of two large bronze and glass doors to serve as a gate over the opening. The 19 foot high statue of

Abraham Lincoln was placed only last year. It was covered with sheets and tarps.

Later, we walked to the Washington Monument. The two were within view of each other, approximately 3600 feet apart. There was some kind of construction being done along the line between the two monuments. We walked up the 897 steps to the top. We did stop and read each and every one of the plaques on the way up. The view from the top was spectacular. The walk down the stairs was far easier than was the walk up.

Once we departed from the Washington Monument, it was just a short walk (thankfully) to the Jefferson Pier Stone. The pier stone marks the second prime meridian of the United States. When M. Pierre L'Enfant laid out his "Plan of the city intended for the permanent seat of the government of the United States" in 1791 (later renamed "City of Washington"), he called for the Capital to be based on a right triangle with the President's house (White House) as the vertex to the north and Congress house (the Capital) as the vertex to the west. At the 90 degree vertex was to be at an equestrian statue of George Washington. The Washington Monument now stands near that point and the Jefferson pier stone stands on the exact point, originally surveyed by then Secretary of State Thomas Jefferson in 1793.

We returned to the hotel, completely exhausted.

November 9, 1921

We, Mother, Father, Annette, Frederick and I, spent the day, to-day, visiting several of the important and historical buildings of our nation. We went to the White House, the Department of the Treasury building, and the Library of Congress. The first two buildings were next to each other. The Library of Congress was down the road, next to the Capital.

The White House was first built between 1792 and 1800 and has been the residence of every President since John Adams. There have been several additions and remodeling, including reconstruction in 1814 after being set ablaze by the British in the War of 1812. The white painted Aquia sandstone used in the neoclassical architectural design by James Hoban is a wonder to behold for all times.

Next to the White house, we visited the Department of the Treasury building. Architecturally, it complements the White House. Imagine for us to stand so near all of our nation's wealth.

A short walk down Pennsylvania Avenue brought us to the Old Post Office Pavilion. The Romanesque style is much more ornate and busier that the Treasury building, but very similar. There is an overall feeling of continuity to all of the structures on the entire street. We tried to enter the Post Office only to be informed by the guard that the building was used for storage. The Post Office had moved to its current location near Union Station only 15 years after this building had opened. What a waste.

We traveled further down the Avenue, past the Capital to the Library of Congress. Again, there is a strong, Romanesque design to the structure. This appears to be the over-all architectural theme for the entire city. The main reading room inside the Library of Congress is well beyond imagination and description. I would not have believed that such grandeur and beauty existed until I witnessed this structure.

Seeing so much of our nation's capital was absolutely awe inspiring, the buildings, the history, the grandeur and majesty of it all! It's enough to take your breath away.

November 10, 1921

We ventured to the Smithsonian Institution, to-day.
I thought that all of the different architectural
styles of buildings that we saw yesterday were
magnificent. But, the Smithsonian, in my opinion,
is the crowning glory. The red stone, castle style
design only whets your appetite for all of the
wondrous treasures that lie within. I am still in
awe over the ponderous selection of artifacts there.
Annette was also taken aback by what we saw. We,
all, could have spent more time at the Smithsonian
Institute. Unfortunately, we had to return to the
hotel to rest and prepare for to-morrow.

November 11, 1921 Armistice Day

We arose early, crossed the Potomac River, and
went to the dedication site. The number of
spectators started low, but steadily grew throughout
the morning. Father and I were able to find a good
position to observe the ceremony at the newly
constructed Memorial Amphitheater at Arlington
National Cemetery. I was surprised and pleased at
the number of people who came to witness this
dedication. The majority of spectators, as best as I
could tell, were not veterans.

I read, in the ceremony pamphlet, of the steps that were taken to select these remains. From across the battlefields in France, the remains of four unknown American Soldiers were placed in four identical caskets and brought together in the city hall in Chalons-en-Champagne. To make the final selection, a decorated veteran of the Great War, Sergeant Edward F. Younger, was selected. On 24 October, Sergeant Younger chose one of the four caskets to be the Unknown Soldier by placing a spray of white roses on a casket. He placed the roses on the third casket from the left. The remaining three caskets were then interred in the Meuse Argonne American Cemetery. The chosen remains were transported back to America aboard the USS Olympia and lay in state in the Capitol Rotunda until to-day.

The ceremony was very good. The remains were transported from the Rotunda to the Amphitheater with full military honors. Once placed in position, several speeches and presentations followed. President Harding made the key note speech. Among the presentations, the Unknown Soldier was awarded the Medal of Honor as well as the British Victoria Cross. Admiral of the Fleet Lord Betty presented the Victoria Cross on behalf of King George V.

By the end of the day, Father and I were exhausted. It was a very draining and rewarding day. I am very pleased and so honored to be here to witness these proceedings.

November 12 to 13, 1921

Father, Mother, Annette, young Frederick and I packed our luggage, loaded the automobile, and headed back to Fort Myer and then back home to Fort Howard over the long, often bumpy, and dusty roads. The journey home was almost as exhausting as the week that we spent in Washington D.C. This has been a most exhilarating vacation for all of us.

November 14, 1921

We finally made it back to our home. We had an absolutely wonderful vacation in our nation's capital. And to share this adventure with my family was an especially enjoyable new experience for me.

November 15 to 23, 1921

The return to the normal routine of life at the post was pleasantly augmented and even drowned out by the memories from our trip to Washington D. C. I can scarcely comprehend all that we saw, the buildings, the people, the ceremony, the entire experience. Annette also enjoyed herself. I know that she is proud of her French heritage. But, she is equally proud of her newly adopted nation and is eager to see and experience as much as she can.

November 24, 1921 Thanksgiving Day

Annette, Frederick, and I journeyed to celebrate the day at Andrew's home in Philadelphia, Pennsylvania. It was only 90 miles away. We made it in less than four hours. We were joined by our parents and Leah with her family. We had a most enjoyable time.

Father entertained everyone with his recounting of our recent trip to Washington D. C. Two things, I could discern from Father's story telling; one, the accuracy of his description matched my recollections exactly. So the events meant the same to both of us as we remembered the same details. And two; from the tone and excitement in his voice, he really enjoyed himself. I can not recall ever hearing so much emotion in his voice. From their expressions, everyone enjoyed Father's telling, almost as much as we enjoyed experiencing it.

November 25 to December 24, 1921 Christmas Eve

We are back to the routine of every-day work at the post. Annette and Frederick bring light into my otherwise dark days.

December 25, 1921 Christmas Day

This was young Fredericks' first Christmas. Annette made every effort to make it enjoyable for him, though I doubt that he will remember anything. I think that Annette is taking advantage of the opportunity to indulge herself. I don't object as I enjoy it, too.

December 26 to 31, 1921 New Year's Eve

This week was spent basking in the warm glow of Annette's company. We both enjoyed watching young Frederick.

January 1, 1922 New Year's Day

The year begins anew. 155 Dry Agents were employed to enforce the eighteenth amendment. In addition, dozens of guns were fired by excited celebrants at midnight in the Italian quarter of the city. One woman was wounded by a stray round and taken to the hospital, as reported in the Tribune to-day.

Additionally, an interesting article that I read in the newspaper, dealt with a series of treaties and agreements. The four power Pacific treaty (Great Britain, United States, Japan, and France) was signed to respect each other's rights as to islands in the Pacific Ocean. A five power agreement (Great Britain, United States, Japan, France, and Italy) will limit the total amount of capital ship tonnage and aircraft carriers of each nation. And a six nation treaty (Great Britain, United States, Japan, France, Italy, and Holland) that is to divide Germany's cables in the Pacific. The cables awarded are:

Yap-Guam cable to the United States
Yap-Shanghai cable to Japan
Yap-Menado cable to Holland

The first question that came to my mind was "What and where is Yap?" I'll have to research that when I return to work.

Two other items of note caught my attention. First was that diplomatic relations between the United States and Germany officially resumed when Karl Lang, charge d'affaires from the Berlin government, presented his letters of credence to Secretary of State Hughes. The Austrian charge d'affaires, Edgar A. Prochnik, had presented his credentials to Secretary Hughes earlier this week.

The other item was the announcement of a finance plan for Europe to the extent of twenty million British Pounds Sterling. The amount of reparations is 132 billion German Gold Marks. As best as I can surmise, the finance plan is about one tenth of the reparations. That is to say, I give you a dollar and you give me back a dime. Why not just cancel to two out? And while I'm thinking about this subject, I'm not really certain that I understand the whole reparations concept. I understand the desire to charge the Triple Alliance for the cost of the war as they were defeated. But to charge Germany the full amount because they are the only government left intact, does not make any rational sense. Germany was not the instigator of the hostilities, Serbia was. Why not charge them? There is a definite resentment and hostility afoot here that goes far beyond reasonable and rational actions. Because of this underlying hatred, I do not feel that it will end well for Germany.

January 2 to 5, 1922

The pressures of the world have faded from view as I am of sole mind and purpose.

January 6, 1922 Annette's Birthday

The celebrations lasted throughout the day and into the evening!

January 7 to 21, 1922

The return to the normal daily activities was inevitable, but necessary. At nearly every opportunity, I attempted to learn more about Yap. This proved to be more elusive than I had originally imagined. I presumed it was in the Pacific. After searching through several documents, atlases, and pouring over many globes, I finally found the knowledge that I sought. I finally found it in the western Pacific, part of the Caroline Islands between New Guinea and the Philippines. I see why it was chosen for all of the cables. It is certainly centrally located for that region of the Pacific.

In searching for Yap, I was struck by another startling fact: the Pacific is large! Also, there are a tremendous number of islands. When I traveled across Europe and Asia, I did so by train or truck. However, the only means to travel across the Pacific is by ship. True, that was how we traveled across the Atlantic. But the Pacific is three to four times the size of the Atlantic. The daunting task of defending it must be horrendous! I am in awe of the Navy and the fine work that they do protecting our shores.

January 22, 1922

Pope Benedict XV died to-day. He had been ill with pneumonia for several days.

January 23 to February 6, 1922

The economy appears to be improving. I am thinking of investing some of our savings in the Stock Market.

I have read several articles that refer to several powers, including the United States, demanding that Japan withdraw from Siberia. I didn't realize that they were still there. I thought that they pulled-out of Siberia when we left. In all of the dealings that I have had with the Japanese, I have learned one thing: you can not trust them. They will say and do whatever it takes to get what they want.

February 6, 1922

Cardinal Achille Ratti, Archbishop of Milan, has been elected to succeed Pope Benedict XV to-day. He has chosen the name of Pius XI. His coronation is set for February 12.

February 7 to 11, 1922

The news these days seem to center around two issues:

One - the treaty among the five major powers in the Pacific, limiting the size of the Navy each country may have. It also limits the number of submarines and their usage.

Two - the conference that will be held in Genoa, Italy, is to be attended by most of the nations of the world. Their purpose is to discuss monetary economics and to formulate strategies to rebuild post-war Europe. There has been a good deal of debate over which of the new nations would be invited to attend and which would not. There have also been concerns as to whether or not the United States would attend.

February 12, 1922 Lincoln's Birthday

Since this day of Lincolns' birth falls on a Sunday, the observance of this holiday will be held to-morrow. It is curious that the observance of Lincoln's birthday is not a Federal holiday. It remains to the States to declare this day to be a holiday or not. I suspect this has to do with the temperament of the southern states. As we are in New York, we will be observing this holiday.

February 13, 1922

This was a pleasant way to spend a Monday. I enjoyed relaxing about the house with Annette and Frederick. Also, I received one of the new "peace" silver dollars. This is the first chance that I have had to see the new coin up close. It is a very good design.

I read in the paper that an estimated 60,000 people attended the coronation of Pope Pius XI in St. Peter's Cathedral, yesterday. An additional 200,000 waited to see him and receive his blessing in the courtyard outside. I'm certain that it was a splendid celebration.

Another article that caught my attention was the announcement of the placing in custody of

Raymond Bischoff of Chicago for swindling 6,000 investors out of an estimated $4,500,000. This financial operation rivaled that of Charles Ponzi of Boston who also swindled investors out of an equal amount after the war. He went to prison, November 1st, 1920. The newspaper referred to this kind of a swindle as a "Ponzi scheme". No matter what you call it, it does not inspire confidence in me to invest in the stock market. I must be careful should I decide to jump in with what little savings we have managed to set aside. I must endeavor to be very careful.

<u>February 14, 1922 Valentine's Day</u>

There was, in the paper to-day, an inordinate amount of space devoted to the discussion on a bill to authorize a Soldiers' bonus. The bill would authorize a bonus for those who served in the Great War. In my opinion, there should be no question or doubt. The major concern is that the estimated cost could be as much as $5,000,000,000. President Harding is concerned as to how it will be financed. He wants to neither raise taxes, issue bonds, nor use foreign debt to pay the bonuses.

Senator Borah of Idaho is leading a group of at least fifteen Senators who are against the bill. Senator Borah has stated in a speech that he gave to the Senate that this bill would be economically unwise. Additionally, he stated that it was contrary to good principles of government. He also connected the bonus to the nation's responsibility to its' disabled veterans, stating that the money needed to pay for the bonus would take away from the estimated $100,000,000,000 needed to discharge the nations obligation to the disabled soldiers. Personally, I do not understand why Senator Borah sees these two issues as mutually excluding. He appears to suggest that the bonus would be paid with the funds needed to take care of the disabled. Senator Jones of New Mexico asked Senator Borah if he considered the bonus a gratuity. Senator Borah said that he would rather view it as a gratuity than as compensation. Talk about adjusted compensation – adjusted to what? The woman who scrubs the floor of the Capital receives more money than this bill is willing to pay the man who risked his life. Senator Borah would rather call the bonus a gratuity than to insult the soldier by telling him that he was not worth more than the charwoman who scrubs the Capitol steps.

Miss Robertson, a member of Congress from Oklahoma, while addressing the Women's Republican Club, stated her opposition to the bonus bill. She stated in her speech that she remembered Civil War times and that her relatives have served in every war that has ever been fought in this country, but never before had United States soldiers demanded a bonus. Relatives of mine have also served in every war in our country's history. But, in no way does that ancestral fact make a person an expert in the hardship and grief of war. It is true that the men of '61 and '98 did not receive a bonus for their service. Instead, they were paid a pension. Perhaps Miss Robertson is suggesting that those who served be paid a pension, too. To do that would certainly cost more than the bonus that is being proposed. Miss Robertson also stated that opposing the bonus and the Russian relief bills made it difficult for a member of Congress who wanted to be re-elected. Miss Robertson needs to remember that she was elected to represent the people. She can vote her conscience. However, if the people do not agree, she should not expect to be re-elected. The power of the vote belongs to the people, not the politicians.

In support of the bill, Representative MacGregor of Buffalo, New York argued that the manufacture of beer and light wine be allowed and that the proceeds derived from the tax on these be used to pay the bonus.

Mr. Fall, Secretary of the Interior, also supports the bill. However, to pay for the bill, he suggests the liberalizing of law to permit the opening up of Alaska. The revenue from the development of the territory's vast coal, oil, and phosphate fields would not only pay for the bonus, but the entire war debt.

In a related article, a questionnaire recently sent through the War Department and several units of the Army, down to the Regimental level, determined that the doughboy with a bayonet is still war's best "engine of death". All of the new equipment of the modern battlefield; planes, tanks, machine guns, cannons, merely are valuable auxiliaries for the Infantry. The foot soldier in bulk armed with rifle, bayonet, steel helmet, and his own agility is still the deadliest arm of the Army. I would have been in total disbelief if the questionnaire had returned any other results.

February 15 to 21, 1922

It's been a bitter cold of late. There's been a good snow fall, too. The news continues to be dominated with the discussion over the bonus bill. Unfortunately, with reference to the bonus bill and how Congress conducts business, the more that I read, the less I understand.

February 22, 1922 Washington's Birthday

Tragedy struck yesterday.

The U. S. Army dirigible, Roma, burst into flames and plunged 1,500 feet while flying over the Army supply base at Norfolk, Virginia. 34 of the 45 crew members died. Several of those who died were burned to death. Many of the other crew members fell to their death when they jumped from the burning ship. The pilot, Captain Dale Mabry, died at his post.

This is such a tragic accident and loss of life.

February 23, 1922

The Army conducted an inquiry into the cause of the Roma disaster. They determined that a rudder accident caused the dirigible to plunge to the ground where it crashed into a power line and burst into flames. I don't suppose that it matters all that much what caused the accident, men still died.

February 24 to March 8, 1922

The days march on in a normal, orderly manner. I decided to invest some of our savings into the stock market. I didn't think that I could afford to invest very much. The broker told me about buying on margin. It is a way to buy stocks without using money. You use the profits that you expect to earn when your stock goes up as collateral. I am not entirely certain that I understand exactly how that works. But, I was able to purchase more stocks than I had thought possible.

March 9, 1922

The United States announced that they will not participate in the Genoa conference. Secretary of State Hughes sent a letter to the Italian Ambassador stating that the United States sees this conference not as an opportunity to bring economic recovery to Europe. But rather we see it as a means to discuss European political questions. That would not be in our best interest. Although I'm certain that our elected officials are well versed in these matters and are making well informed decisions, I can't help but think that, ideally, we are missing an opportunity to help several European countries economically. And thereby help ourselves.

March 10, 1922

Life continues on in an orderly manner. My squad continues to improve and develop into a cohesive unit. Young Frederick is growing day-by-day. Annette is looking more beautiful every day. Even the attitude of the country has moved to optimistic. Everything in life is going exceptionally well.

It is curious that amidst this improved outlook in life, I hear of unrest in the rest of the world. There is constant violence in Ireland. Rumors persist of the killing of untold numbers of people in the Ottoman Empire. And the unrest in India grows ever worse. This grand discrepancy seems most ironic.

<u>March 11, 1922</u>

To-day's paper confirms the news that I heard on the radio, yesterday. Without the United States participating in the economic conference in Genoa has rendered the conference useless. This will leave the European countries economically adrift. This can not be good for any one. President Harding has offered to hold a similar economic conference in the United States. I am uncertain as to what the difference is between the two.

There was also a news report of growing unrest in India. A non-co-operation movement has been gaining in size and strength. They have a different way of displaying their discontent, through non-violence. Their leader, Mahatma Gandhi, has been arrested. Edwin Montagu has already resigned as Secretary of State for India. It is thought that the Viceroy of India, the Earl of Reading, might also resign.

I also read where Germany has placed a ban on all portraits of the ex-Kaiser and all insignia of the former monarchy is to be removed from public buildings where ever possible.

<u>March 12 to 19, 1922</u>

It is almost inconceivable all of the violence in the world these days. The United States has taken the position to not assist Europe financially. That decision will almost certainly throw several countries into a deep quagmire rather than recover from the war.

There are rumors of war in the Pacific amid charges of hostilities that were asserted by the Four-Powers Treaty and accusations of a secret understanding between Great Britain and Japan.

Mr. Mahatma Gandhi was sentenced to six years for sedition. There have been riots in India ever since his arrest. Around one hundred people have been killed and thousands more have been arrested.

There were also riots in Belfast and Cairo further adding to the general feeling of unrest in the world.

March 20 to 21, 1922

The question of weather or not to grant a bonus to veterans of the Great War continues to be debated in Congress. I'm certain that they feel that they are doing what they think to be right. It just seems to me that it must be wonderful for them, from the comfort of a safe and secure nation, to debate the merits of rewarding those who risked their lives to give them that freedom.

On a related news item, all U. S. Troops are to return from the Rhine by July 1, with half of the 4,000 troops to return by April.

March 22 to April 1, 1922

I find it increasingly difficult to believe what I hear on the radio and read in the newspaper. The same information is reported over and over and over. The end result is the impression that nothing ever gets completed. Perhaps it would be better for my piece of mind if I did not pay such close attention to the day-to-day affairs of the world and concentrate more on my troops and family.

The larger picture of the world should suffice for the time being.

April 2, 1922

Just when I think that there is nothing new, something happens. American Telephone and Telegraph Company, operating the Bell System, announced that they intend to start operation of a radio toll service in the city. In an agreement from 1919, the Radio Corporation of America and American Telephone and Telegraph Company resulted in a division of radiophone and radio-telegraphy fields with the radio corporation being given international communication between ship to ship and ship to shore, and the telephone company being limited to continental communication. The new station sports two 100 foot towers above the Walker-Lispenard Building. This will make the total height more than 500 feet above the ground. A second similar station will be opened soon in St. Louis and several more across the country. The telephone company's new radio station will be known as the Public Service Radio Station and will be available at any hour. In the near future, radio fans will be able to pick up broadcasts from anywhere. The telephone company has no intention to permit subscribers to receive radio broadcasts over the telephone.

Additionally, I read where the former Emperor of Austria and King of Hungary, Charles I, died of pneumonia. Upon completion of reading the several articles, two pieces of information stand out in my mind. Firstly, I was struck by the devotion and genuine sorrow of the people when they learned of the passing of their former leader. Secondly, I had not realized that nearly all, if not every, royal family in the world is related to each other. Certainly all of the European countries, Mexico, Central and South America are related to each other. I cannot help but consider that all of those millions of men died because of a family argument.

April 3, 1922

The Tribune began a fifteen article series on Russia, to-day. I will keep my eye on this series. I have some very deep opinions on this subject.

Mr. William Jennings Bryan spoke at the Hippodrome, yesterday. Having listened to his lectures, I am not convinced that his argument is the correct conclusion. I consider myself to be a religious man and I have seen many things in my life. But Mr. Bryan argued against Darwinism, saying that he preferred mud to monkeys because he is familiar with mud, makes no logical, rational sense to me. I am not certain what the correct answer is. But there should be a reasonable solution.

April 4, 1922

Four immigration inspectors were arrested in a graft ring. They are accused of taking bribes to allow the illegal admission of immigrants into the country. I am certainly pleased that Annette and I did not resort to that method of gaining her citizenship.

April 5, 1922

Mr. Eugene K. Martin, an inventor, killed himself by inhaling illuminating gas in his home. Of interest to the newspaper was the fact that he wrote down his thoughts as he died. Of interest to me is that someone would be so down that they would take their own life. I realize that it most likely occurs often. But until I am confronted with it, I prefer not to think about it.

April 6 to 12, 1922

Annette has put in her application to attend Nursing College. This should be no great difficulty for her as she was a Nurse in France for years. As I understand, she needs to complete her accreditation. In all probability, she could take her exams. However, Annette prefers to go through the training as it will be in a second language for her. I support her whole-heartedly in this venture.

April 13, 1922

I read to-day of the testimony given by General Graves and Lieutenant Colonel Morrow to a Senate committee as to the character of General Semenoff. I remember Semenoff from when I was in Siberia. The fact that he calls himself a General does not impress me in the least. He is nothing but a low-life, odious, contemptible human being. I have seen with my own eyes what he and the men under his command did. Reading General Graves' account of confrontations that he had had with Semenoff brought back many memories, including that of Private Horace. I am not certain if it was Semenoff's men that executed Private Horace and those passengers on the train that day. But, it would not surprise me to find out that Semenoff was involved. I do not understand how he was allowed passage into the United States. Considering the recent bribery scandal with immigration inspectors, I would not doubt that some sort of bribe was involved.

April 14, 1922

Testimony continued to-day in the case of Semenoff. In typical fashion for him, he tried to bribe his way out of jail. Bond was not allowed and he was incarcerated at the Ludlow Street Jail. Crowds of people gathered outside the prison yelling, "That's Semenoff. He ought to be shot in the street like a mad dog!" I must say that I agree with the crowd.

In related news, Princess Xenia Sedamon-Eristoff arrived at New York from Constantinople. She is one of very few of nobility to have escaped from Petrograd just before the collapse of the Russian Empire. She hopes to secure a position as a secretary here in America. The irony is not wasted. To be born to royalty and privilege, only to lose everything. Now her future depends on obtaining work, no matter the type.

April 15 to 21, 1922

Our lives and work continue to improve. The small amount of money that we have managed to set aside we have invested into the stock market. We have been able to invest more into the market than the actual value of our available money due to a policy the brokers have to purchase stocks on margin. As I understand, I can purchase $100.00 worth of stocks and it will cost only $10.00. The broker will hold the note or debt for the balance. I was taught to pay my way through life. If I cannot afford something, then I do not need it. I am leery of purchasing these stocks and owing such a large sum of money. The broker assures me that there is nothing wrong, illegal or immoral in doing this. To offset the debt, I could use the dividends from the stocks to pay back the broker or to purchase additional stocks. Despite the broker reassuring me that this is the standard method used by everyone to purchase stocks, I am not comfortable. I have purchased some stocks on margin, but only as much as I feel that we can afford. I must say, though, that it does appear to be working. Maybe this will not be that bad of a venture after all.

April 22, 1922

There was an odd article in the newspaper, to-day. A professor at Princeton University has been working for 8 years on developing a continuous cold light. Professor Harvey declared that he has achieved this. Two points stood out in my mind; first, the protein substance called luciferin comes from a small crustacean and is imported from Japan, burns out quickly. It is only speculated that the luciferin can be intensified and prolonged to the point that it would be of any use. The second point is that Dr. Harvey stated that he had no practical purpose in mind when he began his experimentation 8 years ago. I find it difficult to comprehend the motivation that would drive an individual to pursue an idea for 8 years with neither use nor purpose, only the belief that it could be done. Still, I can well imagine that it was this kind of dedication that has lead to the wondrous inventions and marvels that enhance our lives.

April 23 to 30, 1922

Good news! Annette has been accepted to the Bellevue Hospital School of Nursing. Because she had been a nurse in France, the school is willing to waive many of the required courses. In fact, they have arranged for Annette to take a placement exam to assess her level of knowledge and skill. I am confident that she will do exceptionally well.

May 1, 1922

It appears that there is more unrest in China. Two war lords, General Wu Pei-fu and General Chang Tso-lin are fighting near the capital of Peking. Each General is believed to have 100,000 in forces. The number of casualties is unknown but believed to be in the thousands. A third leader, Dr. Sun Yat-sen, has joined with General Chang.

Foreign intervention has been requested and Britain, France, and the United States have sent gunboats to near-by Tientsin. The London Times reported that an airplane dropped a bomb on a train carrying a detachment of American Marines heading toward Peking. The bomb had no effect on the train.

It would appear that all of this fighting is over the unification of China. And, perhaps more importantly, who will control the nation. It does not appear to be a fight for independence nor separation.

All of this is occurring a relatively short distance from where I was located in Vladivostok. The Japanese province of Korea lies between Vladivostok and Peking. I often suspected that the Japanese harbored desires to rule the entire region. I am surprised that they have sent neither troops nor ships into the area. Perhaps they have and it has not yet been reported.

<u>May 2 to 22, 1922</u>

All is well. My platoon continues to perform in an acceptable manner. Annette has begun her classes. And, despite her early fears, is doing exceptionally well. Young Frederick continues to grow and explore. He has been walking around the house and getting into everything.

<u>May 23, 1922</u>

Father and I have made plans to attend the dedication of the Lincoln Memorial in Washington, D.C. next week. Annette will be unable to join us due to her course work. Mother will stay with her and watch young Frederick while we are away.

May 24 to 29, 1922

The trip to Washington, D.C. was a pleasant one, much like the one that we took last November for the dedication and burial of the Unknown Soldier. The roads are little improved. And at least, this time, we have a better idea of the route that we need to take.

May 30, 1922 Decoration Day

That was a stirring ceremony, to say the least. The memorial itself was simple, yet classical. It is an impressive rectangular structure measuring 190 feet by 119 feet and standing 99 feet high. It looks much like a Greek temple. It is faced with 36 columns on all sides, one column for each state in the Union at the time of President Lincoln's death.

Inside and centered, is a statue of a seated Abraham Lincoln. It is a most impressive figure that rises 19 feet from bottom to top. The walls of two side rooms are carved with the words from his Gettysburg Address and his second inaugural speech.

The president of the Memorial Commission, former President of the United States of America, President William H. Taft, dedicated the Memorial and presented it to current President of the United States of America, President Warren G. Harding, who accepted it on behalf of the American people. President Lincoln's only living son, Robert Todd Lincoln, was present for the ceremony. He is 79 years old.

<u>May 31 to June 6, 1922</u>

Father and I remained in Washington D.C. for another day before beginning our journey home. We toured the city, looking at the many monuments and buildings.

This trip also afforded me the opportunity to visit with Father, without the distractions of work and everyday life.

It was a very enjoyable and rewarding trip.

<u>June 7 to 11, 1922</u>

The home life continues to go well. Annette is gaining confidence in herself as well as English. Young Frederick continues to grow and investigate everything. And I am starting to relax and enjoy life. The dreams persist, but their frequency is diminishing.

June 12, 1922 William's Birthday

I am coming to enjoy my birthday again. Not for my sake. Rather for the joy that I see in Annette. She does so enjoy these celebrations!

June 13 to 30, 1922

It was a bit of a rough time at the unit, recently. On the one side, Private Collins has been performing exceptionally. He has excelled at every task given to him. His marksmanship has improved. And his appearance and bearing is outstanding. I had no reservations in recommending him for promotion. Captain Grange agreed and Private Collins is now Corporal Collins. I am very excited for him. He has earned it.

On the other side, Private Harper has not fared as well. His heart is not in his work. He can do good work when he puts his mind to it. More often than not, he chooses not to put his mind to it. He's a good soldier and I do not want to put him out of the service. But, if his record does not improve, I will have no choice. I am placing him in Corporal Collins' team. Perhaps that will make a difference.

July 1, 1922

400,000 rail shopmen plan to strike over wages, to-day. This will affect every railroad in the country. Additionally, the President met with representatives of the striking coal miners to try, what the paper calls, "moral suasion". I suppose that it is better than a club over the head.

July 2, 1922

Good news. 6,000 Marines took part on a re-enactment of General Pickett's charge at Gettysburg, Pennsylvania. This reproduction, done 59 years after the actual event, was done for the President and his party along with the public. I imagine that it was a spectacular sight.

July 3, 1922

No activity to-day. Everyone is preparing for to-morrow's festivities.

July 4, 1922 Independence Day

What a wonderful day! Annette, young Frederick and I had a picnic in the park. Then we went for a stroll and listened to the various bands playing. We returned home and played a round of croquet on the lawn. Later, after dark, we sat on our front porch and watched a most splendid aerial display of fireworks. I'm afraid that young Frederick was not able to get his normal sleep this night. He did appear to be most fascinated with the fireworks, though.

July 5 to 15, 1922

The railroad strike continues to worsen. The Governors of at least six states have ordered the Militia in to protect the interests of the railroad and keep the trains moving. The President has ordered us to stand-by should we be needed.

July 16, 1922 Second Anniversary

I am thankful for this momentary distraction from the current events. Annette can always put a smile on my face.

July 17 to 25, 1922

The President has asked all of the state Governors to take steps to protect the railroads and coal mines. He has ordered us to stand ready in the event that the states do not succeed in their mission. Rationing plans have been drawn up should the situation get completely out of hand.

231

July 26, 1922

The government has taken emergency control of the railroads and coal mines. They have established a priority list of food and fuel to be delivered to the areas needing it the most. At this time, the states are providing adequate protection.

July 27 to August 1, 1922

Negotiations continue but neither side is giving. Everyone remains confident that an agreement will be reached soon.

August 2, 1922

The agreement has been rejected as completely unacceptable. I wonder if everyone is still confident about finding a solution.

August 3 to 11, 1922

Negotiations for a settlement of the railroad and coal mine strikes continue. I cannot see improvement or advancement.

On the other side of the world, Germany has been pleading for assistance in paying the war reparations. Their inflation rate is so high that it takes 563 Marks to buy one U.S. Dollar. They have asked for a moratorium on payments. That was rejected by Britain and France. France has moved to occupy the Ruhr region of Germany and seize German property and assets in Alsace-Lorraine, valued at about 800,000,000 gold marks. If you remove a nation's industry and ability to produce goods, how can you expect them to sustain an economy?

In Italy, five provinces have been placed under martial law due to rioting by a political party called Fascisti. Fighting between the Fascisti and the Communists and Socialists in Genoa, Milan, Parma, Acona, and Leghorn have forced the government to declare martial law until order is restored.

August 12, 1922 Frederick's First Birthday

What joy! Our son is one year old to-day. Annette is having the time of her life.

To add to the festivities of the day, Annette's parents have arrived for a visit. We went to New York to meet them and bring them back to the house. They arrived aboard the Zeeland out of Antwerp. The Zeeland is part of the Red Star Line. They said that they had a very nice crossing.

My parents also came over this evening to join in the celebration of Frederick's birthday.

August 13 to 14, 1922

This has been a very enjoyable time with M. e Mme. d'Arcy. We had much to talk about. They were very pleased with Annette's decision to get her nursing degree. It was wonderful to see Annette's parents and have a moment to visit with them.

August 15, 1922

The time for the d'Arcys to board their ship and return to France has arrived. We drove them to the city and watched as they boarded the ship. They boarded the West Inskip of the Black Diamond line, bound for Antwerp. We stood on the dock and waved until we could no longer see the ship. We then returned home.

August 16 to 22, 1922

The tension and unrest in the world continues. There appears to be no end in sight. It has even reached the level that the President has asked Congress to make strikes impossible. I find it difficult to comprehend this level of madness.

August 23, 1922

The madness continues. General Michael Collins, the leader of the Free Irish State, has been assassinated, yesterday. This came only two day after escaping from an earlier attempt on his life. All of this happened only 10 days after Arthur Griffith, the founder of Sinn Fein, died leaving Collins the sole leader of the Free Irish State. I can see no good coming from any of this.

August 24 to September 2, 1922

Private Harper is showing some improvement. Not as much as I would like to see. But, it is an improvement, none the less. Corporal Collins is to be congratulated. If this continues, I will be pleased to recommend him for promotion to Sergeant.

September 3, 1922

The coal strike is over! At least that part is done. Now there is the railroad strike with which to contend.

September 4, 1922 Labor Day

It was so relaxing to stay at home with nothing to do, save be with my family. This has been a truly wonderful day.

September 5 to 13, 1922

Everything continues as it has for recent days. The railroad strike continues with no end in sight. Turkey has invaded Greece. The King of Greece, King Constantine, has fled the country. The First Lady, Mrs. Harding, is ill. The only bright spot, outside of my family, is that the stock market continues to rise.

September 14, 1922

The Shopmen railroad strike is over. All parties have come to an agreement. And Mrs. Harding is doing well.

September 15 to 27, 1922

The British have now moved in to stop the Turks. Also, the President has vetoed yet another bill granting bonuses to the veterans of the Great War. By the time that they finally approve a bonus, if they ever do, most of the veterans will be gone. Or, maybe that is their plan.

September 28, 1922

King Constantine of Greece has abdicated and Crown Prince George is the new King of Greece.

September 29, 1922

Now, it is reported that the Sultan of Turkey, Mohammed VI, has abdicated. Additionally, Turkish forces have occupied nearly the entire neutral zone on the Asiatic side of the Dardanelles. This is an interesting turn of events.

September 30 to October 3, 1922

Little else has changed in the world.

October 4, 1922

The World's Series between the Giants and the Yankees will be broadcast for the first time on the radio. It was interesting to hear the battle for the baseball championship as it happened, rather than waiting to read about it in the next day's newspaper. The radio reception was clear as

Annette and I listened to the Giants beat the Yankees, 3 to 2.

October 5, 1922

Game 2 was called on account of darkness after 10 innings. The score was tied, 3 all. Apparently, the fans were not pleased with the decision by the umpires. We, of course, could not tell what the conditions were as we could only hear the game.

October 6, 1922

The Giants won game 3, 3 to 0.

October 7, 1922

Game 4 belongs to the Giants. Even though it was played in a drizzling rain, Babe Ruth, Bob Meusel and all of the Yankees couldn't best the Giants who won the game, 4 to 3.

October 8, 1922

The Giants have won the championship! They beat the Yankees 5 to 3.
That was a very enjoyable event to be able to listen to the games as they happened. Annette and I enjoyed it greatly.

October 9 to 10, 1922

There is nothing of note worth reporting, happening in the world.

October 11, 1922

Turkish hostilities have ended. All powers concerned have signed the agreement ending all aggression.

October 12 to 30, 1922

Things appear to be coming along splendidly. Annette is doing very well in her studies. Young Frederick is getting into everything. The platoon is accomplishing all of their missions. I did read about an Army pilot, 1st Lieutenant Maughan, setting an airplane speed record of 248.5 miles per hour out in Michigan. It is amazing what these new machines can do.

There seems to be some trouble in Italy. Apparently, the Fascisti party is on the move towards Rome.

October 31, 1922

The King of Italy, King Victor Emmanuel, has asked the leader of the Fascisti party, Benito Mussolini, to form a Cabinet, thus giving all power to the "Blackshirts". They are so named for the black shirts that they wear as their uniform.

I also read where the Red Army has occupied Vladivostok. That stirs up many memories.

November 1 to 4, 1922

There is a great deal of turmoil in Turkey, again. It appears that the Sultan, Mohammed VI, has abdicated, again. Another report says that he will fight his forced abdication. I am still unclear if Turkey is an independent country of a part of the Ottoman Empire. I thought that the Sultan of the Ottoman Empire was Mehmed VI Vahdettin. Perhaps my information is incorrect.

The German Mark was devalued, again. It now takes 6,600 Marks to purchase one U. S. Dollar. Along with that, the stock market continues to climb.

November 5 to 6, 1922

Still no clear understanding of what is happening in Turkey. Back in America, people are preparing for the National Elections.

November 7, 1922 Election Day

I had scarce time to remember to vote on this Election Day. Annette had to remind me to do so.

I did read this evening that the District of Columbia Court of Appeals ruled to-day that the minimum wage law was unconstitutional. Judge Josiah A. Van Orsdel stated that "no greater calamity could befall the wage earners of this country than to have the legislative power to fix wages upheld." The Minimum Wage Board will appeal the ruling to the Supreme Court.

November 8, 1922

The Republican Party has held on to control in the Senate and the House of Representatives. The Democratic Party did gain a few seats, but not enough to gain control.

November 9 to 10, 1922

As I pondered the Turkish question, I received some assistance and clarification from a soldier of mine. I also received some very disturbing information.

Private Gorky was born and raised in that part of the world. He informed me that the Ottoman Empire still ruled that region. But that there was Turkish revolt going on and had been since 1919. Also, the Turks were involved in a war with Greece over the regions of Smyrna, Thrace, and Bosporus. Private Gorky told me that Sultan Mehmed VI Vahdettin is the present leader of the Ottoman Empire. He said that he had not heard of a Sultan Mohammed VI of Turkey that the newspaper reported. And that Turkey does not have a Sultan.

The disturbing news came when Private Gorky told me of his life growing up in the Ottoman Empire. How during the war, all of his people, the Armenians, were taken out of the armed forces and put into unarmed labor battalions. Several members of these labor battalions were later executed by the Turks, his father and two uncles included.

Private Gorky also told me of how his entire village was forced to move to another location. They did not know where they were going. There were no provisions for them along the way and the meager amount of food that they had with them soon gave out. Most of the people did not survive the ordeal. The road was strewn with the bodies of the fallen. His Grandmother, Brother and two Sisters were among those who did not make the journey. Once they arrived at what they were told was their new location, there was no food, no water, no shelter, and no means of protecting themselves against the harsh, open environment that they were in. Many more perished, including his Mother and younger Brother.

An opportunity arose for a few to go to a new country. Private Gorky and his only remaining Brother were fortunate to get on the list and that was how they came to America.

I am horrified to learn of this great injustice and admire Private Gorky for having endured it. I would never have known of any of this had he not informed me. To his credit, Private Gorky has performed very well and has never displayed any outward signs of the hardship that he has endured.

November 11, 1922 Armistice Day

I have included Private Gorky's family and all who have perished unjustly in my remembrances.

November 12 to 18, 1922

Not much has changed.

November 19, 1922

Crown Prince Abdul Medjid Effendi has reportedly been elected Caliph of the Ottoman Empire by the Angora Assembly. The Crown Prince is cousin to the exiled Sultan Mehmed VI Vahdettin.

November 20 to 29, 1922

Things continue to proceed without incident. It has been cooler temperatures with some snow. Annette's classes continue to go well.

November 30, 1922 Thanksgiving Day

Annette, Frederick, and I enjoyed an absolutely splendid day, to-day.

December 1 to 24, 1922 Christmas Eve

Issues around the country and the world continue to be the same. The Turks continue to ignore all of the other countries. Greece is in total chaos. France is accusing Germany of preparing for war and plans to occupy the Ruhr. Germany cannot meet its reparation obligation. The newly formed Irish Free State is still fighting.

In America, politicians continue to be ineffective. Louisiana is trying to eliminate the Ku Klux Klan. There is a growing movement to repeal the 18th Amendment and allow the manufacturing, sale and imbibing of alcohol.

At home, my soldiers are doing well. Even Private Harper is showing improvement thanks to the excellent work done by Corporal Collins. Annette has finished her exams and is awaiting her results. Frederick continues to be quite the young man.

December 25, 1922 Christmas Day

We enjoyed spending the day together, by ourselves, as a family. The weather was very pleasant.

December 26 to 31, 1922 New Year's Eve

Annette received official notification from the Bellevue Hospital School of Nursing that as a result of her experience, knowledge, exam results and interviews, the School Board is conferring upon her certification as a Registered Nurse. She will begin applying for a position next month. I couldn't be more proud of her!

January 1, 1923 New Year's Day

What a bright prospect this New Year brings!

January 2 to 5, 1923

That did not take long.

Annette went to the post hospital to inquire as to a position and was hired immediately. She begins next week.

I, too, received some new information. I am being reassigned to the Recruiting Station here on post and begin my new duties next week. As a parting recommendation, I put Corporal Collins in for promotion to Sergeant and Private Gorky for Promotion to Corporal. I wish them well.

January 6, 1923 Annette's Birthday

We certainly have much to celebrate this year.

January 7 to 11, 1923

The training that I am receiving for this new position has, thus far, been enjoyable. It is a complete diversion from what I am use to doing. However, I am confident that I will soon master it.

January 12, 1923

The French Government has carried through with their threat to occupy the Ruhr. French and Belgium troops moved into the Ruhr area of Germany yesterday in order to force Germany to make its reparation payments. As the Ruhr area is the industrial heart of the nation, I fail to understand how taking it from Germany will enable them to pay a debt that they cannot pay with the area. I hope for the best, but fear that it will not end well for anyone.

January 13 to February 11, 1923

I am exhausted! With Annette working at the post hospital, I am trying to help by doing more around the house. However, my new assignment requires much more of my time and energy than my former position. The result being that I haven't had the time to do all of the pleasures that I use to do. I scarcely have any time available to read the newspaper or even listed to the radio. We haven't gone for an evening walk in weeks. That part is not as bad since the winter weather has arrived. Even so, we would not have the time to walk if the weather was pleasant enough to allow. I scarcely have the time to write this entry.

It is obvious to me that some re-organization and time management is necessary.

February 12, 1923 Lincoln's Birthday

A well deserved respite. Annette had to work for part of the day. But I had a chance to relax, if only for a little while.

February 13, 1923

I had imagined that this new assignment would be easy. At present, my days are filled with meetings and following other recruiters at the station to learn what I can from them. For something as simple as enlisting a new recruit into the Army, there is a lot of work to be done.

February 14, 1923 Valentine's Day

Annette and I went out to celebrate. We had a marvelous dinner at a very nice Italian restaurant called Giuseppe's. It was an absolutely wonderful day.

February 15 to 21, 1923

I am still unsure of myself. I feel as though I might be gaining a fair understanding. Then again, I could be mistaken.

February 22, 1923 Washington's Birthday

Another welcomed brief respite.

The German Mark has been devalued again. It now takes 17,000 German Marks to exchange for one U.S. Dollar. This has to be a result of the occupation of the Ruhr.

February 23 to April 25, 1923

The days are long and the hours are hard. But, I do believe that I am getting to understand this new work of mine. One half of the job is getting out into the public and talking with all of the potential candidates and persuading them to join the Army. Another half of the job is filling out all of the forms and papers necessary when they do join. The other half is taking care of the new recruits and attending all sorts of meetings and events. And the last half is for me.

April 26, 1923 Royal Wedding Day

Prince Albert, Duke of York married Lady Elizabeth Bowes-Lyon to-day in Westminster Abbey, England.

Annette is absolutely obsessed with this. She listens to the radio for any news of the ceremony. When the evening paper arrived, she poured over it, studying every picture and reading every article. This is a very big occasion to her.

April 27 to May 9, 1923

Annette continues to scour the newspapers for information on the Royal wedding. Even when we go to the movie theater, she insists on being early in hopes the newsreel will have some new images.

As for me, I am hopeful that I am finally getting control over the situation at work. It feels as if the work flow is moving easier. I do not wish to be too optimistic, though.

May 10, 1923

There was a record snow fall in Michigan, yesterday. Detroit and all of southeastern Michigan was covered with up to 6 inches of snow. That is very unusual for this time of the year.

May 11 to 29, 1923

Life in our household continues as before. Annette works at the hospital and I work at the Recruiting Station. We appear to be settling into a rather normal routine.

May 30, 1923 Decoration Day

This should have been a pleasant day of relaxation. Instead, Annette had to work and I spent the majority of my time catching up on my paperwork. That does not seem to me to be a very good way to spend a holiday.

May 31 to June 11, 1923

And so the days continue. We scarcely have any time for ourselves.

June 12, 1923 William's Birthday

I had nearly forgotten that to-day was my birthday. Fortunate for me, Annette remembered. She and Frederick are the bright spot of these dark days. I hope that they shall always be that way.

June 13, 1923

Yesterday was a most enjoyable respite from the toils of the day. But now, it is back to that daily drudge.

June 14, 1923

The fighting in China that has been going on for more than a year has resulted in President Li abandoning his residence. It appears that this fighting among the different warlords will continue until all have perished.

June 15 to July 3, 1923

The daily drudge continues.

July 4, 1923 Independence Day

To-day was a very welcomed relief. Annette, Frederick, and I spent the day together. We had an enjoyable afternoon listening to the band in the park and walking around the post. We had a wonderful dinner and in the evening, watched the fireworks from our front porch. It was just as we had done, years before.

July 5 to 15, 1923

Playtime is over, back to work.

July 16, 1923 Third Anniversary

This was one day that I would not let slip by, unnoticed. I arranged to have a quiet evening alone with Annette. It seemed to me that she needed a break as much as I did.

July 17 to 20, 1923

And so we return to our jobs. I have no time to read the newspaper these days. I hardly have any time to listen to the radio. Every now and again, I hear about something, or happen to pick up on some piece of information. I do miss being in touch with what is happening in the world.

July 21, 1923

Here's a piece of news that I was glad to hear. Pancho Villa was assassinated at Hidalgo del Parral, Chihuahua Mexico by a group of gunmen. I recall Father leaving in 1916, after Villa destroyed Columbus, New Mexico, to capture him. I did not see Father again for several years as we were both caught up in the Great War by 1917. I called Father on the telephone to see if he had heard the news. He had, and we talked for a while. Mostly, we talked about the family and how everyone was getting along. It was good to talk with my parents.

July 22 to 24, 1923

This was an enjoyable weekend. Soon enough it ends and the workweek begins.

July 25, 1923

I heard on the radio that the Treaty of Lausanne was signed yesterday in Switzerland. This treaty establishes the boundaries of the new nation of Turkey. It is hoped that this will bring an end to the fighting in that part of the world. This also marks the beginning of the end of the Ottoman Empire.

July 26 to August 2, 1923

Back to work.

August 3, 1923

President Harding has died. He was on a speaking tour of the far west and was in San Francisco, California when he fell ill with some kind of a respiratory infection. At 7:35 p.m. California time yesterday, he passed away. His body will be brought back to the capital where he will be kept until his state funeral. Vice President Calvin Coolidge will soon be sworn in as President of the United States of America.

August 4, 1923

Vice President Coolidge was visiting his parents in Vermont. Their home has no electricity. So Mr. Coolidge's Father, a Notary Public, swore him in as President by the light from a kerosene lamp, on August 3, 1923 at 2:47 a.m. Vermont time. It is reported that President Coolidge is on his way back to Washington D. C.

August 5 to 7, 1923

President Harding's funeral train made its way back across the nation. All along the route, scores of people gathered to get a glimpse of the train and to pay their final respects.

August 8, 1923

The state funeral for President Harding was held to-day. Thousands gathered at the Capital. Mother and Father were there. Father had been assigned to the funeral detail. Alas, Annette and I were not able to attend.

August 9, 1923

President Harding's funeral train made its way to Marion, Ohio where he will be buried to-morrow.

August 10, 1923

President Harding was buried to-day in the Marion Cemetery, Marion, Ohio. Thousands gathered to pay their final respects.

August 11, 1923

There is a general feeling of loss and mourning across the land.

August 12, 1923 Frederick's Birthday

Annette and I are determined to not let this solemn time interfere with the joy of Frederick's second birthday. We have made it as festive as we can.

August 13, 1923

Our spirits are up. But, there is still a feeling of gloom everywhere.

August 14, 1923

There is hopeful news from Germany. Yesterday, Gustav Stresemann was named Chancellor of Germany and has formed a coalition government for the Weimar Republic. He certainly has his work cut out for him. The exchange rate is now 4,600,000 Marks for one U. S. Dollar.

<u>August 15 to September 2, 1923</u>

The mood of the country has improved as everyone returns to their jobs.

<u>September 3, 1923 Labor Day</u>

This day of rest could not have come at a more opportune time. Annette, Frederick and I were able to relax and enjoy a day at home enjoying each other's company.

<u>September 4 to 8, 1923</u>

Everything appears to be running normally.

<u>September 9, 1923</u>

There has been a terrible accident in California. Last night, while on maneuvers, seven U. S. Navy destroyers ran aground at Honda Point, near Santa Barbara. Lost were the U.S.S. Delphy, U.S.S. S. P. Lee, U.S.S. Young, U.S.S. Woodbury, U.S.S. Nicholas, U.S.S. Fuller, and U.S.S. Chauncey. Damaged were the U.S.S. Farragut, and U.S.S. Somers. There is no word on how many Sailors lost their lives. How this happened is under investigation. This is such a tragic loss of life and equipment. And, for it to have happened during a time of peace is almost beyond comprehension.

September 10 to 26, 1923

We return to our daily tasks at hand.

September 27, 1923

There is disturbing news from Germany. Bavaria has declared martial law and placed Gustav Ritter von Karl Staatskomissar (state commissioner) with absolute power over the police and military. This action was done due to all of the recent assassinations, turmoil, and political unrest. This does not bode well.

September 28 to 30, 1923

This was a most enjoyable weekend. We were able to relax at home.

October 1, 1923

There is more unrest in Germany. A group, called the Black Reichswehr, led by Major Ernst von Buchrucker, has seized control of several forts around Berlin. They are calling this type of overthrow by force, a "putsch".

October 2, 1923

Our work continues.

October 3, 1923

Yesterday, in Germany, Major Buchrucker and his forces have surrendered to government forces.

October 4 to 23, 1923

And so, we return to our jobs. There is a lot of news concerning the number of tropical storms in the Gulf of Mexico. I certainly am glad that we are stationed in Pennsylvania.

October 24, 1923

There are more reports of another putsch in Germany. This one is in Hamburg and it is led by the Communist Party. There are reports of heavy fighting in the streets.

October 25, 1923

There is no report of any reduction in the fighting in Hamburg.

October 26, 1923

The fighting in Hamburg has ended with the Communists being defeated and the putsch ending in failure.

October 27 to 29, 1923

Our work, as does our lives, continues.

October 30, 1923

The Ottoman Empire has officially dissolved. An Empire that had ruled for over 600 years, ended yesterday with the official establishment of Turkey as a republic. The Empire had lost most of its lands and nearly all of its power after the Great War.

October 31 to November 10, 1923

There was yet another putsch in Germany over the previous two days. This one was in Munich. The group causing the putsch is called the National Socialist German Worker's Party, or Nazi Party, led by Adolf Hitler. As with the putsches before, this one failed.

November 11, 1923 Armistice Day

As always, we should take a moment to remember those who gave their lives during the Great War and all wars.

November 12 to 17, 1923

Recently, the German currency exchange was 4,200,000,000,000 Marks to one U. S. Dollar. I had to count the zeros several times to be certain that I had it correct. Yesterday, the German government did away with the old Papiermark currency, and established a new currency called Rentenmark. It is hoped that this new currency will help stabilize the German economy.

November 18 to 28, 1923

There is nothing going on in the world that is different. I did read in the newspaper that the coalition government that Herr Stresemann, the German Chancellor, had assembled, has failed. There is no word as to how this will affect the German government. Most likely, they will have to form a new coalition under new leadership.

November 29, 1923 Thanksgiving Day

Annette had to work to-day. So, it fell upon me to prepare our feast. I am not nearly as talented in the culinary arts as she is. But, I did my best, and if I do say so, produced a rather tasty meal. When Annette returned home, she was pleasantly surprised, to say the least.

November 30 to December 24, 1923 Christmas Eve

The days are cooler, as it is to be expected. It does provide a good reason to sit by the fireplace in the evenings.

December 25, 1923 Christmas Day

What a most wondrous day it is to-day! Young Frederick is beginning to notice the tree and all of its lights. The look of surprise and joy on his face is priceless.

December 26 to 31, 1923 New Year's Eve

This time that we have had together as a family has been simply wonderful. I must keep it in my mind not to let the toils of the day make me forget what is truly important, this family.

January 1, 1924 New Year's Day

Annette and I tried to see the old year out and welcome the new year in. But, we were so exhausted that we fell asleep long before midnight.

January 2 to 5, 1924

Somehow, the world seems a little better. Even trudging through the snow to get to the Station is not so bad. Perhaps this new year brings the promise of hope and renewal. Perhaps I am just a hopeless romantic.

January 6, 1924 Annette's Birthday

What better way to hail in this new year than to celebrate Annette's birthday. Maybe they are not connected. But, to me, it is a wonderful reason to continue the celebration of the past month. Any reason for me to shower gifts on Annette is perfectly acceptable to me.

January 7 to 21, 1924

The euphoric elation of the recent holidays is slowly drawing down as the pace of our everyday lives takes over. Even with that in mind, there does seem to be an elevation in the general mood of the nation. The news from abroad is ripe with despair. And yet, at home, the economy continues to improve as the stock market seems to climbs to new heights every day. The average of the stock prices has gone over $100.00 for the first time since 1920. The price for a gallon of gasoline has gone down to 20 cents. It would appear that prosperity has arrived.

January 22, 1924

Vladimir Lenin, the leader of the Bolshevik Revolution and the new Russia, has died. The news agency out of the Soviet Union has announced the Lenin died yesterday and that Joseph Stalin is now the Head of State. My experience with the Bolsheviks has left a very bad taste in my mouth. I doubt that I will ever forget it.

January 23 to 24, 1924

The days have been crisp. That is to be expected for such a fine winter as we have had.

January 25, 1924

The International Winter Sports week has started to-day in Chamonix, France. These are very similar to the Olympics that will be held in Paris, later this year. Annette's parents, M. e Mme. d'Arcy are attending. Annette and I wanted to join them. However, with our responsibilities, we were unable to make that a reality. We are hoping to take some vacation time later and join M. e Mme. d'Arcy for the Olympics in May.

January 26 to 27, 1924

In the winter sports, Charles Jewtraw of the United States won the first gold medal in the 500 meter speed skate. In Russia, Lenin was buried in a mausoleum in Moscow. Also, the city of Petrograd (Saint Petersburg) was renamed Leningrad. We were to go to Petrograd to link up with the Expeditionary Force there. Those plans were changed once we found out that the troops there had already left.

January 28 to February 11, 1924

We are continuing to enjoy a most splendid winter. The winter sports are finished and Norway won the most medals; 17 in all. As it turns out, the first gold medal awarded was the only gold medal won by the United States. The United States won a total of 4 medals.

There was mentioned in the newspaper of the State execution of a prisoner in Nevada where they used gas for the first time. I do not understand why anyone would want to use that horrid product for anything. I saw too much of its effects in the trenches of France.

February 12, 1924 Lincoln's Birthday

As a surprise, I took Annette to a concert to-day. We drove into New York City, to Aeolian Hall, to listen to Whiteman's Orchestra. The program "An Experiment in Modern Music" was extremely entertaining. There was a suite of music by Victor Herbert and a piece called "Rhapsody in Blue" by George Gershwin. Mr. Gershwin played the piano himself for that piece. The performance was crowned with "Pomp and Circumstance Military Marches" by Edward Elgar. It was a most enjoyable event. Annette and I had a wonderful time. This new Jazz music is really quite enjoyable. We were told that this was the first performance of Mr. Gershwin's piece, "Rhapsody in Blue".

February 13, 1924

I don't want to return to work, to-day. But, it is Wednesday and duty calls.

February 14, 1924 Valentine's Day

What better way to celebrate to-day than with my wonderful wife.

February 15 to 21, 1924

The days roll on. The dock workers have gone on strike. I certainly hope that this does not last as long as the railroad strike did back in 1922.

February 22, 1924 Washington's Birthday

It was an interesting evening, to-day. President Coolidge, "Silent Cal" as he is called in the newspapers, was not very silent. The president spoke to the nation from the White House, over the radio. The content of his speech was of interest. In particular was his calling for a quick end to the dock strike. What was of greater interest, to me, was the ability for everyone in the nation to listen to the President speak. This was the first time any Presidential address has been heard over the radio. These are truly wonderful times that we live in.

February 23 to 26, 1924

The dock strike is over. Fortunately for the nation, that did not last long.

February 27 to March 3, 1924

Caliph Abdul Mejid II of the Ottoman Empire has been deposed. The last Caliph and remnant of the 1,400 year old regime has been swept away and replaced with the new Republic of Turkey and its President, Kemal Ataturk.

March 4 to 25, 1924

Along with the end of the Ottoman Empire, Greece has now declared itself to be an independent Republic. I am certain that many of the lands of the former Empire will now declare themselves to be independent nations.

March 26 to April 1, 1924

Annette and I continue with our plans to visit her parents this summer. We hope to have the dates of the visit coincide with the Olympics to be held in Paris. This should be a marvelous vacation.

April 2, 1924

Of minor interest was the news from Germany that the instigator of one of the putsches last year, Adolph Hitler, has been sentenced to five years in prison. Hopefully, this will be the last that anyone hears of this.

April 3 to 6, 1924

The Fascist Party has won a two-thirds majority in the Italian elections, to-day. This is of little surprise since Mr. Mussolini has had complete control of the Italian government since he was made Prime Minister in 1922. According to Italian law (Acerbo law), the party that receives the majority of the votes is awarded two thirds of the Parliamentary seats. The National Bloc (Fascists) received a clear majority and therefore the two thirds majority of the Parliament.

April 7 to 24, 1924

We have been spending the majority of our time, these days, preparing for our upcoming trip to France. Annette is absolutely elated! She has gone over her packing list several times to be certain that nothing is forgotten. Young Frederick is aware that something is happening. But he is not certain what it could be. I dare say that he is in for the surprise of his life!

We have booked passage aboard the S.S. Nieuw Amsterdam. It was Annette who remembered that this is the same ship that her parents sailed on when they came to visit us in 1920. We should do well. We are scheduled to arrive in Calais, France on Thursday, May 2. This should be plenty of time before the opening ceremony for the Olympics on the 4th.

At this moment, we are relaxing in our room at the Plaza Hotel. That is, we are relaxing as much as is possible. Annette has checked our boarding passes and passports several times. She has gone through the luggage a dozen times, mentally and physically. I'm exhausted just watching her. I do not fault her for this. In fact, I praise her for it. It is her attention to detail that will enable us to have a most enjoyable journey. I only hope that she will take the time to enjoy the trip, herself.

We sail in the morning.

April 25, 1924

As I expected, our boarding went extremely smooth. Annette is relaxing, for the moment. Young Frederick is amazed at these new surroundings. Annette and I have not been aboard ship since we sailed to America, some four years ago. I am glad that we could have this time together as a family.

271

April 26 to May 1, 1924

This has been a most wondrous trip. Annette and I feel much more relaxed.

The ship's newspaper reports of a mine explosion that happened on April 29th in West Virginia. It is unknown how many men the Wheeling Steel Corporation in Benwood, West Virginia were lost. It is believed to be over a hundred. It is such a terrible loss.

May 2, 1924

We docked at Calais, France at 2:40 p.m. There was a brief delay as we went through the port authority, but no real delay. M. e Mme. d'Arcy were waiting near the docks to greet us. It was a joyous reunion. They were thrilled to see Frederick. After securing our luggage, we then proceeded back to their home. It took only a bit over two hours to get there. Much of the countryside has returned to normal since the war. Some areas have not changed at all. It brings back some old memories that would be best forgotten.

May 3, 1924

We slept! I did not realize just how tired we were. Once awake, we proceeded to visit and get ourselves organized. M. e Mme. d'Arcy had the schedule of events for the Olympics and their location. We decided upon which events that we would like to see and prepared an itinerary. This should be a most enjoyable time.

May 4, 1924

We traveled to Paris to watch the opening ceremony to the Games of the VIII Olympiad. The raising of the drapeau tricolore (French Tricolor) and the playing of Le Marseillaise was very stirring. M. e Mme. d'Arcy and Annette were quite moved as was I. Even young Frederick was enjoying the moment. The theme for the Olympics, Citius, Altius, Fortius (Faster, Higher, Stronger) was performed next in the artistic portion of the ceremony. Again, we were enchanted. The parade of participants was next and was most splendid. Greece was first, being the origin of the games. This year, for the first time in modern history, Greece stood as an independent nation. The remaining participating nations entered the stadium in alphabetical order. The end of the ceremony and the beginning of the games was marked by the lighting of the cauldron with the Olympic torch. By the end of the day, we were exhausted and exhilarated!

May 5 to 29, 1924

We were able to attend several events in tennis, water polo, and rugby. The U.S.A. took gold in all five tennis events. In water polo, France defeated America, 3 to 1, in the first round. In the final, France won gold and U.S.A. won bronze. The final rugby competition, France played against the United States. That was a most different game. I could cheer when France scored. I could also cheer if America scored. No matter who scored, I could cheer! In the final score, U.S.A. won, 17 to 3.

May 30, 1924 Decoration Day

On this day of decoration of the graves of our fallen brothers-in-arms and remembrance, we thought that we would go to the battlefield around the Argonne forest. We made it as far as Verdun. We laid flowers on many of the graves of American and French Soldiers. I could not remain any longer. My hands and arms were trembling to the point that I could no longer hold the flowers. Annette was in tears. We returned to M. e Mme. d'Arcy's home.

May 31, 1924

We packed our luggage and prepared to depart in the morning. Our stay with Annette's parents has been a wonderful one. M. e Mme. d'Arcy were thrilled to see Frederick and to spend some time getting to know him.

June 1, 1924

We rose early and proceeded to the docks at Calais. The boarding process went very smoothly. In no time at all, we were on board our ship and waving farewell to Annette's parents. Soon we were on our way back to the United States of America.

June 2 to 7, 1924

Our crossing went very smoothly. This was an excellent time to relax and spent some time together. I am troubled by old memories and some restless nights. Hopefully, this will pass soon.

June 8, 1924

We docked, disembarked, and made it to our hotel room in good order. We will rest here for the night and proceed home in the morning.

June 9, 1924

It was very enjoyable and uneventful trip home. It took us nearly two hours to unpack and put everything away. Frederick was thrilled to see his room again. And I suspect that Annette was happy to be home. I know that I am. I think Annette's parents are wonderful, but I would much rather be in my own home.

June 10, 1924

Annette and I returned to work, to-day. It is good to return to our normal routine. I do feel that a few more days of rest might be beneficial, even though we were just on a "vacation". There is no point in delaying the inevitable. We must return to work at some time. We might as well do it now and be done with it. Postponing the inevitable will only make it harder.

June 11, 1924

It will take me a month of Sundays to get through this mountain of mail and newspapers that accumulated in our absence. The vast majority of it was of little or no consequence.

One item that did come to my attention was an article and a letter. The article in the newspaper spoke of the enactment, on June 2nd, of the Indian Citizenship Act. This act declared that all non citizen Indians born within the territorial limits of the United States are now citizens. The letter, from my Father, was to inform me of the same news. Although this does not affect us directly, as we already have our citizenships, it does affect other members of our family.

June 12, 1924 William's Birthday

Annette planned and carried out a most splendid celebration for me. I am always deeply moved by all that she does for me and our family.

Birthday celebration aside, an interesting item came to my attention. In addition to the Indian Citizenship Act, I came across an official notification from the War Department that the Renegade Period of the Apache Wars was officially declared over. This officially ends all of the Indian Wars. I suppose that now members of every tribe are citizens, they are not renegades. And any crimes that anyone makes are not acts of defiance. It only makes the perpetrators outlaws. That is so much more convenient for the Government.

June 13 to 23, 1924

It has been some rather nice, warm, summer days. The days have been most enjoyable. Occasionally, we have been able to attend a concert or take in a motion picture show.

On the National news, the Republican Party has concluded their convention. It was held in Cleveland, Ohio. It was no surprise to hear that they have nominated President Calvin Coolidge to run for President. It was of interest to find out who the Vice Presidental nominee would be, as there has been no Vice President since President Harding's death. Charles G. Dawes of Marietta, Ohio, was announced as the Vice President candidate. Mr. Dawes is the great-great-grandson of William Dawes who rode with Paul Revere to warn the Colonists of the impending approach of the British Army in 1775. Mr. Dawes is also the son of Brigadier General Rufus Dawes, commander of the 6th Wisconsin Regiment of the Iron Brigade during the Civil War. Mr. Dawes himself was a Brigadier General of the Seventeenth Engineers during the Great War. He is also a lawyer and businessman. He has served in many political offices and appointments.

June 24, 1924

The radio announced the news of a remarkable feat, yesterday. 1st Lieutenant Russell L. Maughan, a test pilot in the U. S. Army Air Service, has flown across the United States during the hours of daylight. This "Dawn-to-Dusk" flight was accomplished through a series of "hops". The Lieutenant took off from Mitchel Field on Long Island, New York at 3:58 a.m. and flew to McCook Field in Dayton, Ohio. He then flew to St. Joseph, Missouri, North Platte, Nebraska, Salduro Siding, Utah, and finally landing at Crissy Field at the Presidio of San Francisco, California at 9:46 p.m., local time, a minute before dusk. This was truly an outstanding accomplishment. 1st Lieutenant Maughan was also the pilot that set the airplane speed record back in 1922. What a wondrous time this is that we live in.

June 25 to July 3, 1924

The days continue to be warm and wonderful. Recruitment has been steady. The economy has been improving as of late. This has started to have an adverse effect on those wishing to enlist in the Army. The better the civilian world becomes, the less appealing the military world becomes. I just have to work harder to fill my quotas.

July 4, 1924 Independence Day

To-day was another glorious celebration of our Nation's birth. Frederick, Annette and I had a very enjoyable and relaxing day, ending with a splendid display of fireworks above the parade field.

July 5 to 15, 1924

Life goes ever forward during these warm summer days.

The Democratic Party has completed their convention. It was convened in New York City, New York. They have announced their candidates for the office of President of the United States. There was much heated debate and arguments from the delegates such as to include or condemn the support of the Ku Klux Klan. This debate threatened to split the Party. Such noted delegates as William Jennings Bryant and Wendell Willkie spoke on the subject over several days. Neither of the two front running candidates, William G. McAdoo of California nor Al Smith of New York, could gain the two-thirds majority required to receive the nomination. The debate lasted for so long that Will Rogers commented that "New York invited the Democratic delegates to visit the city, not to live there". After 100 ballots, a decision could not be reached. A compromise was finally reached on the 103rd ballot, in John W. Davis of West Virginia. Charles W. Bryan of Nebraska, brother of William Jennings Bryan, was selected as the Vice Presidental candidate.

July 16, 1924 Fourth Anniversary

It is hard to believe that Annette and I have been married for four years, now! That day is still as clear in my memory as if it had happened yesterday. Ah, what wonderful memories those are. I took Annette out for dinner at her favorite restaurant. I don't think that she notice anything around us. She looked so divine, much like she did that day that I first saw her in the Hospital. She does appear to be much happier now, than she did at that time.

July 17 to August 11, 1924

We return to our normal lives. But the memories of recent events and celebrations, and the joy that they bring, carry on.

August 12, 1924 Frederick's Birthday

Young Frederick is three years old, to-day! He is becoming quite the strapping young man.

August 13 to 15, 1924

The days continue to be warm and sultry.

Will Rogers quipped recently "I'm not a member of any organized political party. I'm a Democrat".

To add to that sentiment, Robert M. La Follette of Wisconsin announced the creation of a new political party, the Progressive Party. Their platform is based on pro-labor union and anti-big business. They are for the nationalization of cigarette factories, large industries, and the public ownership of railroads. They support increased taxation on the wealthy and the right of collective bargaining for factory workers. The Progressive Party has gained the support of the American Federation of Labor, the Socialist Party of America, several labor unions and railroad brotherhoods.

This is the same Progressive Party that Mr. La Follette had attempted to form in 1912.

The Progressive Party has chosen Robert M. La Follette to run as their candidate for President. This comes as no surprise. Burton K. Wheeler of Montana was selected as the Vice Presidental candidate.

 August 16, 1924

The final results from the Olympiad have been announced:

Country	Gold	Silver	Bronze	Total
United States	45	27	27	99
Finland	14	13	10	37
France	13	15	10	38
Great Britain	9	13	12	34
Italy	8	3	5	16
Switzerland	7	8	10	25
Norway	5	2	3	10
Sweden	4	13	12	29
Netherlands	4	1	5	10
Belgium	3	7	3	13

Some notable athletes were;

Johnny Weissmuller (U.S.A.) won 3 gold medals in swimming and 1 bronze medal in water polo.

Roger Ducret (France) won 3 gold medals and 2 silver medals in fencing.

Harold Osborn (U.S.A.) won 2 gold medals and set Olympic records in both the high jump (6' 6") and the decathlon with a total score of 7,710.775 points.

Harold Abrahams (Great Britain) won 1 gold medal in the 100 meter dash and 1 silver medal in the 4x400 meter relay race.

Eric Liddell (Great Britain) won 1 gold medal in the 400 meter run, setting an Olympic record (47.6 seconds) and 1 bronze medal in the 200 meter dash.

August 17, 1924

A plan to solve the economical problems of Germany was adopted yesterday. The Dawes Plan calls for the withdraw of foreign troops from the Ruhr, reparation payments would begin at 1 billion marks and increasing annually to a total of 2 1/2 billion marks at the end of 5 years, reorganize the Reichsbank (under Allied supervision), and increase the sources to pay the reparation.

This plan was created and proposed by Charles G. Dawes before he was chosen as the Republican Vice Presidential candidate.

This does appear to be a good plan. Only time will tell if it will work.

<u>August 18, 1924</u>

There is cautious optimism across Europe as we wait to see if the Dawes Plan will be accepted.

The stock market, too, is waiting for an answer. Trading is expected to be down, to-morrow, when the stock market opens.

<u>August 19, 1924</u>

That didn't take long. France has begun to withdraw her forces from the Ruhr. This is a hopeful indication of good things to come.

The stock market went up on this good news from Europe.

August 20 to 31, 1924

I am alarmed over the increasing violence across the country. The majority of the violence appears to be connected to organized crime, chiefly fueled by illegal alcohol production and sale or bootlegging and rum-running. There has always been violence and crime associated with alcohol since the enactment of prohibition. Until recently, the crime has been small and localized. Lately, the scope and intensity has been increasing. Ever more gangs are being created and growing larger and stronger. There have even been reports of Thompson sub-machine guns being used by these gangsters.

September 1, 1924 Labor Day

It was a cool autumn day, to-day. It was a wonderful day for us to relax and enjoy being together as a family.

September 2 to 9, 1924

Fall temperatures are starting to arrive. As are the fall colors to the trees.

September 10, 1924

There is sad news these days, indeed. Riots are happening in two different lands.

The first was in the territory of Hawaii. Twenty died yesterday and several more injured when police and Filipino workers clashed at the McBryde sugar plantation on Hanapepe Island. Of the dead, four were policemen and sixteen were Filipinos. It appears that the police were ordered to shoot the strikers. The strikers must have been armed. Otherwise, how could you explain the deaths of the four policemen?

The other fighting is going on at this time in British India. The reports are not very clear and there are little details. It appears that Hindus are being attacked in a northern province of British India. There is no information on the causes or how many people are injured or killed. There should be more information as this event develops.

September 11 to 28, 1924

The riot in Kohat, British India has ended. 155 Hindus and Sikahs have died during the three days of fighting. Several thousand, nearly all of the Hindu and Sikah population, have fled for their lives. The Muslims are the instigators of this violence. Mahatma Gandhi has been fasting until the Hindus and Muslims agree to stop fighting. The last that I recall hearing of Mr. Gandhi was that he had been arrested and sentenced to six years in prison for sedition back in 1922. It appears that he has been released as there is no mention of him being in prison.

September 29, 1924

Another amazing aeronautical feat has been accomplished! Two Army Aviators, 1st Lieutenants John Harding and Erik Nelson have flown around the world! It took them 175 days and 74 stops to fly from Seattle, Washington, all the way around the world and return to Seattle, Washington. It seems as if there is nothing that these aviators cannot do.

September 30 to October 14, 1924

The days continue to grow cooler and more colorful as the autumnal season passes.

October 15, 1924

We welcomed a new member to our family, to-day. Angelica Rudolf was born at 6:04 A.M. She is an absolute joy and delight. I named her Angelica because she looks just like her mother and Annette always looks like an angel to me.

October 16 to 21, 1924

Annette and I introduced Angelica to her brother, Frederick. He seemed most interested in his little sister.

October 22, 1924

Mother and Father came up from Fort Myer, Virginia for a visit and to see their new grand-daughter.

We spent some time talking of family matters. But the majority of time was spent on Angelica.

October 23 to 25, 1924

It was a pleasure having my parents visit and help get things moving smoothly throughout the house. The extra assistance has been greatly appreciated.

October 26, 1924

Mother and Father left for Fort Myer, to-day. As they were leaving, Frederick had a curious look on his face. I asked him what was wrong. He said grand-mommy and grand-daddy were forgetting the baby. He thought that Angelica was staying with them. I had to explain that Angelica was going to stay with us. From the look on his face, I would say that he was none too happy with that decision. He'll just have to get use to the idea of having a little sister.

October 27 to November 3, 1924

I am tired! I know Annette has to be even more so.

November 4, 1924 Election Day

With all of the excitement of recent weeks, I had nearly forgotten that we need to vote to-day. Annette and I bundled the children and went to the polling place to cast our votes.

The choice for President is between;

Republican: President Coolidge and Mr. Dawes, continued prosperity.

Democrat: Mr. Davis and Governor Bryan, change.

Progressive: Senator La Follette and Senator Wheeler, socialist labor.

Something of greater interest to me is the fact that with the enactment of the Indian Citizenship Act earlier this year, this is the first time that all American Indians will be allowed to vote.

November 5, 1924

The results are in. President Coolidge and Mr. Dawes have been elected to serve as President and Vice President with over half of the nation voting for them. Mr. Davis and Governor Bryan carried twelve states, all of them in the south. Senator La Follette carried his home state of Wisconsin. It is curious to observe that Mr. Davis did not carry his home state of West Virginia.

November 6 to 10, 1924

Of greater importance to me than the election, is watching my family grow. Our new addition, in the form of this tiny angel, has brought great joy into our lives. She has also created a sense of wonderment to Frederick.

November 11, 1924 Armistice Day

To-day is a time to pause and reflect. I remember them all.

November 12 to 26, 1924

The long autumn days have been very enjoyable. Between work and home life, there is little time to do anything else. There has been much advertising in the newspaper of a parade in New York City on Thanksgiving Day. R. H. Macy & Co. claims that their Christmas Parade will be a spectacular sight to behold. I am of the opinion that we could use a small family outing. That is, if Annette and Angelica are feeling up to the adventure.

November 27, 1924 Thanksgiving Day

We traveled to New York City, yesterday, in order to be here in time when the Macy Christmas Parade began at 9:00 A.M. Being that this was the first such parade, we did not know what to expect. The turn-out was tremendous. Throngs of people lined the parade route, from 145th Street up in Harlem, down to 34th Street in mid-town. We had to search for a suitable place to observe the parade. We finally found an area near the Macy's store. The parade itself was wonderful with flags, marching bands, costumed entertainers, floats, and even some wild animals in cages. From our location, we could see the front of R. H. Macy's. Throughout the entire parade, Santa Clause was sitting on a big chair on a balcony above the front doors. He was waving and applauding as the people in the parade passed by in front of him. Finally, after the parade was finished, an official came out onto the balcony with him and crowned him King of the Kiddies! Frederick was squealing with joy the entire time. I am not at all certain if Angelica will remember any of this. Later that same day, we returned to our home and feasted on a marvelous dinner that I prepared.

November 28 to December 24, 1924 Christmas Eve

These cold winter days are a splendid reason for us to stay at home by the warm fire. Frederick seems to feel otherwise. He cannot spend enough time outside in the snow. Whenever possible, I'll join him. We'll go sledding down the hill, build snowmen, build a snow fort and have a snowball fight, make snow angels, all sorts of fun activities. Several of his friends will join us from time to time. I am grateful for the support. It allows me the opportunity to go into the house and warm-up.

December 25, 1924 Christmas Day

I don't think that I will ever get tired of the joy that I receive when I see Frederick come down the stairs to see what Santa has brought him. And now, Angelica will soon learn of the wonder of

Christmas. The wide-eyed expression of anticipation and excitement is absolutely precious! Much to my surprise, Santa brought me a new camera. It is a travel model so we can take it on our trips with us. Annette was also thrilled with the gifts that Santa brought her. By the end of the day, the children were asleep, amongst piles of wrapping paper. Annette and I were happy and exhausted from the day's festivities.

December 26 to 31, 1924 New Year's Eve

What a wonderful week this has been. Mother and Father stopped by for a visit. They brought with them some gifts for the children. Frederick's face lit up anew. He has still a twitter over what Santa had brought him and now Grand-mommy and Grand-daddy. The joy never ceases.

January 1, 1925 New Year's Day

Life continues to improve. Our family is healthy. My work at the Recruiting Station and Annette's work at the hospital continues to go well. Our investments in the Stock Market are doing fine. The Dow Jones Industrial Average is over $120.00. All things considered, life is very good.

January 2 to 5, 1925

A fresh snow fall has renewed Frederick's arctic activities.

There were two pieces of interesting news that I read about recently.

The first was about an astronomer by the name of Edwin Hubble declared that the Andromeda Nebula was in fact a galaxy. Additionally, he claimed that our galaxy, the Milky Way, is but one of several galaxies in the universe. It boggles my mind to comprehend the scope of that concept.

The other piece of news comes from Italy. There, Mr. Mussolini has announced that he has taken complete power of the government. This new Fascist form of government appears to have everything, nationalism, socialism, corporatism, expansionism, and anti-communism. They have one person in charge as dictator, and a ruling monarch. They appear to have something for everyone. I will reserve comment for now, preferring to wait and see how they handle themselves.

January 6, 1925 Annette's Birthday

What better way to forget about the worries of the world and beyond than to celebrate Annette's Birthday! Everyone had a wonderful time.

January 7 to February 1, 1925

This has been a most enjoyable time for us. Frederick has been enjoying the winter wonderland. Angelica has been enjoying the world around her. Annette and I have been enjoying every moment that we have together.

There has been news on the radio and in the newspaper, of an outbreak of diphtheria in the territory of Alaska, in the city of Nome. The disease threatens to eliminate the entire population of the area, about 10,000 inhabitants. The entire city is under quarantine. The weather is too cold for the three open cockpit bi-planes in the area. Also, the farthest that they could fly under good conditions would be around 260 miles. That would not be nearly enough to cover the 674 miles distance to fly the needed antitoxin into Nome. The sea ports are iced in and are closed. The only way to get the life saving serum to the infected people is by dog sled. They have been racing across the frozen landscape since January 27th. Everyone is waiting for news of the outcome. Annette is very concerned. She has seen those infected with diphtheria. She knows how fast it can spread. And what a terrible disease it is.

February 2, 1925

They made it! The final team made it into Nome yesterday. They took the antitoxin 674 miles from Nenana to Nome, in a little over five days.

One report stated that the original plan was to use only two dog sled teams, one heading east, and the other heading west. They would meet in the middle, hand-off the serum, then the one team would return to Nome. The plan was later modified by adding 18 more dog sled teams to the route. This would make each segment of the relay easier on the teams and the precious cargo can proceed without stopping.

Unfortunately, this information was not told to Leonhard Seppala, the original musher who was going all of the way to the mid-point. He did get the cargo sooner than the mid-point. But, he and his team covered 91 miles before they were through. The other teams usually covered 20 to 30 miles. Mr. Seppala and his team, lead by Togo, crossed treacherous ground in blizzard conditions.

The temperature was 20 to 30 degrees below zero. They even drove over the ice floats of Norton Sound to save some time. This was a trek that was truly, a remarkable feat.

The serum was finally brought into Nome by Gunnar Kaasen and his team, lead by Balto. They took the serum the last 53 miles of the journey.

The manner in which this entire race was organized and executed was truly of epic proportions. It certainly captured the hearts and imaginations of everyone across the land. I know that it did Annette and me.

February 3 to 12, 1925 Lincoln's Birthday

My word, it is cold! This has been a brutal winter storm. I read in the newspaper where the Hudson River has frozen. If this is anything like the weather those poor dog teams had to endure, they are even braver than I had thought. I do not see how they did it.

February 13 to 14, 1925 Valentine's Day

The weather continues to be icy cold. Even Frederick does not want to venture out into it for long. This is an excellent reason to stay inside by the warm fire place.

February 15 to 22, 1925 Washington's Birthday

The severe cold weather continues.

February 23 to March 3, 1925

The weather has been a little bit warmer. It is still rather cold, though. There was a report of an earthquake on February 28th, in Canada, along the Saint Lawrence River. We felt some shaking here. But, did not know what it was until the next day.

March 4, 1925 Inauguration Day

President Coolidge was sworn in for a new term as President of the United States, to-day. Father's unit was selected to be part of the ceremony. So Mother and Father were in Washington D.C. for the festivities. Annette and I stayed home and listened to the inauguration and the President's speech on the radio. This was the first time a President's inauguration has ever been broadcast on the radio. These are truly wondrous times that we live in.

March 5 to 18, 1925

There has been a warming trend of sorts. Father stated that he would have enjoyed the inauguration more if the weather had been a little warmer. I refrained from telling him how warm we were by the fireplace.

March 19, 1925

Disaster has struck in the mid-west. A tornado has cut its' way across three states, Missouri, Illinois, and Indiana. The death toll is unknown, but believed to be over a thousand. The total damage is estimated to be in the millions of dollars. There were several other tornadoes born from this same storm.

March 20 to May 5, 1925

Blizzards, earthquakes, tornadoes, this has certainly been a most unusual year, weather-wise. They were able to finalize the death toll from that tornado that tore across three states, 695 died and 2,027 were injured. What a massive amount of destruction caused by nature. The remainder of this spring has been relatively normal. Let us hope that the worst of the weather has passed.

May 6, 1925

There was an article in the newspaper, to-day, also an announcement on the radio. A biology teacher, John Scopes, in Dayton, Tennessee was arrested yesterday for teaching Mr. Darwin's theory of evolution. The Butler Act, making it illegal to teach such theories in public schools, had been signed into law by Governor Peay only a month ago, on March 21st. I feel certain that there is more to this story than what I have read. From what I have read, this makes no reasonable sense, certainly nothing worthy of receiving this amount of attention.

May 7 to 29, 1925

The weather continues to be very pleasant. Mr. Scopes has been indicted and will stand trial.

May 30, 1925 Decoration Day

My Recruiting Station was given the assignment to decorate the cemetery. We went early to place the flags upon the graves of our fellow Soldiers. To us, it was an honor, not a burden, to perform this task. Later in the day, Annette and the children joined us, as did the families of several members of the station. After we had completed our mission, the

Station Commander, 1LT Thomas, called everyone together. He explained, mostly for the benefit of the family members, why we were there and why we decorate the graves. This was followed by a moment of silence for the fallen. We then had a splendid outing and remainder of the day. It was very enjoyable to spend time with my family and the families of the men at the station.

May 31 to June 11, 1925

This has been a most enjoyable spring. The weather has been very pleasant.

June 12, 1925 William's Birthday

Another year has passed me by. And yet, I feel exhilarated. Annette and the children are a constant source of joy and inspiration to me. The gifts are nice, too.

June 13 to 29, 1925

The days are getting warmer.

I was given a promotion on June 15th. 1LT Thomas announced that he was making me First Sergeant of the Recruiting Station. In addition to my normal recruiting duties, I am now in charge of all of the other Recruiters and all of the administrative duties that entails. I am humbled by Lieutenant Thomas' confidence in my abilities. But, I am not certain that I can handle the added responsibilities. I am reminded of a quote from Mr. Lincoln when asked how he liked being President. He likened it to a man being run out of town on a rail who said;

"If it wasn't for the honor of it, I'd rather walk".

June 30, 1925

There was terrible news on the radio, to-day. There was another earthquake, yesterday, in Santa Barbara, California. The extent of the damage and loss of lives is not yet known.

This does appear to be a year of natural disasters.

July 1 to 3, 1925

Reports continue to come in from California. 13 have died and nearly the entire town of Santa Barbara has been destroyed. In addition, the earthquake caused the near-by earthen Sheffield Dam to collapse. The rushing water flooded the lower part of the town up to two feet deep. The railroad tracks were severely damaged.

<u>July 4, 1925 Independence Day</u>

What better way to forget about the worries of the day than to enjoy some time with your family! I do look forward to this holiday.

<u>July 5 to 9, 1925</u>

We have had some very nice, warm days as of late.

<u>July 10, 1925</u>

The State of Tennessee versus John Thomas Scopes, or Monkey Trial as the news reporters like to call it, began to-day in Dayton, Tennessee. Mr. William Jennings Bryan appears for the prosecution, while Clarence Darrow is heading the team of lawyers appearing for the defense. I still do not understand why this trial is getting so much attention.

<u>July 11 to 15, 1925</u>

The more that I hear and read about this trial, the more confused I get. As I understand it, the Butler Act, which was signed into law earlier this year, makes it illegal to teach evolution in public schools in the State of Tennessee. The textbook that teachers are required to use has a chapter in it that explicitly charts and teaches evolution. So the

November 26, 1925 Thanksgiving Day

To-day was truly a splendid celebration. Mother, Father, Andrew and his family arrived early. Everyone worked together to put on a spectacular feast. It was good to see Andrew and his family under happier circumstances. It was very enjoyable to spend some extra time with everyone. We had all spent so much time with our own lives that we forgot to stay in touch with each other. It would be a shame to lose track of each other over so minor of a thing such as work.

November 27 to December 24, 1925 Christmas Eve

Winter is definitely here!

On a different subject, there is mention of another treaty in Europe. This one, formulated in Locarno, Switzerland, is a mutual peace-pact between France, Belgium, and Germany with enforcement guaranteed by the United Kingdom and Italy. Simply stated, should any of the first three nations attack either of the other two; the remaining country will come to the attacked country's defense along with Britain and Italy. Although this treaty does define the national boundaries of Western Europe, it does not clearly define the borders for the new nations of Poland and Czechoslovakia. I

<u>June 27, 1926</u>

To-day was a good day to stay at home. It rained for most of the day. We have planned to visit my parents at Fort Myer, next week and to take in the sights there. I do hope that the weather will be nice.

<u>June 28 to July 3, 1926</u>

It did rain for a while on our journey to Washington D.C. But, it soon cleared up and remained pleasant for the rest of the week. We visited several of the monuments and sights in and around Washington D.C. M. and Mme. d'Arcy were very excited and thrilled. They remarked at how much it felt like Paris.

<u>July 4, 1926 Independence Day</u>

Mother and Father joined us, to-day, to celebrate our nation's birthday. We watched the parade down Pennsylvania Avenue and visited a few more sights around the Capital. The evening fireworks display was spectacular! Everyone had a wonderful time. M. and Mme. d'Arcy felt a part of the celebration through France's support of the young colonies that made our dream of independence a reality. They also felt a connection teachers are required to break the law. Mr. Scopes is not a full-time teacher. He is a substitute Math and Biology teacher. He was not arrested for teaching evolution, he was not even teaching at the time. Rather, he was arrested for having taught it in the past. As have every other teacher in the State of Tennessee. The American Civil Liberties Union is the organization behind this trial. They talked Mr. Scopes into pleading guilty and are paying all expenses. That explains how a substitute teacher can afford these famous lawyers. But, it does not explain why there is so much attention given to this trial in the newspaper and on the radio. I feel as if this entire affair is being orchestrated by someone.

<u>July 16, 1925 Fifth Anniversary</u>

This is truly a welcomed island of joy and happiness in a sea of trouble. It seems as if the only news in the world is happening in Tennessee. I prefer to take this opportunity to enjoy the company of Annette and the children.

<u>July 17 to 20, 1925</u>

The trial, and the heat, continues. After many long orations by two very learned men, the matter now rests with the jury. To me, the matter is simple; did Mr. Scopes break the law? If the answer is no, then he is innocent. If the answer is yes, then he is guilty. As he has already pleaded guilty, then the verdict has already been reached. And yet, the past ten days have spent leading to this simple conclusion. I am still confused.

July 21, 1925

The verdict is in, Mr. Scopes is guilty. He has been fined $100.00. As I said earlier, this was the only conclusion possible. Perhaps now, we can put this behind us and get on with our lives.

July 21 to August 7, 1925

The days proceed.

August 8, 1925

There was a large rally, to-day, in Washington D.C. The Ku Klux Klan held a parade down Pennsylvania Avenue. The news reporter on the radio estimated 40,000 men and women marched in the parade. I suppose that they did this as a show of strength. They claim to have 5 million members.

August 9 to 11, 1925

The photographs in the newspaper of that parade are very impressive. There were a large number of men and women that participated in the parade.

August 12, 1925 Frederick's Birthday

Frederick turned four, to-day! We had a splendid celebration for him.

August 13 to 25, 1925

I am not certain if the reason why is the increased work and strain at my unit, our newborn girl, or maybe the heat. But, I am so very tired of late. I scarcely have time to spend with my family when I come home at night. Annette is tired, too. Although she has not voiced it, I can see it in her eyes and in her every move. I believe that we need a vacation.

August 26, 1925

In accordance with the Dawes Plan, the last French troops have left the Ruhr area of Germany. It is good to see that the French Government is true to their word. Let us hope that this will be the end of trouble in that region.

August 27 to September 3, 1925

We have discussed several vacation destinations and ideas. So far, we have not come up with a good workable plan. We will continue.

September 4, 1925

There is terrible news, to-day. There are reports that the U.S. Navy dirigible, the USS Shenandoah, has crashed near Caldwell, Ohio. It is believed that it went down due to bad weather. 14 crew members, including the Commander, died. There were 29 survivors. I recall seeing the USS Shenandoah on one of my trips to the Naval Air Station Lakehurst. It is next to Fort Dix in New Jersey. The Shenandoah was very massive and very impressive. That must have been a powerful storm to have brought down that airship.

September 5 to 7, 1925 Labor Day

This was a very welcomed respite. Although we have not yet decided on a vacation plan, the opportunity to stay at home, relax, and spend time together has been most enjoyable and greatly appreciated.

<u>September 8 to October 14, 1925</u>

Through much discussion and analysis, we could not arrive at a consensus of opinion as to what to do for a vacation. We could neither decide on a destination, nor a feasible time schedule. Therefore, we shall remain at home.

<u>October 15, 1925 Angelica's First Birthday</u>

Our little girl turns one to-day! We had a splendid celebration for her. The wonder and amazement in her eyes is a joy to behold.

<u>October 16 to November 10, 1925</u>

The cool fall days are a welcome relief from the hot summer days. The foliage is most splendid. We did decide to take a few short trips around the area to enjoy the wondrous autumn colors.

<u>November 11, 1925 Armistice Day</u>

We did spend the day in both reverential silence and joyous laughter. We shall never forget the sacrifices that others have made for us. However, it is good to laugh, too.

<u>November 12 to 13, 1925</u>

The crisp fall air is upon us. Winter cannot be far away.

<u>November 14, 1925 Grandpa Benjamin's Death</u>

We have just received word that Grandpa Benjamin has died. I recall that he was born in 1862, during the Civil War and had a very long and distinguished career in the service. He was, in my memory, quiet and a bit aloft. Perhaps he was just tired most of the time. But, when he would tell a story, he could make the whole room light up with the glow from his face and his smile! Annette and the children never had a chance to know him. Service will be held for him in Arlington National Cemetery. He was 63 years old. I shall miss him.

<u>November 15 to 17, 1925</u>

Since Father is stationed next to Arlington Cemetery at Fort Myer, they invited us to stay with them. It took some effort, but we managed to get packed and on the road in short order. During our travels, I tried to inform and impress upon Annette and Frederick the kind of man Grandpa was. Annette understood. I am not so certain about Frederick.

He may be too young to understand. We made the trip in good time. The service is to-morrow.

November 18, 1925 Grandpa Benjamin's Burial

The service and ceremony was very nice. Andrew, Jean, and Leah were there along with their families, Grandma Ellen, of course, and several other relatives and friends of Grandpa's. Afterwards, everyone returned to Mother and Father's home. It was good to have the whole family together to reminisce and get caught up on what's happening with everyone, now. It is just sad that such a sorrowful event had to happen to cause such a gathering.

November 19 to 25, 1925

Jean and Leah and their families left to return to their homes on Thursday. Andrew and I remained an extra day. Annette and I invited everyone to our home for Thanksgiving. Leah and Jean had to decline as they had prior arrangements. Mother, Father, Andrew and his family accepted. We returned home and prepared for the upcoming holiday.

cannot help but remember the pacts and treaties that contributed to the Great War. I certainly hope that we are not going down the same road again.

December 25, 1925 Christmas Day

A wonderous day was to-day. Angelica was too young to understand the events of the day. She was mesmerized by all of the lights and festive atmosphere. Frederick, however, fully understood the day. The present portion for certain. Annette and I had nearly as much fun as Frederick!

December 26 to 31, 1925 New Year's Eve

It is hard to believe, but another year has passed. This last year has had so many changes, too.

January 1, 1926 New Year's Day

A new day dawns, a new year begins. The ruckus celebration at mid-night was loud enough to awaken Angelica. Frederick, however, could hardly keep his eyes open. He nearly made it. Try as he did, when the hour struck, Frederick was fast asleep.

<u>January 2 to 5, 1926</u>

Being stationed on the waterfront does have its advantages and disadvantages. In the summer, we don't have far to go to enjoy a relaxing day at the beach. The weather is conducive for growing many different flowers and plants which makes for a splendid and colorful spring and fall. The snow and ice of winter, however, leaves a bit to be desired. I have had my fill of the cold, blustery stuff. Frederick, on the other hand, cannot seem to get enough of it. It is almost as if he lies in a dormant, altered state, waiting for the first snow. Then he comes to life and lives until the final traces of the white powder are swept away with the advent of spring. There, he returns to his cocoon, waiting for winter's return.

<u>January 6, 1926 Annette's Birthday</u>

What a wondrous, spectacular day, it is to-day! To celebrate the birth of Annette is always a cause for great rejoicing to me. She is as beautiful, now, as she was that day when I first saw her in the field hospital.

January 7 to February 12, 1926 Lincoln's Birthday

It has been an interesting start to this new year. The Dow Jones Industrial Average momentarily rose above an all time high of 160. Theodoros Pangalos has declared himself dictator of Greece. Abdul-Aziz ibn Saud has been crowned King of Hejaz. Belgium has accepted the Locarno Treaties. And England and Belgium have moved their troops out of Cologne, Germany. It is a rather quiet beginning for this year. Perhaps it will continue throughout the year.

February 13 to 14, 1926 Valentine's Day

This has been a wonderful weekend. The majority of the day was spent relaxing by the fireplace, the occasional romp through the snow with Frederick, then warming up by the fireplace. The weekend culminated in a quiet dinner with Annette on Sunday. That is, as quiet and uninterrupted as our children would allow.

February 15 to 22, 1926 Washington's Birthday

It has been another pleasant, and cold, week. There has been very little news of any major event around the world. This comes as a welcomed relief.

February 23 to May 29, 1926

It has been a very nice spring, cool breezes, beautiful flowers and trees. It has been a splendid time.

At home, the children are doing well. Annette is considering returning to her position at the Hospital. I am kept busy running the recruiting station. We are anticipating a visit from Annette's parents in June. They are planning on staying with us for a while. We are planning several activities for their visit.

In other events around the world, in April, the dictator Theodoros Pangalos elected himself President of Greece. There was an assassination attempt against Prime Minister Mussolini in Italy. It failed. In May, a coal miners' strike in England expanded into a general strike across Britain. Martial Law was declared. It lasted nine days. Admiral Byrd and Floyd Bennett flew over the North Pole. Three days later, Roald Amundsen of Norway and his team also flew over the North Pole. Jozef Pilsudski seized power in Poland. And there was news to-day of some unrest occurring in Portugal.

May 30, 1926 Decoration Day

We spent this Sunday together as a family. We started the day by helping to decorate the graves in the post cemetery, followed by a moment of remembrance and prayer. Later, after church service, we enjoyed a picnic and stroll around the grounds. There were several activities going on around the post. It was a very enjoyable and relaxing day.

May 31 to June 11, 1926

The warm days of summer have arrived. M. and Mme d'Arcy have set sail and will be joining us soon. In Poland, Ignacy Moscicki has been named as President. There is still unrest in Portugal. The government appears to have collapsed. The news reports are still very sketchy. General Gomes de Costa started a revolt that was defeated and he surrendered. Other revolts around the country were more successful. Several members of the Government, including President Berdardino Machado and Prime Minister Antonio Maria da Silva have resigned. Jose Mendes Cabecadas Junior had become both President and Prime Minister. The National Assembly has been dissolved. We can only hope that things will get better.

<u>June 12, 1926 William's Birthday</u>

What a welcomed relief from all of the depressing news from Portugal. M. and Mme. d'Arcy's ship will be arriving next week.

<u>June 13 to 17, 1926</u>

Last minute preparations and looking over our plans have filled this time. The excitement and anticipation is high.

<u>June 18, 1926</u>

We drove to New York City and checked into our Hotel room. To-morrow, we will go to the docks to greet Annette's parents.

<u>June 19, 1926</u>

We arrived at the docks in time to watch their ship arrive. After a brief wait as they passed through the Port Authority, we were able to greet them and introduce them to their Granddaughter. They were very excited. We gathered up their luggage and proceeded home. We offered to take them to a restaurant. But, they declined. They said that there would be time enough for that later. They would rather go to our house and get unpacked, first.

We made excellent time going home. It took us just under five hours. Once we arrived at home and we all unpacked, we sat in the front room and talked for an extended period of time. It was wonderful to hear all about what was happening in France. And they were just as interested in what was happening in America. But, what they really wanted to hear about was the children. They couldn't get enough of Frederick and Angelica. We had a wonderful dinner, prepared by Annette, and continued to talk until it was time to go to sleep.

What a day!

June 20, 1926

After church service, we strolled around Fort Howard. Very little has changed, here, since their visit in 1922.

June 21 to 26, 1926

We spent the week visiting many of the sights in and around Baltimore, took in a show and a movie. Everyone had a great time.

and a favor returned from our support in the Great War. But most importantly, they feel a strong and personal connection through Annette, me and their Grandchildren. Whatever the reason may be, they enjoyed the celebration.

July 5, 1926

Having finished our visit with my parents and saying our farewells, we left Washington D.C. and traveled to Philadelphia, Pennsylvania. It is a bit of a drive, being a little over 150 miles away. But, the U.S. Highway System has opened several sections of its' newly constructed U.S. Route 1, which makes much of the trip quick and easy. We were able to travel along smooth roadways at speeds of up to 40 miles per hour! There weren't any signs along the way. But it wasn't too hard to figure out the right way. It took us just under 5 hours to make the journey. Once in Philadelphia, we located our hotel and proceeded to get organized.

July 6 to 15, 1926

There were many wondrous sights for us to see. Of course we had to go to Independence Hall and all of the other buildings that played such a prominent role in our nation's birth. To see where the Declaration of Independence was signed, where the

321

Continental Congress sat, Benjamin Franklin's grave, and so much more was quite inspiring. Everyone enjoyed it greatly.

We also visited the Philadelphia Zoo or Garden Zoological Society as the entrance gate proclaims. It was and is an absolutely remarkable place. Also of interest, in addition to viewing the animals, was viewing the people and over-hearing some of the new small talk that the younger people use. I've heard some of it while recruiting new soldiers, but not as much as I have heard of late. I know that a "fliver" or "tin lizzie" is a car, that "H2O" is water, and that a "flapper" is a young lady. M. and Mme. d'Arcy noticed this need for younger people to be different, too. They told us that it's the same way in Paris. M. d'Arcy said that they call these days Les Annees folles (the crazy years).

We heard on the radio and read in the newspaper of a massive explosion that happened in New Jersey. It appears that lightning started a fire at the Lake Denmark Powder Depot, next to the Picatinny Arsenal. The Navy uses this facility to store their powder and ammunition. The fire spread to one of the powder storage buildings and set off a series of explosions that destroyed the depot. The fire and explosions lasted for two or three days. Several people lost their lives.

This is such a terrible tragedy. Still, I cannot let these events dampen our glad times and splendid visitation with M. and Mme d'Arcy.

July 16, 1926 Wedding Anniversary

It is difficult to believe, but Annette and I have been married for six years! It was an especially nice celebration, this year. M. and Mme d'Arcy and my parents planned a wonderful party. Annette and I were quite overwhelmed. They took us to a Broadway Show, The Cocoanuts with the 4 Marx Brothers, Harpo, Groucho, Chico, and Zeppo. It was an absolute delight! I remember seeing the 4 Marx Brothers, years earlier, in a Vaudeville Show. It was Chico, Harpo, Groucho, and Gummo at that time.

Later in the evening, we were taken to dinner. My head is spinning, still, from all of the excitement.

July 17 to August 11, 1926

It has been a real delight, having Annette's parents here. Frederick and Angelica are taking advantage of the opportunity and getting to know them, though Frederick more than Angelica.

The d'Arcy's visit has made me think of a few things, such as space. Our automobile is sufficient for our needs, but nothing more. To accommodate the d'Arcy's for a trip makes it a bit cramped. Even though our "tin lizzie" is adequate for our needs, there is no room for expansion. I have begun looking into purchasing a new vehicle. The Dodge Brothers offer a very nice sedan that would meet our growing needs. There is talk, however, of a new design being released next year. I might wait to see what that looks like. Ford continues to offer the same models. A larger sedan might do us for the moment. I do like the size, style, and power of the Duesenberg. However, the asking price of $6,500.00 makes it unaffordable. There are several other makes and models available. But, for one reason or another, they just do not fulfill our needs. I will continue to search.

<u>August 12, 1926 Frederick's Birthday</u>

Fredrick celebrated his fifth birthday, to-day! From the smile on his face, I would say that he had a wonderful party.

<u>August 13 to 23, 1926</u>

There is a new craze in film making, talking pictures. Warner Brothers recently released a "talkie", 'Don Juan'. It is said that Fox Films will be releasing a "talkie" of their own, soon. The other film studios appear to be waiting to see how the public reacts to this new sensation. We will have to see what all of the fuss is about. I saw a talking picture, not that long ago. It was interesting and somewhat entertaining. Too often, though, the recording and the picture did not match-up correctly. That, too, was very entertaining, but not for the reason that the film makers had intended.

August 24, 1926

As we prepared to take M. and Mme. d'Arcy to the Port of Authority, we heard of the passing of Rudolph Valentino. He was 31 and had been ill for several days. Valentino was a very popular actor of the silver screen. There are news reports of large out-pouring of grief across the Nation. Indeed, across the world. Personally, I don't understand it. So much sorrow over one man. And little to none felt for the millions who lost their lives in the defense of freedom.

August 25 to September 5, 1926

Warm, sunny, summer days fill our lives. In Greece, Pavlos Kountouriotis announced that he was no longer a dictator. Now, he's the President of

Greece. And Lebanon is no longer under French rule. They are now a Republic and have elected Charles Debbas as their first President.

The Congressional investigation into the fire and explosions at the Lake Denmark Powder Depot has published their findings that no one was to blame for the incident. They concluded that no laws were broken, that everything was done according to regulations. The depot commander, Otto Dowling, was commended for his actions. As a result from the investigation, though, Congress has directed the establishment of the Armed Forces Explosives Safety Board. Their purpose will be to provide oversight on every aspect of explosives in the military.

Here at home, Frederick and Angelica continue to be a delight. They are certainly a handful for Annette and me.

September 6, 1926 Labor Day

What a grand day this was. There was a slight coolness in the air. Just enough to let us know that fall will soon be upon us. Annette had to work at the hospital this morning. She was able to join us for a wonderful evening meal. Frederick and Angelica played in the yard for the majority of the day. I did manage to catch-up on some reading and do a few chores about the house. When all was said and done, it was a very enjoyable day.

September 7 to 14, 1926

The days continue to grow cooler.

Germany has become a member of the League of Nations. Three days later, Spain withdrew from the League of Nations.

September 15, 1926

News has come from Geneva, Switzerland that yesterday the Locarno Treaties had been ratified and went into effect. It has been nearly a year since their signing in London. With the problems that the beleaguered nations are having, I wonder if these treaties will be enforceable.

September 16 to 18, 1926

There is terrible news of a hurricane hitting southern Florida. It is said that the force of the winds and the water destroyed bridges, picked ships up and threw them onto dry land. Several people are missing and feared dead. One account said that there may be as many as a hundred people dead.

<u>September 19 to October 14, 1926</u>

Fall is definitely upon us now. The leaves on the trees are turning colors. There is a crispness in the air. And the days are growing shorter.

There are increasing news reports of the gangster violence. A great deal of it seems to be happening in Detroit, Michigan and Chicago, Illinois. I do hope that all of this violence will end soon.

<u>October 15, 1926 Angelica's Birthday</u>

Angelica turns two to-day! We had a splendid party in celebration of her special day. One of Angelica's gifts was a new book titled "Winnie-the-Pooh", by Alan Milne. I'm sure that we'll have a wonderful time reading it to her.

<u>October 16 to 30, 1926</u>

These fall days have been splendid. The news of the world continues to be a mixed bag of hate and hope. The more that I read and hear, the less that it concerns me.

Still, I cannot help but wonder, what will come from all of this? Will we destroy our very existence? Will we learn to live together? Or will we just continue on as it has been? I tend to believe that the latter is the most probable.

October 31, 1926

Sad news that does concern me, magician Harry Houdini died to-day. I recall watching him perform his act and being absolutely mystified! To this day, I have not a clue as to how he was able to do them.

November 1, 1926

I continue to be a bit melancholy to-day. It is strange to me that I should feel this way.

November 2, 1926 Election Day

Annette and I rose early to cast our ballots. She is so thrilled with the election process. Her excitement is contagious.

November 3 to 10, 1926

The crisp fall weather is most enjoyable. It reminds me of a time in my youth when I would anxiously await the first snowfall of the season. Those were some wonderful times.

November 11, 1926 Armistice Day

We went to the cemetery, here on post, to mark the graves of those who served this great nation of ours and to remember those that we lost in the Great War. My darkness continues.

November 12 to 24, 1926

The weather continues to be cooler and this little black cloud hanging over me continues to follow me wherever I go.

November 25, 1926 Thanksgiving Day

To-day comes as a momentary respite from our normally busy lives. And it is a welcomed relief. It is a time to relax and reflect on all that we have to be thankful. I have but to look at my wonderful family to realize how splendid my life is.

And yet, I continue to have this feeling of sadness.

November 26 to December 24, 1926 Christmas Eve

I have had enough of this feeling down. I must stop this self-pity.

I cannot allow my sadness to put a damper on these glad times. Annette has gone to great lengths to have a marvelous celebration, as she does every year.

December 25, 1926 Christmas Day

What a joyous time for the entire family! This was truly a wonderful day. It snowed the night before, giving us a beautiful white Christmas.

December 26 to 31, 1926 New Year's Eve

The snow continues to fall. It is most serine and peaceful.

January 1, 1927 New Year's Day

As the old year leaves and the new one begins, many things come to mind. Not only those friends and acquaintances forgot, as in the song "Auld Lang Sine", but for all that has happened over the past year to our family and everywhere.

The stock market average climbed above $160 for the second time over the past year. There have been many improvements in the fields of communications and transportation. The new highway system is ever expanding across the land. Even with the rise of crime in the larger cities and the crime bosses such as Al Capone, there is an overall feeling of excitement and happiness. This is truly a wondrous time that we live in.

January 2 to 5, 1927

Perhaps I was a little premature in my optimism. Violence has erupted in Mexico. A group calling themselves "Cristeros" has fought back against the Government's oppression of the church. What had been a series of peaceful protests has now become violent. There is no way of knowing how or when this will end.

January 6, 1927 Annette's Birthday

This is always a marvelous time of the year. I don't need an excuse to give presents to Annette. But, since I have a good reason, I'm going to take advantage of it.

January 7 to February 12, 1927 Lincoln's Birthday

The cold winter winds certainly do blow hard.

I received an assignment order, yesterday, stating that as of 1 March 1927, I will be reassigned back to the 12th Infantry Regiment. My tour of duty as an Army Recruiter is over. I must say, after four long years, I am ready to return to a regular unit.

February 13 to 14, 1927 Valentine's Day

Annette and I enjoyed a very nice dinner and evening together.

February 15 to 22, 1927 Washington's Birthday

Things are moving along at a normal pace. I am preparing to depart the recruiting station. Annette is working hard at the hospital. The children continue to have a wonderful time.

There is some unrest in Shanghai. There are news reports of a general strike throughout the city in protest of the presence British troops.

February 23 to 28, 1927

A new regulatory commission has been created. The Federal Radio Commission is charged with regulation of the air waves. It would seem that there are now so many radio stations that they need to be regulated. I recall hearing the news last October of Westinghouse, General Electric, and the Radio Corporation of America joining together to form the National Broadcasting Company Network, joining together radio stations across the country. I suppose that it was only a matter of time before the air waves would need to be regulated.

March 1, 1927

What a day! I returned to the 12th Infantry to report in, but they were unaware that I coming. I was then sent to the 16th Infantry Brigade Headquarters. They changed my assignment order to the 34th Infantry Regiment. Upon arrival at the Regimental Headquarters, they assigned me to A Company as the 2nd Platoon Sergeant. After all of my meetings with the Regiment and Company Commanders, and all of the administrative work that needed to be done, the day was over. I'll meet with my troops to-morrow.

During all of this, at the Brigade Headquarters, I recall the comment that the clerk made while he was looking for a place to assign me. He mentioned that there were two other places that he could send me; the 15th Ordnance Company and the 8th Tank Company. Neither of which were very appealing to me. I suppose that I should be grateful for any assignment.

March 2, 1927

I really must learn to expect anything. I reported in to my new platoon, only to find that the position was filled. We went back to the Company Headquarters to straighten out the situation. The clerk had no idea. So, we went to the Regimental Headquarters. We were greeted with the same confused faces. After visiting the Brigade Headquarters, the conclusion was that the other Sergeant's assignment order had not been processed correctly or completely. Since his assignment date was before mine (by a week), I was to be re-assigned. I am now assigned to the 8th Tank Company (light). I'll meet with the unit commander in the morning. Hopefully, the position will still be available.

March 3, 1927

That position was still open. However, after my meeting with the Commander, he decided to assign me as the Company First Sergeant. This may not be a good assignment. The Company is currently at about half strength, which works out well because only about half of the tanks are operational. Besides the Headquarters platoon, there are three tank platoons. Each of those platoons has six tanks assigned, for a total of 18 tanks in the Company. We have been outfitted with the French Renault FT-17 tanks. I remember seeing these tanks in the fields of France, mostly stuck in the mud.

This assignment is certain to be a different set of problems for me.

March 4 to 11, 1927

And so it has become.

When I first formed-up the unit, I thought to myself, "that's one platoon, where's the rest?" Then I realized that this was the Company! After the morning assignments, I met with the Platoon Sergeants to get to know them. That was a bit of a surprise, too. Instead of four Sergeants, I had one

Corporal and three Privates. Two of whom had been assigned to the unit at the same time as me.

I was told that some of the soldiers knew how to operate the tanks. The rest of the soldiers would learn as they go. None of the soldiers have ever fired the cannon.

I had a meeting with the Regimental Sergeant Major to get some more men and equipment. The response that I got was: "Be thankful for what you have." And I was given the direct guidance that there would be no more time or money wasted on this "passing fling". It is clear that there will be no help coming from the command.

Later, I spoke with the Commander, Capt. Ross, and told him about the meeting. He did not seem to be surprised. He told me that he was given very much the same speech from the Regimental Commander. We are, for all intents and purposes, on our own. I asked the Captain what he planned to do. He said, fight with what he has for what he can get. I asked him if he would ask any questions if things happened. "Just don't put me in the stockade" was all that he said. I have a few thoughts.

First of all, I need a true assessment of the men and equipment. Then I can establish what needs to be done to improve and what items we need to acquire. Finally, we will build the best Tank Company in the United States Army.

March 12 to 13, 1927

This was a fine weekend. It did rain for a while on Saturday. But, the time spent at home with the family was most enjoyable.

March 14 to 18, 1927

The work begins.

I stopped by my old recruiting station. My intent was to attempt to divert some new recruits to the 8th. My friends were happy to comply. With good fortune, I will soon have sufficient soldiers to fill the rank and file of the company.

Later in the week, the company went to the firing range. The results were as expected, less than impressive.

March 19 to 20, 1927

The weekend was a welcome time of rest and a chance to spend some time with my family.

March 21 to 25, 1927

I had the Platoon Sergeants concentrate on maintenance of their FT-17s. I also had the Platoon Sergeants work on their soldiers' discipline.

There was a report in the newspaper of an incident in China on the 24th. Communist forces in Nanking were rioting, looting and killing foreign residents. Marines were landed to evacuate American citizens. U. S. and British destroyers fired on the city to break up the rioting mob. I do hope that this ends without too much loss of life.

March 26 to 27, 1927

It was another splendid weekend. The temperature was a bit cool.

March 28 to April 1, 1927

We continued to work on basic soldiering skills. I used the current event in China to illustrate how we must always be ready. There is no way of knowing when or where we might be called to action.

April 2 to 3, 1927

It rained this weekend.

April 4 to 8, 1927

The continuing rain restricted our activities to indoor training and cleaning this week.

April 9 to 10, 1927

The rain finally let up by Sunday.

April 11 to 15, 1927

The men worked on company area beautification this week, police call, mowing the grass, painting the buildings, and such activities.

April 16 to 17, 1927

This was another fine weekend. There were occasional rain showers.

April 18 to 22, 1927

I had the men concentrate on their tank maintenance. We were able to utilize parts off of disabled tanks to get other ones operational. I have talked with Sgt. Woolsey, our Supply Sergeant, about replacement parts. He told me the main problem is low supplies throughout the Army and also that we are low priority for receiving them. I told him to give me a list of everything that we needed to get everything running, quantities, and priority of importance. I have a few ideas that I will try.

An article in the newspaper reported the large scale flooding of the Mississippi River. The melting snows of winter and the rains that we have had this spring have caused the river to go over its banks. The article mentioned several levees on many of the tributary rivers had broken, adding to the already swollen Mississippi River. There is no end in sight.

April 23 to 24, 1927

The rain has let up, here. This made for another splendid weekend.

April 25 to 29, 1927

The men worked on their basic soldiering skills this week. Sgt. Woolsey gave me the list of parts and materials in short supply. Many of the items were non-existent. I must admit, it is a bigger list than I had though. I called Father to see if he might have anything in his unit that we could have. He said that he would see what he could do for us.

The flood waters of the Mississippi continue to rise.

April 30 to May 1, 1927

I needed to do a little bit of maintenance around the house this weekend. It finally stopped raining long enough for me to cut the grass.

May 2 to 6, 1927

Things are beginning to improve around the company.

The first of our new recruits have arrived. We started their integration into their sections and the unit.

We have managed to get 12 of our tanks running, which is much better than the 8 when I came to the unit. I remember hearing a joke about that's how we got our name as the 8th Tank Company, we only had 8 tanks that worked.

The men are beginning to look and act like soldiers. It's a good beginning.

May 7 to 8, 1927

This was another fine weekend to relax and spend time with the family.

May 9 to 13, 1927

This was a week for surprises. Two delivery trucks arrived. Both of the trucks were full of boxes and crates. One truck was full of the parts that Sgt. Woolsey had ordered. The other truck came from Fort Myer, Virginia. I recognized what that was about. Father was able to get a lot of the supplies that we needed. And with the other supplies that we received, we are able to have all 18 of our tanks fully operational. And with new troops coming in every day, we also have enough soldiers to man all of the tanks.

I guess we'll have to rename ourselves the 18th Tank Company. On second thought, we'll stay with the 8th. The men are making quite a name for themselves. I think that they are ready for the next step.

May 14 to 15, 1927

Again, this was a most enjoyable weekend. I called Father to let him know that his shipment had arrived. He did find it humorous that both of us are in tank units.

May 16 to 20, 1927

Capt Ross and I arranged for the men to take their tanks to range for a live fire exercise. For nearly all of the men, this was the first time that they ever fired the cannon. The range is small and we had to take one tank to the firing line at a time. I had the remainder of the tanks do some maneuvers in the near-by field, rotating between firing and maneuvering. The men were like Frederick and Angelica on Christmas morning! They had never done anything like this before. Apparently, no one at Fort Howard had seen anything like this before, either. It appeared as if everyone at the Fort had come out to see the tanks in action. It was a splendid demonstration. And their marksmanship was very good. I was very pleased and proud of their performance.

May 21 to 22, 1927

Lindberg made it! Charles Lindberg has flown, by himself, from New York to Paris! He took off, Friday, from Roosevelt Field on Long Island, New York and arrived at Le Bourget Airport, Paris on Saturday. The flight took him 33½ hours to complete. That was a fantastic feat of flying. For him to stay awake and fly his plane, the Spirit of St. Louis, the entire time is just fantastic! I can remember having to stand watch for 24 hours and how hard that was for me. I have a difficult time imagining what he must have gone through to complete this flight. It is just phenomenal!

May 23 to 27, 1927

Everyone is still excited over "Lucky Lindy". It seems as though this is all anyone can talk about.

May 28 to 29, 1927

Annette and Frederick listen to the radio to see if there is any new news of Lindberg. Angelica is too young to understand. However, she is aware that something exciting has happened.

May 30, 1927 Decoration Day

Annette and I took our family on an outing, to-day. We took a moment to visit the cemetery and pay our respects to our fallen soldiers. It was most inspiring to see all of the decorated graves. We then proceeded to the commons for our picnic. Unfortunately, the wind was blowing so hard that we decided to postpone our venture and return home. Not before we all had a grand time playing on the grass, however.

May 31 to June 10, 1927

My men have completed the repairs to their tanks. Fortunately, there were no major break-downs. What damages that did occur, we were able to repair with the spare parts that we have on hand. The men are taking a great deal of pride in their equipment and in themselves. I will have to talk with Capt. Ross about some promotions. There are a couple of potential leaders out there.

June 11, 1927

We drove to New York City, to-day, in part for my birthday. Also, we came here for the parade on Monday for Lindberg. Capt Ross gave me a two-day pass for the training exercise. I thought that this would be an excellent use of that pass.

We booked a room on 5th Avenue where the parade is supposed to take place. We can see the street from our room window. This turned out to be a very fortunate turn of events. Annette had made the reservation a while ago when she was planning this celebration. When we heard about the parade, we decided to stay the extra day. And a good thing it was that we had our reservation. As soon as the parade was announced, there wasn't a room available for miles! I suppose that this is a birthday bonus.

June 12, 1927 William's Birthday

This has been a wonderful day! Annette planned everything down to the last detail. There were a few inconveniences because of the parade tomorrow. But they were nothing worth mentioning. Frederick and Angelica were excited and very impressed with the big city.

June 13, 1927

What a spectacular parade! We were able to see everything from our hotel room. We listened to the radio in our room.

We listened to the broadcaster described the event until we could see it. Although, there was so much confetti and streamers being thrown from the buildings that it was difficult to see anything. It was good that we were able to watch from our room. The street below was so crowded that I doubt that we would have been able to see anything.
I remember watching the Christmas Parade in the past. But that does not compare to this parade.

June 14, 1927

We returned home. Everyone was still a buzz from the weekend. That was a birthday to remember.

June 15 to July 1, 1927

The company continues to improve, and grow. I no longer need to go to my friends at the recruiting station to beg for new soldiers. Several soldiers are requesting to transfer in. We have received so many requests that Capt. Ross and I have decided to start reviewing the requests to determine if we have an opening for them and would they be a good fit for the company. We are still having issues getting all of the supplies that we order. We are receiving some supplies. Not enough to sustain us, though. For now, I will need to rely on my outside sources.

July 2 to 4, 1927 Independence Day

This was a fine day, a fine weekend, and a fine celebration of the birth of a fine Nation.

July 5 to 15, 1927

It rained for several days. The rain hampered our training with the tanks. We attempted some maneuvers on Wednesday. The ground proved too wet and soft to support our tanks. It reminded me of that day in France when I first saw them in action. In fact, it was almost exactly like that day in France. Except that we were not being shot at. It seems to me that we should have learned how to do it better. I'll look into ways to improve our tactics.

July 16, 1927 Wedding Anniversary

Annette planned a wonderful day together and dinner for us. I did assist her, as it is her anniversary, too.

July 17, 1927

This was a most splendid Sunday.

July 18 to August 11, 1927

There was some disturbing news from Austria. It seems that a group of Socialist Democrats clashed with Catholic Church groups in Vienna. A protest, a general strike, started on the 15th of July. Apparently, this was in response to a jury verdict from a murder charge over the deaths from an earlier clash between these groups. The defendants were acquitted. There are reports of hundreds of people injured or killed. These deaths and injuries happened when the police shot into the protesters. I am certain that they have their reasons for their actions, but there must be a better way to resolve them short of violence and bloodshed.

August 12, 1927 Frederick's Birthday

Frederick is becoming quite the young man. We had a splendid party for him this evening.

The 12th Infantry Regiment was reassigned from the 8th Infantry Division to the 4th Infantry Division, to-day. As far as I can tell, they will remain stationed here at Fort Howard.

August 13 to 14, 1927

The rain put an end to any plans that we had to work outside this weekend.

August 13 to September 2, 1927

The building of our company continues at a satisfactory rate. We have a marksmanship range scheduled for later in the month.

September 3 to 5, 1927 Labor Day

What a wonderful weekend. Annette and I had the entire time to spend with Frederick and Angelica. We had a most enjoyable time.

September 6 to 27, 1927

Our range went well. I would have liked to have seen my soldiers score higher. However, there average score was better than the last time we were at the range. Over all, I am pleased with their improvement.

September 28, 1927

The newspaper and radio are filled with the reports of a massive tornado near St. Louis. The reports of 70 to 80 deaths and 500 to 600 injuries make this, one of the deadliest tornadoes in history.

September 29 to October 14, 1927

I worked on our tank tactics. Father had nothing more than what we had. A meeting with my platoon sergeants did not yield any workable results. It would appear that I will need to create these tactics from scratch. I challenged each platoon to come up with at least two combat tactics.

They have three weeks to finish their challenge. I hope that they will come up with some interesting solutions.

October 15, 1927 Angelica's Birthday

Our little girl turned three, to-day. We had a dinner-party for her. Everyone had an enjoyable time.

October 16, 1927

The remainder of the weekend was cold, but pleasant.

October 17 to November 10, 1927

After losing the World Series last year to the St. Louis Cardinals, the New York Yankees swept the Pittsburgh Pirates in four games. Their Murderers' Row of Earle Combs, Mark Koenig, Babe Ruth, Lou Gehrig, Bob Meusel, and Tony Lazzeri proved to be too much for Pittsburgh. New York's Murderers' Row proved to be too much for almost everyone as the Yankees went 110-44.

Back here, I reviewed the tactical proposals. The majority of them was a restatement of our current operating procedures; escort the infantry close to the enemy and then fall back to the start line.

One of the suggestions from 3rd Platoon was to use the tanks as a form of light artillery. The plan suggested to use the mobility of the tank to position them within range of the enemy, fire in support of the attack, and then follow or withdraw as needed. It also proposed the use of the tanks in defensive actions. Again, they utilized the mobility and fire power in order to weaken the enemy's attack.

However, 2nd Platoon submitted a different idea. Instead of using the tanks in a supporting role, use them as an attack weapon. I showed the plans to Capt Ross. He, too, liked the potential of 2nd Platoons' plan. There are a few problems with the logistics and execution. We feel that there is enough promise in this plan to warrant further development. We are going to try to work out as many issues as we can.

<u>November 11, 1927 Armistice Day</u>

Annette and I spent the day relaxing after a moment of silence and remembrance. It was a good day.

November 12 to 13, 1927

This was a very relaxing and cold weekend.

November 14 to 23, 1927

Capt Ross and I worked on the new tactic concept. There may be more problems than we anticipated. For now, instead of trying to solve the entire problem, we are going to take one aspect, work on it, test it in field maneuvers, and see where we are at that time.

November 24, 1927 Thanksgiving Day

We are very thankful this day and every day. News reports of violence in Colorado remind us of this. It is disheartening to read about how several unarmed, striking mine workers were killed by the State Police in Colorado. It is reports such as this that make us appreciate all that we have.

November 25 to December 24, 1927 Christmas Eve

Ford released their new model, the Model-A. That seems unusual, considering their last model was the Model-T. The Model-A has several body styles, from a coupe to a Tudor sedan. They also come in a variety of colors including black, gray, and green.

The price is from $350 to $500. This might be the answer to our car question.

December 25, 1927 Christmas Day

What a joyous day! Watching the glow and wonder on Frederick and Angelica's face is a source of enjoyment for Annette and me. The children were exhausted before dinner. Annette and I were not far behind.

December 26 to 31, 1927 New Year's Eve

The snow was lovely, but cold, heavy to shovel, and it makes driving and walking very dangerous.

Capt Ross and I continue to work on the new tank doctrine. We are making progress.

January 1, 1928 New Year's Day

As another year ends and the new one begins, this Sunday seems like a good time to take stock of a few things.

Speaking of stocks, the Dow Jones average climbed above $200. My stocks continue to do well, too.

Annette, Frederick, and Angelica are healthy and continue to flourish.

Capt Ross and I are working on refining the tank doctrine. The Tank Company is growing stronger and stronger.
All things considered, 1928 looks to be a good year.

January 2 to 5, 1928

Cold. The New Year has started off cold.

January 6, 1928 Annette's Birthday

To-day was a cold and snowy celebration of Annette's birthday. The whole family went out for dinner at Antonio's. Afterwards, we returned home for some birthday cake and gifts.

January 7 to February 10, 1928

Our tank doctrine is ready for field testing. Capt. Ross and I discussed our options. We talked about waiting until the spring to test our doctrine. However, we decided to take advantage of the cold weather to see if that might have any effect on operations. We will hold our maneuvers later in February.

February 11, 1928 Winter Olympics Begin

The 1928 Winter Olympics begin to-day in St. Moritz, Switzerland. These are winter games just like the ones that we saw in Paris four years ago. This time, they are Olympic Games on their own and not a part of the Summer Olympic Games.

The newspaper reports that the opening ceremony was held in blizzard conditions. I'm glad that we did not go to see these games.

February 12, 1928 Lincoln's Birthday

To-day was a cold and snowy Sunday. It is an excellent day to stay inside.

February 13 to 14, 1928 Valentine's Day

On Monday, I told the platoon sergeants about our upcoming maneuvers. I also issued a copy of our doctrine to each of the platoons so that they could study, plan, prepare, and rehearse. I expect great things from them.

For dinner, Tuesday, Annette and I had a nice, quiet time together.

February 15 to 19, 1928 Winter Olympic Games End

The Winter Olympic Games have ended. Although they began in a blizzard, the rest of the time the weather was warm. The temperature reached as high as 77 degrees forcing several events to be canceled.

Of the 25 nations that participated, 12 won medals. They were:

COUNTRY	GOLD	SILVER	BRONZE	TOTAL
Norway	6	4	5	15
United States	2	2	2	6
Sweden	2	2	1	5

COUNTRY	GOLD	SILVER	BRONZE	TOTAL
Finland	2	1	1	4
Canada	1	0	0	1
France	1	0	0	1
Austria	0	3	1	4
Belgium	0	0	1	1
Czechoslovakia	0	0	1	1
Germany	0	0	1	1
Great Britain	0	0	1	1
Switzerland	0	0	1	1

Clearly, Norway dominated the event. The United States of America took both Gold and Silver in the Bobsleigh and Skeleton events. The Skeleton was also the event that Great Britain received their only medal. The two Bronze medals that American athletes received were for Ladies' Figure Skating and the Men's 500 meter Speed Skating.

On a sad note, Eddie Foy died on February 16th. I remember going to see "Eddie Foy and the Seven Little Foys" when I was younger. I believe it was in 1912 or 1913. The radio broadcast said that he was appearing in a show in Kansas City, Missouri when he died. He was 71.

February 20 to 22, 1928 Washington's Birthday

Frigid temperatures continue. We have scheduled our maneuvers for next Wednesday, February 29, Leap Day. It will be for only two days. That should be enough to test our doctrine.

February 23 to 28, 1928

The temperature has been in the low 20s. There is snow on the ground. Terrible conditions to work in. Excellent conditions to train in, though.

1st and 2nd Platoons will the Red Team while 3rd and 4th Platoons will be the Blue Team. Headquarters will be the Referees. Red Team will use the new tactics while Blue Team will employ conventional tactics. The objective is to capture the opponents' flag.

February 29, 1928 Leap Day

Both Teams deployed to their respective Base Camps. They set their battle lines and prepared for action. Unfortunately, weather conditions have forced a delay in the attack.

March 1, 1928

The battle was over in less than two hours. Red Team used the weather conditions to pre-position their tanks ahead of the start line. They also used half of their team as infantry and hid them throughout the contact area. When the Blue Team began their assault, they were quickly out flanked and over-whelmed. It was exciting to watch.

From the evaluation point of view, there were a few problems. The cold weather made it difficult for the tanks to move, not only physically through the snow, but also mechanically with the oil and fuel. When the engines did run, they provided much needed warmth for the crew. This, however, will cause problems in the summer.

Another large problem was with communication. In poor visibility, signal flags are useless and messengers are too slow. For the moment, the only way to communicate from tank to tank is to use another vehicle to drive between them. This tends to give away your position. If only we could connect field phones to each tank, or even a wireless. But, that is just not possible.

For now, we need to return to the barn, clean-up, and get ready for the next exercise.

<u>March 2 to April 9, 1928</u>

We cleaned-up and warmed-up. The men did a great job during the exercise. Red Team was rewarded with a three-day pass.

Capt. Ross and I went over our observations and the reports from the teams. Using that information, we continue to revise our doctrine.

Elsewhere in the world, on March 15th, Japan made a mass arrest of all known Communists and suspected Communist sympathizers. Over 1600 people were arrested.

April 10, 1928

The primary election was held to-day in Chicago, Illinois. It was not so much about the election as it was about the killings that preceded the election. The dispute appears to be over organized crime and bootlegging. Politicians have been gunned down or blown up. Apparently, the gangsters like their chances on the street better than at the polls. One report was calling it the "pineapple primary", pineapple being the hip term for hand-grenade. That is a very sad comment on the affairs of the country these days.

April 11 to May 3, 1928

The spring thaw has been very good this year. Nearly all of the tanks are operational. The men are anxious for a re-match on the field. There are a few details that Capt. Ross and I need to work out. But, we should be ready by next month. We have requested the use of the training area for June 4 through 8.

In other news, as they say on the radio, there was a bomb attack on Benito Mussolini in Milan, Italy, on the 12th of April. 17 people were killed. Mr. Mussolini was unharmed. It would appear that bombs are the weapon of choice these days.

May 4, 1928

There are news reports of fighting in China, in Jinan. Japanese forces along with some Chinese warlords have attacked Kuomintang forces. The reports don't have many details.

May 5 to 29, 1928

Preparations for the field exercise continue. Everyone is in high spirits in anticipation of the "battle".

May 30, 1928 Decoration Day

This Wednesday, the weather was excellent for our task of placing flags on the graves of our Soldiers who have died.

May 31 to June 11, 1928

The field exercise is over. As earlier, 1st and 2nd Platoons were the Red Team; 3rd and 4th Platoons were the Blue Team. Headquarters served as the referees again.

The results were different. Blue Team was better prepared. Red Team did not have the advantage of the weather. We were able to observe the advantages and disadvantages of the tactics.

Red Team used deception in lieu of the weather. They made a faint deployment much like how they set-up previously. Blue Team took the bait and attacked. This time, though, they did protect their flanks. When Red Team tried to spring their trap, Blue Team was ready and able to hold their line. It looked to be a draw, when a force of Red Team tanks appeared, as if from nowhere, and smashed through Blue Teams line in a good old fashion cavalry charge style. Blue Team had nothing left and soon collapsed.

The remainder of our time in the field was spent in combined maneuvers. There were very few break-downs and no injuries. This was an excellent training tool and exercise.

June 12, 1928 William's Birthday

This was a different birthday for me. We just completed an excellent field exercise and I received a wonderful birthday present. Actually, the family received the present. We sold our old fliver and bought a new Model-A Ford Sedan. After the sale of our tin lizzie, the new car cost us $350. This has been a swell birthday.

June 13 to July 3, 1928

We made a few more minor adjustments and re-worded some parts of our doctrine. We also have begun expanding and including support elements. The bottom line of a successful operation remains the ingenuity of those carrying out the mission.

Elsewhere around the world;

On June 15, the Republican National Convention in Kansas City, MO, nominated Herbert Hoover, the Secretary of Commerce, as their candidate for President. President Coolidge declined to run for a second full term.

Amelia Earhart became the first woman to make a trans-Atlantic flight, June 17 to 18.

On June 29, the Democratic National Convention in Houston, TX, nominated Al Smith, the Governor of New York, as their candidate for President.

Back at home;

I could not help but notice that my financial worth is doing very well. However, when we went to purchase our automobile, it was difficult to gather the required funds. The majority of my "worth" is in stocks and bonds. They do have value, but are not readily available for purchases. Is it truly a value if you can't readily access it when you need the funds? Perhaps I need to re-evaluate this situation.

July 4, 1928 Independence Day

To-day, we celebrated our Nations' birthday. We relaxed, had a wonderful picnic and walk around the parade grounds. Later, we watched the fireworks. It was an excellent day.

July 5 to 15, 1928

I told Father about our Field Exercise. He enjoyed hearing about it.

Also, he was very interested when I mentioned the new doctrine that we were developing. I mailed a copy of it to him. He showed it to his commander. They are going to begin using it. This is very exciting to me.

July 16, 1928 Wedding Anniversary

This is a wonderful beginning to the week. The weather is nice, work at the unit is proceeding very well, and the family is doing fine. And as a crowning glory, we celebrate our 8th wedding anniversary. This is really the "bees' knees" as the young people like to say.

July 17, 1928

What an interesting event. When Father introduced our doctrine to his commander, it was sent to the regiment command for approval. The commander, Col. Patton, came from Fort Myer to Fort Howard, immediately, to meet with Capt. Ross and myself.

At first, Col. Patton was very agitated and upset. I did not understand why. He repeatedly asked where we got this manual. After producing earlier versions and several of the notes and drafts, he began to believe that we had written it ourselves. Col. Patton's entire personality began to change and he became much more relaxed. He then showed us a manual that he had written on tank tactics. I looked through it quickly and began to understand why the Colonel was so upset. His manual was very similar to ours.

Once everything was understood, we had an excellent meeting. We talked about many things. At one point, the upcoming Summer Olympics was mentioned. Col. Patton told us how he had competed in the Modern Pentathlon in the 1912 Olympics. It was quite exciting to hear.

We also talked about our manuals. We took a few moments to go over them. Upon closer examination, we found many features in common. We also found some differences. Col. Patton became very interested. Capt. Ross and I told him of our recent field exercise. He especially enjoyed it when we told him about Red Team's cavalry charge.

When we ended our meeting, Col. Patton told us to continue with our tactics development, and that we would be hearing from him. Despite his initial stern, command presence, Capt. Ross and I had an excellent meeting with Col. Patton.

<u>July 18 to 27, 1928</u>

We took Col. Patton's advice and have been continuing to refine our doctrine. Mostly, I have been reviewing his manual and locating what we can incorporate into ours.

We did receive word and I read it in the newspaper that on July 25th, we removed all U.S. Troops out of China. Considering recent and on-going events there, that seems to be the right course of action.

July 28, 1928 Summer Olympics Begin

The Summer Olympics began to-day in Amsterdam, Netherlands. 46 Nations will compete in 109 events. Germany will be participating for the first time since 1912. The parade of nations was lead by Greece, for the origins of the Olympic Games, and ended with Netherlands, the host nation. All other nations were in alphabetical order. This was different from the parade that we saw in Paris. Also different was the lighting of an Olympic Flame. A giant flame atop a tower at the stadium was lit. It is a symbol taken from the ancient games in Greece.

July 29 to August 11, 1928

Col. Patton said that we would hear from him. He was correct. Capt. Ross and I are being transferred to the 3rd Cavalry Regiment at Fort Myer, Virginia. Apparently, Col. Patton was impressed with our work. We have a report date of September 10, 1928. Annette and I have begun to pack our belongings. I told Father of our transfer. He is looking into housing for us on post.

369

August 12, 1928 Frederick's Birthday and Summer Olympics End

Young Frederick is 7 years old, to-day. We took time from our hectic schedule to celebrate.

Our packing and preparing continues. I am amazed at how many things that we own. The furniture, the dishware, the books, the clothes, there is a lot of things. I'm glad that someone else will be doing the actual moving. I would hate to have to load everything into our automobile and drive off.

From Amsterdam, the top 12 Olympic medal count is:

COUNTRY	GOLD	SILVER	BRONZE	TOTAL
United States	22	18	16	56
Germany	10	7	14	31
Finland	8	8	9	25
Sweden	7	6	12	25
Italy	7	5	7	19
Switzerland	7	4	4	15
France	6	10	5	21
Netherlands	6	9	4	19
Hungary	4	5	0	9
Canada	4	4	7	15

COUNTRY	GOLD	SILVER	BRONZE	TOTAL
Great Britain	3	10	7	20
Argentina	3	3	1	7

In all, 33 nations brought home a medal.

India won its first ever gold medal in Field Hockey. It was also India's only medal.

Johnny Weissmuller won 2 gold medals in swimming. One for the 100 meter Freestyle, and the other for the 200 meter Freestyle Relay. I remember Johnny Weissmuller winning 3 gold medals and a bronze medal at the Paris Olympics. This brings his total count to 5 gold medals and a bronze medal.

Paavo Nurmi of Finland won a gold medal in the 10,000 meter and 2 silver medals in the 5,000 meter and the 3,000 meter Steeplechase. This brings his total medal count to 9 gold medals and 3 silver medals.

A big surprise was Percy Williams of Canada who won 2 gold medals. One medal was for the 100 meter Sprint and the other for the 200 meter Sprint.

Mikio Oda of Japan won the gold medal for the Triple Jump. He is the first athlete from an Asian country to win a gold medal.

Another first was Halina Konopacka of Poland. She is the first woman to win a gold medal in Track and Field. She won it in the Woman's Discus Throw.

<u>August 13 to September 3, 1928 Labor Day</u>

Our packing is complete. In addition, we have made all other preparations. Clearing the unit and the post, giving notice at the hospital, changing schools, are just a few of the outside tasks that we must accomplish prior to our move. I believe we have done everything. The movers arrive tomorrow to pick-up our things.

<u>September 4 to 9, 1928</u>

The movers arrived, picked up our belongings and headed out.

We loaded up the automobile and did the same.

The trip to Fort Myer was a smooth drive. The roadways have improved recently. We stopped at my parents' house to say hello and to find out what they had learned about our housing. They had found out much. Our quarters had already been assigned when Father first looked into the matter. He gave me the address and showed me where it is. It is located in the Command Area. We were both surprised.

September 10, 1928

I signed-in to the unit and received another surprise. I have been assigned to the Regimental Headquarters and promoted to Sergeant Major. Capt. Ross has also been assigned to the Headquarters and in now Major Ross. We are on the Regimental Staff and are to work on refining Tank Tactics. This should be exciting.

September 11 to October 14, 1928

We moved into our new home and began unpacking. This new house is larger and nicer than our former home. Annette was able to get a position at the hospital and the children are enrolled in school. This has been a very smooth transfer. Col. Patton stopped by to check on us and to make sure that everything was going well.

October 15, 1928 Angelica's Birthday

Angelica is 4 years old to-day. This is our first celebration in our new home.

October 16 to November 5, 1928

We are settling into our new home and our new surroundings very well.

November 6, 1928 Election Day

Herbert Hoover was elected to be the next President of the United States of America. He won over Al Smith by a large margin, 444 electoral votes to 87. Anti-Catholic and anti-prohibition were the main campaign themes. Al Smith, being Roman Catholic, suffered from the anti-Catholic sentiment. And his anti-prohibition stance finished him off.

President-elect Hoover almost took the majority of the Democratic solid south. He did carry several of the former Confederate States, such as Virginia, North Carolina, Tennessee, Florida, and Texas.

November 7 to 10, 1928

The weather has turned colder.

November 11, 1928 Armistice Day

On this cold and bleak Sunday, the weather has matched the solemn occasion.

We observed a moment of silence for all who have gone before us.

November 12 to 28, 1928

As we continue to get settled into our new positions and surroundings, I am reminded of all that we have done and gone through. Especially, as we approach Thanksgiving, it puts me in mind of how much I have to be thankful for.

November 29, 1928 Thanksgiving Day

This feeling of gratitude continues through to this national day of thanks.

We had a splendid meal with my parents. It is much easier, now that we live so close together.

November 30 to December 24, 1928 Christmas Eve

We continue to get settled in. Nearly everything has been put away. Mother and Father have been a great help in getting everything done.

Col. and Mrs. Patton invited us to the Regimental Holiday Dinner. It was wonderful. Annette enjoyed herself and the Colonel seemed to be quite taken with her. Maj. Ross and his wife were there, too. It was a magical evening.

December 25, 1928 Christmas Day

Watching the excitement and joy on Frederick and Angelica's faces on this special day continues to be a source of great joy to me.

December 26 to 31, 1928 New Year's Eve

The snow finally arrived, and with it the cold air. Still, it is not enough to dampen our spirits.

January 1, 1929 New Year's Day

A new year has begun. It is filled with the promise of great and wondrous things to come! These years of late have been most wondrous and concerning. All of the fun and gaiety of the young folks with their jazz music, their Charleston and Lindy Hop dances, and even with their flappers, is off-set by the organized crime violence.

The stock market average climbed over the $300 mark.

I have a good position, money in the bank, a wonderful family, and everyone is healthy. Life is good.

<u>January 2 to 5, 1929</u>

Life may be good, but it is also cold! It is to be expected, this being winter. Still, it seems to be a harsher winter this time. Perhaps that feeling is due to the unfamiliarity of our new location.

<u>January 6, 1929 Annette's Birthday</u>

I took Annette to her favorite restaurant to celebrate her day. Later, back home with the children, she opened her gifts. It was a joyous time.

January 7 to February 12, 1929 Lincoln's Birthday

The cold continues, as does our work. Maj. Ross and I have been working on the tactics for tanks. The level of detail and depth that Col. Patton requires is substantial. It is not that we have to write down exactly what each soldier must do. Rather, we must consider every conceivable possibility and situation, and a few inconceivable possibilities, too. There is more to this than meets the eye. Col. Patton will occasionally review our work and offer guidance and some personal insight. We have accomplished a great deal. However, I fear that we still have much to do.

The news reported of two interesting events that happened recently. Firstly, the Litvinov's Protocol was signed on February 9 by the Soviet Union, Poland, Romania, Latvia, and Estonia. It is basically a non-aggression pact between the nations. Secondly, the Kingdom of Italy and the Sancta Sedes of the Catholic Church signed the Lateran Treaty on February 11. This is to establish the Vatican City as an independent sovereign enclave within Rome. Both documents need to be ratified by all parties concerned before they can be put into effect.

February 13 to 14, 1929 Valentine's Day

The radio announcer informed us of some gangster violence in Chicago, Illinois. It would seem that seven gang members were killed in a garage. The announcer was calling it the Saint Valentine's Day massacre. The reports were incomplete at this time. No word as of yet on who committed this crime. Something needs to be done about all of this gang violence.

February 15 to 22, 1929 Washington's Birthday

Our work continues. We are making progress. At times, I feel like not fast enough for Col. Patton's taste. I can see some real advancement, however. There were times when I thought that we were nearly complete. But Col. Patton had other ideas. He is a very detailed oriented man.

February 23 to March 4, 1929 Inauguration Day

Mr. Herbert Hoover was inaugurated as President to-day. Father's unit was in the procession. We also sent a squadron to participate. We listened to the events on the radio. The weather even co-operated for the day.

March 5 to April 12, 1929

Work on our tactics manual is done. We have now gone into the review stage. Once we complete this stage, we will then proceed to the fielding stage. After we are done there, we will gather up our notes and return to the writing stage. At least Maj. Ross and I get a brief rest. This has been quite the learning process.

April 13 to May 16, 1929

The review portion is about to begin. The review committee has been selected. They have been given guidance. We will see what they find.

May 17, 1929

There was an interesting article in the newspaper, to-day. Last night, a new award was presented to the movie Wings. This new award was created by a group referred to as the Academy Awards. It appears that the people who make the movies has established an Academy of their own people. Their sole purpose is to decide what a good movie is. They then proceed to present an award to that effect. As I have little enough time to sit and read about what is happening on the screen, I do not go to the movies often. I don't understand what the rationale is behind this action.

May 18 to 29, 1929

The review committee have completed their preliminary review. On the one hand, they had surprisingly few corrections and recommendations. On the other hand, they considered that entire effort a complete waste of time. Maj. Ross and I are devastated.

May 30, 1929 Decoration Day

Our solemn duty to decorate the graves of those who have gone before us, is exceptionally difficult with the recent ending of the work that so many have done on the tank tactics manual. With our work dissolved, we have only to wait for our next assignment. I will miss Maj. Ross and all of the fine soldiers that worked so feverishly toward the successful completion of this task.

May 31 to June 11, 1929

A dark cloud remains over us as we go about the business of clearing out our office area. Several of the soldiers make light of the situation. But, the moment of levity soon passes and we are faced once again with the crushing reality of our situation. I suppose that I will be assigned to a line unit. Hopefully, I will be able to retain my rank.

Also, I have read of a convention that is taking place in Buenos Aires, Argentina. It is a conference of the Communist Parties of Latin America. I find it impossible to believe that anyone would knowingly accept the communist method of government. I will never forget what they did to Private Horace on that fateful day back in '20.

<u>June 12, 1929 William's Birthday</u>

My mood has not improved. Yet, I was determined not to let my family down. They were aware of my melancholy state and they have worked very hard to cheer me up for my birthday. I will not disappoint them.

As I prepared to leave the office and join in the planned revelries at home, a messenger brought a dispatch for me. It was the orders that I had been dreading. "I am a soldier." I told myself. "I will go where ever they send me." I opened the envelope and awaited my fate. As I read my new assignment, I couldn't believe my eyes. I was to be assigned to Col. Patton's staff with a report date of Monday, June 17, 1929. This should not be a difficult move as it is one building over. I couldn't be happier! I went home with a genuine, joyous heart and told Annette. This was, indeed, a very happy birthday!

June 13 to 16, 1929

These few days could not pass quick enough. I do not believe that it took more than a few hours to move my few belongings to my new digs. In reality, the only item of any importance was the files containing all of the documentation for the Armor Tactics manual.

June 17, 1929

Col. Patton officially welcomed me to my new assignment. The first thing that he asked about was the manual. I had it front and center on my desk. The corner of his mouth turned up giving a slight smile. As if to say, 'I knew you were the right choice'. It made my heart swell with pride.

June 18 to July 3, 1929

This has become a time of rapid learning and joy. Being the Regimental Sergeant Major brought a new set of responsibilities and duties. Working for Col. Patton brought a different set of duties and responsibilities. I couldn't be happier. At the staff meeting, I discovered what became of Maj. Ross. He was transferred to the Regimental S-1, Administration section. Col. Patton has every confidence, as do I, that he will handle this assignment admirably.

July 4, 1929 Independence Day

The post festivities were especially wondrous this year. Troop D was selected to participate in the post parade. Annette, Frederick, Angelica, and I accompanied Col. and Mrs. Patton on the reviewing stand. I don't know which made me prouder, watching my soldiers pass in review, or having my family there with me.

July 5 to 15, 1929

Working for Col. Patton has been a different kind of experience. He will come into a room or situation and observe what is happening. If everything is under control and going smoothly, he will leave. Often, others in the area will not even realize that he had been there. If he is unsure of the situation, he will ask questions. If he is satisfied with the answers, again, he will leave. However, if he comes into a room or situation and he is not satisfied with what he sees or the answers that he receives, God help whoever is in charge. I have seen him relieve commanders on the spot. For me, this is not a difficult mission. I know what he expects and I work my tail off making sure that everything is in order. In turn, I expect no less of my First Sergeants. If they fail me, I replace them with someone who can get the job done. I must be able to depend on them. Just as he must be able to depend on me.

July 16, 1929 Wedding Anniversary

Our 9th wedding anniversary. I put in long days. I come home so tired that I can barely stay awake. And I have never been happier. Frederick and Angelica are eager to show me what they have done. Annette works as hard as I do keeping the house in order and she still manages to smile and take care of me. She deflects the troubles of the day with pleasant conversation. She deserves my complete attention and I give it to her. To-night a different subject was broached. As next year will be our 10th wedding anniversary, Annette would like to bring her parents over for a visit and to help us celebrate. I told her that that was an excellent idea. That we should begin working on the planning. Of course I will assist her any way that I can.

July 17 to 25, 1929

I read in the paper that the Kellogg-Briand Pact went into effect yesterday. It had been signed in Paris, France nearly a year ago. I remember Annette's father writing about it. He was surprised that there was very little fanfare. There was hardly any mention of it in the newspaper. To have 15 of the world's most powerful nations sign an agreement to renounce war as an instrument of national policy is a significant event. And to have 32 more nations sign on would serve to reinforce my point. Let us hope that this will prevent the Great War from happening again.

July 26 to 28, 1929

As if to accent the point of the Kellogg-Briand Pact, a convention held in Geneva, Switzerland was completed yesterday. I'm not certain what the full intent of the convention was. I did read where it was intended to correct some gaps in the Hague Regulations of 1899 and 1907. Apparently something arose from the Great War that needed to be corrected. Doing away with war would be a good beginning. But, that is not in the nature of man.

July 29 to August 11, 1929

The dog days of summer are certainly upon us. Sweltering temperatures have made it very difficult to get any work done.

August 12, 1929 Frederick's Birthday

My little man turns 8 to-day. He is getting so grown-up. He seems to really enjoy watching the soldiers drill and train. Once, I came home to discover him playing with his toy soldiers. He was so engrossed in his activities that he did not notice my presence. He had them all organized by units and standing at attention. He gave his orders. Then he had the figurines carry out his orders. One toy soldier fell over. Frederick laid into that poor little toy soldier so hard that I started to feel bad for him. I wonder where Frederick learned to act that way. I am so proud of my little man.

August 13 to September 1, 1929

The heat has not abated. Neither has our work load. We do have to take into consideration the soldiers' health. Too much heat can harm them. A soldier can do no good on the battlefield if he is ill or dead.

Two recent events have sparked my interest. The first being reports of riots in the British territory of Palestine. Hundreds are reported to be killed or wounded. This in the wake of the Kellogg-Briand pact the Britain signed.

The second, and a much lighter subject, was the news of the successful circumnavigation of the world by a rigid airship. It took the German Graf Zeppelin just 21 days to accomplish the task. It started its' trek from the Lakehurst Naval Aerostation in New Jersey. Beyond the obvious impressive aerial accomplishment, I was struck by the speed with which the task was accomplished. Truly, these rigid airships are the mode of transportation for the future. I mentioned this to Annette, in reference to her plans for her parents to visit us next year. This could reduce the travel time by half. She said that she would investigate it further.

<u>September 2, 1929 Labor Day</u>

The warm days have subsided for the moment. It is a welcome relief.

September 3 to 6, 1929

A matter of great concern weighs heavily on my mind. I have watched with great joy as my investments in the New York Stock Market have steadily grown. What has me more than a little troubled is a piece of information that I heard recently. It appears that a significant portion of the value of the stocks is based on future value. That investors are purchasing stocks on the speculation that the value of the stock will go up and therefore they do not need to provide actual funds to purchase the stock. I believe someone called it "buying on margin". This is all well and good if the stocks do indeed go up. But what if they don't? What if they fall? To me, that is the same as saying, "That trench is mine. I don't need to use any troops to take it". If no one is there, then it would become reality. What about the enemy? Are they going to let me walk over and take control of their trench? I think not. This fallacy in the way that they conduct the stock market has caused enough of a concern in me that I have decided to withdraw from the market. Even though they posted an all-time high on Tuesday last and it could go even higher. I am not comfortable with the overall lack of visible support.

Stephen E. Moss

<u>September 7 to October 4, 1929</u>

What curious times are these?

After selling all of my stocks and losing a sizable portion to the broker, I did manage to come away with a reasonable sum of money. What to do with it is the next question. Perhaps I should just leave it in the bank until I decide what to do.

The Prime Minister of France, M. Aristide Briand, introduced his plan to create a European union, a United States of Europe. M. Briand, along with the former United States Secretary of State Mr. Frank B. Kellogg, co-authored the Kellogg-Briand Pact. This would appear to be the next logical step toward the deterrence of war. If all of the European nations were unified, much like the United States of America, it would reduce the chances of war amongst those nations. This is a bold and ambitious plan.

Seemingly in response to M. Briand's plan the Kingdoms of Serbs, Croats, and Slovenes announced that they are unifying into one nation. They are now to be known as the Kingdom of Yugoslavia. I hope for their success as well as the success of M. Briand's plan.

October 5 to 14, 1929

There appears to be more good news for peace. The Afghan Civil War has ended. In what appears to have been a series of revolts by different factions against whichever government that happens to be in control at that moment for almost the last year, one group has now claimed victory and established the Kingdom of Afghanistan. I pray for peace in the region, but fear that it will not come.

October 15, 1929 Angelica's Birthday

My little Angelica turns 5 to-day. She is such a little lady. She definitely favors her mother. Her wide-eyed wonderment of everything around her in the world is a joy to behold. Often, in the evening, as I sit pouring over the newspaper or the daily reports, she will climb up into my lap to see what I am doing. She will sit and pour over the papers, too. I am not entirely certain that she understands what it is that she is staring so intently upon. It matters not. Her presence is enough to melt my heart.

October 16 to 23, 1929

Cold temperatures are a welcome relief from the dog days of summer that just recently left us. Work continues to proceed as well, if not better than expected. One could almost believe that the nation is on the verge of great things. If not, indeed, the entire world. Peace appears to be breaking out everywhere. Unifications are coming about around the world to ensure that peace. The newspaper delivered a small dark cloud over this bright and shiny future. The Prime Minister of France, M. Briand, and his council government have received a vote of "no confidence". M. Briand will remain on until a new cabinet can be organized and Prime Minister appointed. Annette's father will send me any information that he receives as this is not very news worthy here in America. I do hope that this is not a dramatic foreshadowing...

To be continued in Through The Eyes of a Soldier: A World Gone Mad Part II.

ABOUT THE AUTHOR

Stephen E. Moss is a retired United States Army Master Sergeant with over 37 years of service. He has served in nearly every state in America and over 20 countries. He also served in several combat zones. He received his Master's Degree from University of Louisville and Bachelor's Degree from Purdue University. After retirement, he settled in Louisiana, Missouri where he currently serves on the Boards of Louisiana Historical Preservation Association, Louisiana Public Library, and Louisiana Area Historical Museum.

Stephen E. Moss

ALSO AVAILABLE FROM POLSTON HOUSE

"An inspiring true story."
- Author Woodrow Polston

MIRACLES ON
THE CANCER
JOURNEY

DEBRA YOUNG WALLER

Stephen E. Moss

ALSO AVAILABLE FROM POLSTON HOUSE

Stephen E. Moss

www.ingramcontent.com/pod-product-compliance
Lightning Source LLC
Chambersburg PA
CBHW060812030726
47503CB00002B/453